Brown-Eyed Girl

Also by Lisa Kleypas

Crystal Cove

Dream Lake

Rainshadow Road

Christmas Eve at Friday Harbor

Smooth Talking Stranger

Seduce Me at Sunrise

Blue-Eyed Devil

Mine Till Midnight

Sugar Daddy

WALLFLOWER SERIES

A Wallflower Christmas

Scandal in Spring

Devil in Winter

It Happened One Autumn

Secrets of a Summer Night

Brown-Eyed Girl

Lisa Kleypas

St. Martin's Press
New York

BROWN-EYED GIRL. Copyright © 2015 by Lisa Kleypas. All rights reserved. Printed in the United States of America. For information, address St. Martin's Press, 175 Fifth Avenue, New York, N.Y. 10010.

www.stmartins.com

The Library of Congress Cataloging-in-Publication Data is available upon request.

ISBN 978-0-312-60537-7 (hardcover)
ISBN 978-1-4668-8178-5 (e-book)

St. Martin's Press books may be purchased for educational, business, or promotional use. For information on bulk purchases, please contact the Macmillan Corporate and Premium Sales Department at 1-800-221-7945, extension 5442, or write to special markets@macmillan.com.

First Edition: August 2015

10 9 8 7 6 5 4 3 2 1

For Eloisa James and Linda Francis Lee,
who make me happy when skies are gray.
Love always,
L.K.

Brown-Eyed Girl

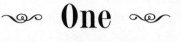

One

As an experienced wedding planner, I was prepared for nearly every kind of emergency that might occur on the big day.

Except for scorpions. That was a new one.

The distinctive movement gave it away, a sinister forward-and-back scuttle across the tiles of the pool patio. In my opinion, there wasn't a more evil-looking creature in existence than a scorpion. Usually the venom wouldn't kill you, but for the first couple of minutes after you'd been stung, you might wish it had.

The first rule for dealing with emergencies was: *Don't panic.* But as the scorpion skittered toward me with its grasping claws and upward-curved tail, I forgot all about rule number one and let out a shriek. Frantically I rummaged through my bag, a tote so heavy that whenever I set it on the passenger seat, the car would signal me to buckle it in. My hand fumbled past tissues, pens, bandages, Evian, hair products, deodorant, hand sanitizer, lotion, nail and makeup kits, tweezers, a sewing kit, glue, headphones, cough drops, a chocolate bar, over-the-counter medications, scissors, a file, a brush, earring backs, rubber bands, tampons, stain remover, a lint roller, bobby pins, a razor, double-sided tape, and cotton swabs.

The heaviest object I could find was a glue gun, which I threw at the scorpion. The glue gun bounced harmlessly on the tile, while the scorpion bristled to defend its territory. Pulling out a can of hair spray, I ventured forward with cautious determination.

"That's not going to work," I heard someone say in a low, amused voice. "Unless you're trying to give him more volume and shine."

Startled, I looked up as a stranger moved past me, a tall, black-haired man dressed in jeans, boots, and a T-shirt that had been washed to near annihilation. "I'll take care of it," he said.

I retreated a couple of steps, shoving the can back into my bag. "I . . . I thought hair spray might suffocate him."

"Nope. A scorpion can hold its breath for up to a week."

"Really?"

"Yes, ma'am." He crushed the scorpion beneath his boot, finishing with an extra grind of his heel. There was nothing a Texan killed more thoroughly than a scorpion or a lit cigarette. After kicking the exoskeleton into the mulch of a nearby flower bed, he turned to give me a long, considering glance. The purely male assessment jolted my heartbeat into a new frenzy. I found myself staring into eyes the color of blackstrap molasses. He was a striking man, his features bold, the nose strong, the jaw sturdy. The stubble on his face looked heavy enough to sand paint off a car. He was big-boned and lean, the muscles of his arms and chest as defined as cut stone beneath the worn layer of his T-shirt. A disreputable-looking man, maybe a little dangerous.

The kind of man who made you forget to breathe.

His boots and the raggedy hems of his jeans were skimmed with mud that was already drying to powder. He must have been walking near the creek that cut through the Stardust Ranch's four thousand acres. Dressed like that, he couldn't possibly have been one of the wedding guests, most of whom possessed unimaginable fortunes.

As his gaze swept over me, I knew exactly what he was seeing: a full-figured woman in her late twenties, with red hair and big-framed glasses. My clothes were comfortable, loose, and plain. "Forever 51," my younger sister Sofia had described my standard outfit of boxy tops and elastic-waist wide-legged pants. If the look was off-putting to men—and it usually was—so much the better. I had no interest in attracting anyone.

"Scorpions aren't supposed to come out in the daylight," I said unsteadily.

"We had an early thaw and a dry spring. They're looking for moisture. Swimmin' pool's going to draw 'em out." He had a lazy, easy way of talking, as if every word had been simmered for hours over a low flame.

Breaking our shared gaze, the stranger bent to retrieve the glue gun. As he handed it to me, our fingers touched briefly, and I felt a little jab of response beneath my lower ribs. I caught his scent, white soap and dust and sweet wild grass.

"You'd best change out of those," he advised, glancing at my open-toed flats. "You got boots? Running shoes?"

"I'm afraid not," I said. "I'll have to take my chances." I noticed the camera he had set on one of the patio tables, a Nikon with a pro-level lens, the metal barrel edged with red. "You're a professional photographer?" I asked.

"Yes, ma'am."

He had to be one of the second-shooters hired by George Gantz, the wedding photographer. I extended my hand. "I'm Avery

Crosslin," I said in a friendly but businesslike tone. "The wedding coordinator."

He gripped my hand, the clasp warm and firm. I felt a little shock of pleasure at the contact.

"Joe Travis." His gaze continued to hold mine, and for some reason he prolonged the grip a couple of seconds longer than necessary. Unaccountable warmth swept over my face in a swift tide. I was relieved when he finally let go.

"Did George give you copies of the timeline and shot list?" I asked, trying to sound professional.

The question earned a blank look.

"Don't worry," I said, "we've got extra copies. Go to the main house and ask for my assistant, Steven. He's probably in the kitchen with the caterers." I fished in my bag for a business card. "If you have any problems, here's my cell number."

He took the card. "Thanks. But I'm not actually–"

"The guests will be seated at six thirty," I said briskly. "The ceremony will begin at seven and finish with the dove release at seven thirty. And we'll want some shots of the bride and groom before sunset, which happens at seven forty-one."

"Did you schedule that too?" Mocking amusement glinted in his eyes.

I shot him a warning glance. "You should probably spruce up before the guests are up and out this morning." I reached into my bag for a disposable razor. "Here, take this. Ask Steven where there's a place you can shave, and–"

"Slow down, honey. I have my own razor." He smiled slightly. "Do you always talk so fast?"

I frowned, tucking the razor back into my bag. "I have to get to work. I suggest you do the same."

"I don't work for George. I'm commercial and freelance. No weddings."

"Then what are you here for?" I asked.

"I'm a guest. Friend of the groom's."

Stunned, I stared at him with wide eyes. The creepy-crawly heat of embarrassment covered me from head to toe. "I'm sorry," I managed to say. "When I saw your camera, I assumed . . ."

"No harm done."

There was nothing I hated more than looking foolish, *nothing*. The appearance of competence was essential in building a client base . . . especially the upper-class clientele I was aiming for. But now on the day of the biggest, most expensive wedding my studio and I had ever orchestrated, this man was going to tell his wealthy friends about how I'd mistaken him for the hired help. There would be snickers behind my back. Snide jokes. Contempt.

Wanting to put as much distance as possible between us, I muttered, "If you'll excuse me . . ." I turned and walked away as fast as I could without breaking into a run.

"Hey," I heard Joe say, catching up to me in a few long strides. He had grabbed the camera and slung it on a strap over his shoulder. "Hold on. No need to be skittish."

"I'm not skittish," I said, hurrying toward a flagstone-floored pavilion with a wooden roof. "I'm busy."

He matched my pace easily. "Wait a minute. Let's start over."

"Mr. Travis–," I began, and stopped dead in my tracks as I realized exactly who he was. "God," I said sickly, closing my eyes for a moment. "You're one of those Travises, aren't you."

Joe came around to face me, his gaze quizzical. "Depends on what you mean by 'those.'"

"Oil money, private planes, yachts, mansions. *Those.*"

"I don't have a mansion. I have a fixer-upper in the Sixth Ward."

"You're still one of them," I insisted. "Your father is Churchill Travis, isn't he?"

A shadow crossed his expression. "Was."

Too late, I remembered that approximately six months earlier, the Travis family patriarch had passed away from sudden cardiac arrest. The media had covered his funeral extensively, describing his life and accomplishments in detail. Churchill had made his vast fortune with venture and growth capital investing, most of it related to energy. He'd been highly visible in the eighties and nineties, a frequent guest on TV business and financial shows. He—and his heirs—were the equivalent of Texas royalty.

"I'm . . . sorry for your loss," I said awkwardly.

"Thanks."

A wary silence ensued. I could feel his gaze moving over me, as tangible as the heat of sunlight.

"Look, Mr. Travis—"

"Joe."

"Joe," I repeated. "I'm more than a little preoccupied. This wedding is a complicated production. At the moment I'm managing the setup of the ceremony site, the decoration of an eight-thousand-square-foot reception tent, a formal dinner and dance with a live orchestra for four hundred guests, and a late night after-party. So I apologize for the misunderstanding, but—"

"No need to apologize," he said gently. "I should've spoken up sooner, but it's hard to get a word in edgewise with you." Amusement played at the corners of his mouth. "Which means either I'm going to have to speed up, or you're going to have to slow down."

Even as tense as I was, I was tempted to smile back.

"There's no need for the Travis name to make you feel uncomfortable," he continued. "Believe me, no one who knows my family is impressed by us in the least." He studied me for a moment. "Where are you headed to now?"

"The pavilion," I said, nodding to the covered wooden structure beyond the pool.

"Let me walk you there." At my hesitation, he added, "In case you run across another scorpion. Or some other varmint. Tarantulas, lizards . . . I'll clear a path for you."

Wryly, I reflected that the man could probably charm the rattles off a snake. "It's not *that* bad out here," I said.

"You need me," he said with certainty.

Together we walked to the ceremony site, crossing beneath a motte of live oak on the way. The white silk reception tent in the distance was poised on a tract of emerald lawn like a massive cloud that had floated down to rest. There was no telling how much precious water had been used to maintain that brilliant grassy oasis, freshly rolled out and laid only a few days ago. And every tender green blade would have to be pulled up tomorrow.

Stardust was a four-thousand-acre working ranch with a main lodge, a compound of guesthouses and assorted buildings, a barn, and a riding arena. My event-planning studio had arranged to lease the private property while the owners were away on a two-week cruise. The couple had agreed on condition the property would be restored to exactly the way it had been before the wedding.

"How long you been at this?" Joe asked.

"Wedding planning? My sister Sofia and I started the business about three years ago. Before that, I worked in bridal fashion design in New York."

"You must be good, if you were hired for Sloane Kendrick's wedding. Judy and Ray wouldn't settle for anyone but the best."

The Kendricks owned a chain of pawnshops from Lubbock to Galveston. Ray Kendrick, a former rodeo rider with a face like a pine knot, had laid out a cool million for his only daughter's wedding. If my event team pulled this off, there was no telling how many high-profile clients we might gain from it.

"Thanks," I said. "We've got a good team. My sister is very creative."

"What about you?"

"I take care of the business side of things. And I'm the head co-ordinator. It's up to me to make sure that every detail is perfect."

We reached the pavilion, where a trio of reps from the rental company were setting up white-painted chairs. Rummaging through my bag, I found a metal tape measure. With a few expert tugs, I extended it across the space between the cords that had been staked out to line up the chairs. "The aisle has to be six feet wide," I called out to the reps. "Move the cord, please."

"It is six feet," one of them called back.

"It's five feet and ten inches."

The rep gave me a long-suffering glance. "Isn't that close enough?"

"Six feet," I insisted, and snapped the measuring tape closed.

"What do you do when you're not working?" Joe asked from behind me.

I turned to face him. "I'm always working."

"Always?" he asked skeptically.

"I'm sure I'll slow down when the business is more established. But for now . . ." I shrugged. I could never seem to cram enough into one day. E-mails, phone calls, plans to be made, arrangements to nail down.

"Everyone needs some kind of hobby."

"What's yours?"

"Fishing, when I get the chance. Hunting, depending on the season. Every now and then I do some charity photography."

"What kind of charity?"

"A local animal shelter. A good photo on the website can help a dog get adopted sooner." Joe paused. "Maybe sometime you'd like to—"

"I'm sorry—excuse me." I had heard a ringtone from somewhere in the abyss of my bag, repeating the five notes of "Here Comes the Bride." As I retrieved the phone, I saw my sister's ID.

"I've been calling the dove handler, and he won't answer," Sofia said as soon as I answered. "He never confirmed which container we wanted for the release."

"Did you leave a message?" I asked.

"Five messages. What if something's wrong? What if he's sick?"

"He's not sick," I assured her.

"Maybe he got bird flu from his doves."

"His birds aren't doves. They're white pigeons, and pigeons are resistant to bird flu."

"Are you sure?"

"Try him again in a couple of hours," I said soothingly. "It's only seven. He may not even be awake yet."

"What if he's a no-show?"

"He'll be here," I said. "It's too early in the day to freak out, Sofia."

"When am I allowed to freak out?"

"You're not," I said. "I'm the only one who gets to do that. Let me know if you don't hear from him by ten."

"Okay."

I slipped the phone back into my bag and gave Joe an inquiring glance. "You were saying something about the animal shelter?"

He stared down at me. His thumbs were hooked in his pockets, most of his weight braced on one leg, in a stance that was both assertive and relaxed. I had never seen anything sexier in my life.

"I could take you along with me," he said, "next time I head over there. I wouldn't mind sharing my hobby until you get one of your own."

I was slow to respond. My thoughts had scattered like a flock of baby chicks at a petting zoo. I had the impression that he was asking me to go somewhere with him. Almost like . . . a date?

"Thanks," I said eventually, "but my schedule is full."

"Let me take you out sometime," he urged. "We could go out for drinks, or lunch."

I was rarely at a loss for words, but all I could do was stand there in baffled silence.

"Tell you what." His voice turned coaxing and soft. "I'll drive you to Fredericksburg one morning, while the day is still cool and we have the road to ourselves. We'll stop to buy some coffee and a bag of kolaches. I'll take you to a meadow so full of bluebonnets, you'll swear half the sky just fell over Texas. We'll find us a shade tree and watch the sunrise. How does that sound?"

It sounded like the kind of day meant for some other woman, someone who was accustomed to being charmed by handsome men. For a second I let myself imagine it, lounging with him on a quiet morning in a blue meadow. I was on the verge of agreeing to anything he asked. But I couldn't afford to take such a risk. Not now, not ever. A man like Joe Travis had undoubtedly broken so many hearts that mine would mean nothing to him.

"I'm not available," I blurted out.

"You're married?"

"No."

"Engaged?"

"No."

"Living with someone?"

I shook my head.

Joe was quiet for a few seconds, staring at me as if I were a puzzle he wanted to solve. "I'll see you later," he said eventually. "And in the meantime . . . I'm going to figure out how to get a 'yes' out of you."

~∾~ TWO ~∾~

Feeling somewhat dazed after the encounter with Joe Travis, I went to the main house and found my sister in the office. Sofia was beautiful and dark-haired, her eyes a rich hazel green. She had a curvy figure like me, but she dressed with flair, having no reservations about flaunting her hourglass shape.

"The dove handler just called back," Sofia said triumphantly. "The birds are confirmed." She gave me a concerned glance. "Your face is red. Are you dehydrated?" She handed me a bottle of water. "Here."

"I just met someone," I said after a few gulps.

"Who? What happened?"

Sofia and I were half-sisters who had been raised apart. She had lived with her mother in San Antonio, while I had lived with mine in Dallas. Although I had been aware of Sofia's existence, I hadn't met her until we were both grown. The Crosslin family tree had a few too many branches, thanks to our father Eli's five failed marriages and prolific affairs.

Eli, a handsome man with golden hair and a blinding smile, had pursued women compulsively. He had loved the emotional and sexual high of conquest. Once the excitement had faded, however, he'd never been able to settle into everyday life with one woman. For that matter, he'd never stayed with one job for more than a year or two.

There had been other children besides Sofia and me, half-siblings and innumerable stepsiblings. All of us had been abandoned by Eli, in turn. After the occasional call or visit, he would disappear for long periods, sometimes a couple of years. And then he would reappear briefly, magnetic and exciting, full of interesting stories and promises that I knew better than to believe.

The first time I met Sofia had been right after Eli had suffered a major stroke, an unexpected event for a man of his age and good physical condition. I had flown down from New York City to find an unfamiliar young woman waiting in his hospital room. Before she had even introduced herself, I had known she was one of Eli's daughters. Although her coloring—black hair, glowing amber skin—had come from her Hispanic mother's side of the family, her fine, sculpted features had unmistakably been inherited from our father.

She had given me a cautious but friendly smile. "I'm Sofia."

"Avery." I had reached out for an awkward handshake, but she'd moved forward to hug me instead, and I'd found myself reciprocating and thinking, *My sister,* with a thrill of connection I wouldn't have expected. I had looked over her shoulder at Eli in the hospital bed, hooked up to machines, and I hadn't been able to make myself let go. That had been fine with Sofia, who was never the first to end a hug.

In the vast accumulation of Eli's offspring and exes, Sofia and I were the only ones who had shown up. I didn't blame any of the others for that: I hadn't even been sure why I was there. Eli had never read me a bedtime story, or bandaged a skinned knee, or done any of the things fathers were supposed to do. In his self-absorption, there had been no attention to spare for his children. Moreover, the pain and fury of the women he'd abandoned had made it difficult to contact their children, even if he'd wanted to. Eli's usual method of ending a relationship or a marriage was to have an exit affair, cheating until he was caught and kicked out. My mother had never forgiven him for that.

But Mom had repeated the same pattern, taking up with cheaters, liars, deadbeats, men who wore their red flags on their sleeves. Among the tumult of affairs, she had married and divorced two more times. Love had brought her so little happiness, it was a wonder that she kept searching for it.

In my mother's mind, the blame lay entirely with my father, the man who had started her on the self-defeating path. As I became older, however, I wondered if the reason Mom hated Eli so much was that they were so similar. I found no small irony in the fact that she was a temp secretary, going from office to office, boss to boss. When she had been offered a permanent position at one of the companies, she had refused. It would become too monotonous, she'd said, doing the same thing every day, always seeing the same people. I had been sixteen at the time, too mouthy to resist pointing out that with that attitude, she probably wouldn't have stayed married to Eli anyway. That had provoked an argument that had nearly resulted in me getting kicked out of the house. Mom had been so infuriated by my comment that I knew I was right.

From what I'd observed, the kind of love that flared brightest also burned out the fastest. It couldn't survive after the novelty and excitement had worn off and it was time to match socks from the dryer, or vacuum the dog hair off the sofa, or organize household debris. I wanted nothing to do with that kind of love: I couldn't see the benefit. Like the slam and fade of a destructive drug, the high never lasted long enough, and the low left you empty and craving more.

As for my father, every woman he'd supposedly loved, even the ones he'd married, had been nothing more than a stop along the way to someone else. He had been a single traveler on his life's journey, and that was how it had ended. The office manager of Eli's apartment complex had found him unconscious on the floor of his living room, after he'd failed to show up to renew his lease.

Eli had been rushed to the hospital in an ambulance, but he had never regained consciousness.

"My mother's not coming," I had told Sofia as we sat together in the hospital room.

"Mine either."

We had glanced at each other in mutual understanding. Neither of us had to ask why no one else had come to say good-bye. When a man abandoned his family, the hurt of it kept bringing out the worst in them long after he'd gone.

"Why are you here?" I dared to ask.

While Sofia considered her answer, the silence was punctured by the beeps from a monitor and the ventilator's constant rhythmic *whoosh*. "My family is Mexican," she finally said. "To them, everything is about togetherness and tradition. I always wanted to belong, but I knew I was different. My cousins all had fathers, while mine was a mystery. *Mamá* would never talk about him." Her gaze went to the bed where our father lay enmeshed inside a tangle of tubes and wires that hydrated, fed, breathed, regulated, and drained. "I only saw him once, when I was a little girl and he came to visit. *Mamá* wouldn't let him talk to me, but I ran after him when he walked out to his car. He was holding some balloons he'd brought for me." She smiled absently. "I thought he was the handsomest man in the world.

He tied the ribbons around my wrist so the balloons wouldn't float away. After he drove off, I tried to bring the balloons into the house, but *Mamá* said I had to get rid of them. So I untied the ribbons and let them go, and I made a wish as I watched them float away."

"You wished that you would see him again someday," I said quietly.

Sofia nodded. "That's why I came. What about you?"

"Because I thought no one else would be here. And if someone had to take care of Eli, I didn't want it to be a total stranger."

Sofia's hand had covered mine, as naturally as if we'd known each other all our lives. "Now it's the two of us," she'd said simply.

Eli had passed away the next day. But in the process of losing him, Sofia and I had found each other.

At the time I had been working in bridal couture, but my career had been going nowhere. Sofia had been working as a nanny in San Antonio, planning children's parties on the side. We had talked about starting a wedding-planning studio together. Now, a little more than three years later, our Houston-based business was working out better than we had even dared to hope. Each small success had built on the next, allowing us to hire three employees and an intern. With the Kendrick wedding, we were on the verge of a breakthrough.

As long as we didn't screw up.

"Why didn't you say yes?" Sofia demanded after I told her about meeting Joe Travis.

"Because I don't believe for one minute that he was actually interested in me." I paused. "Oh, don't give me that look. You know that type of guy goes for trophy women."

I had been voluptuous since adolescence. I walked everywhere, took the stairs whenever possible, and went to a dance class twice a week. I ate healthy food and routinely consumed enough salad to choke a manatee. But no amount of exercise and or dieting would ever shrink me down to a single-digit dress size. Sofia often urged me to buy more body-conscious clothes, and I always told her I would do it later, when I was the right size.

"You're the right size now," Sofia would reply.

I knew that I shouldn't let a bathroom scale stand between me and happiness. Some days I won, but more often than not, the scale won.

"My grandmother always says, *'Sólo las ollas saben los hervores de su caldo.'*"

"Something about soup?" I guessed. Whenever Sofia related some of her grandmother's wisdom, it usually took the form of food analogies.

"Only pots know the boilings of their broths," Sofia said. "Maybe Joe Travis is the kind who loves a woman with a real figure. The men I knew in San Antonio always went for the women with big *pompis.*" She patted her rear end for emphasis and went to her laptop.

"What are you doing?" I asked.

"Googling him."

"Right now?"

"It will only take a minute."

"You don't have a minute—you're supposed to be working!"

Ignoring me, Sofia kept pecking at the keyboard, two-finger style.

"I don't care what you find out about him," I said. "Because I happen to be busy with this thing we've got scheduled . . . What was it? . . . Oh, yes, a wedding."

"He's hot," Sofia said, staring at her monitor. "And so is his brother."

She had clicked on a *Houston Chronicle* article headed with a photo of three men, all dressed in beautifully tailored suits. One of them was Joe, much younger and lankier than he'd been today. He must have packed on at least thirty pounds of muscle since the photo had been taken. A caption beneath the picture identified the other two as Joe's brother Jack and his father, Churchill. Both sons were a head taller than their sire, but they bore his stamp—the dark hair and intense eyes, the pronounced jawlines.

I frowned as I read the accompanying article.

HOUSTON, Texas (AP) In the aftermath of an explosion on their private boat, two sons of Houston businessman Churchill Travis tread water among fiery debris for approximately four hours as they waited for rescue. After a massive search effort by the Coast Guard, the brothers, Jack and Joseph, were located in Gulf waters off Galveston. Joseph Travis was airlifted directly to the level one trauma unit at Garner Hospital for immediate surgery. According to a hospital spokesman, his condition has been listed as critical but stable. Although details of the surgery have not been released, a source close to the family confirmed that Travis was suffering from internal bleeding as well as—

"Wait," I protested as Sofia clicked on another link. "I was still reading."

"I thought you weren't interested," she said impishly. "Here, look at this." She found a Web page labeled "Houston's Top Ten Eligible Bachelors." The article featured a candid shot of Joe playing football on the beach with friends, his body sleek and hard-looking, muscular without being muscle-bound. The expanse of dark hair on his chest narrowed to a dark line that led to the waistband of his board shorts. It was a picture of unself-conscious masculinity, off-the-charts hot.

"Six foot one," Sofia said, reading his stats. "Twenty-nine years old. Graduate of UT. A Leo. Photographer."

"Cliché," I said dismissively.

"Being a photographer is a cliché?"

"Not for an ordinary guy. But for a trust fund baby, it's a total vanity job."

"Who cares? Let's see if he has a website."

"Sofia, it's time to stop fangirling over this guy and get some work done."

A new voice entered the conversation as my assistant, Steven Cavanaugh, walked into the office. He was a good-looking man in his mid-twenties, blue-eyed and blond and lean. "Fangirling over who?" he asked.

Sofia replied before I was able. "Joe Travis," she said. "One of *the* Travises. Avery just met him."

Steven glanced at me with acute interest. "They did a story on him in CultureMap last year. He won a Key Art award for that movie poster."

"What movie poster?"

"The one for the documentary about soldiers and military dogs." Steven looked sardonic as he saw our mystified expressions. "I forgot the two of you only watch telenovelas. Joe Travis went to Afghanistan with the film crew as the stills photographer. They used one of his shots for the poster." He smiled at my expression. "You should read the paper more often, Avery. It comes in handy on occasion."

"That's what I have you for," I said.

Nothing escaped the intricate filing cabinet of Steven's mind. I envied his near total recall of details such as where someone's son had gone to college, or the name of their dog, or if they'd just had a birthday.

Among his many talents, Steven was an interior designer, a graphic design specialist, and a trained EMT. We had hired him immediately after starting Crosslin Event Design, and he had become so necessary to the business that I couldn't imagine doing without him.

"He asked Avery out," Sofia told Steven.

Giving me a dark glance, Steven asked, "What did you say?" At my silence, he turned to Sofia. "Don't tell me she shut him down."

"She shut him down," Sofia said.

"Of course." Steven's tone was arid. "Avery would never waste her time with a rich, successful guy whose name would open any door in Houston."

"Drop it," I said curtly. "We've got work to do."

"First I want to talk to you." Steven glanced at Sofia. "Do me a favor and make sure they've started setting the reception tables."

"Don't order me around."

"I wasn't ordering, I was asking."

"It didn't sound like asking."

"Please," Steven said acidly. "Pretty please, Sofia, go to the reception tent and see if they've started setting the tables."

Sofia left the room with a scowl.

I shook my head in exasperation. Sofia and Steven were cantankerous with each other, quick to take offense, slow to forgive, in a way that neither of them was with anyone else.

It hadn't started off that way. When Steven had first been hired, he and Sofia had become fast friends. He was sophisticated and meticulously groomed and had such an acid wit that Sofia and I had automatically assumed he was gay. It had been three months before we had realized that he wasn't.

"No, I'm straight," he had said in a matter-of-fact tone.

"But . . . you went clothes shopping with me," Sofia had protested.

"Because you asked me to."

"I let you into the dressing room," Sofia had continued, increasingly irate. "I tried on a dress in front of you. And you never said a word!"

"I said thank you."

"You should have told me you weren't gay!"

"I'm not gay."

"It's too late now," Sofia had snapped.

Ever since then, my sunny-natured sister had found it difficult to muster anything more than the barest degree of politeness toward Steven. And he responded in kind, his barbed comments never failing to hit the target. Only my frequent interventions kept their conflict from escalating to an all-out war.

After Sofia left, Steven closed the office door for privacy. He leaned back against it and folded his arms as he contemplated me with an unreadable expression. "Really?" he eventually asked. "You're really that insecure?"

"I'm not allowed to say no when a man asks me out?"

"When was the last time you said yes? When have you gone out for coffee, or drinks, or even had a non-work-related conversation with a guy?"

"That's none of your business."

"As your employee . . . you're right, it isn't. But at the moment I'm talking to you as a friend. You're a healthy, attractive twenty-seven-year-old woman, and as far as I know, you haven't been with anyone for over three years. For your own sake, whether it's this guy or someone else, you need to get back in the game."

"He's not my type."

"He's rich, single, and a Travis," came Steven's sardonic reply. "He's everyone's type."

By the end of the day I felt as if I'd walked the equivalent of a thousand miles, vectoring between the reception tent, the ceremony pavilion, and the main lodge. Although it seemed that everything was coming together, I knew better than to succumb to a false sense of security. Last-minute problems never failed to plague even the most meticulously planned ceremonies.

The members of the event production team worked in concert to handle any issues that cropped up. Tank Mirecki, a burly handyman, was proficient with carpentry, electronics, and mechanical repair. Ree-Ann Davis, a sassy blond assistant with a background in hotel management, had been assigned as the bride and bridesmaid handler. A brunette intern, Val Yudina, who was taking a gap year before starting at Rice, was managing the groom's family.

I used a radio earpiece and clip-on mike to stay in constant communication with Sofia and Steven. At first Sofia and I had felt silly using standard voice procedures for the hands-free radios, but Steven had insisted, saying there was no way he could tolerate both my voice and Sofia's in his ears without some rules. We had soon realized he was right; otherwise we would have constantly talked over each other.

An hour before the guests were scheduled to be seated, I went to the reception tent. The interior had been floored with eight thousand feet of rare purpleheart hardwood. It looked like a fairy tale. A dozen twenty-foot-high maple trees, each weighing half a ton, had been brought inside the tent to create a lavish forest, with a scattering of LED fireflies winking among the leaves. Strands of unpolished rock crystal hung in loops from a row of bronze chandeliers. Luxuriant live moss crossed the long tables in organically shaped runners. Each place setting had been accented with a wedding favor of Scottish honey sealed in a tiny crystal jar.

Outside, a row of ten-ton Portapac units pumped nonstop, chilling the air inside to a blissful sixty-eight degrees. I breathed deeply, relishing the coolness as I looked at my final countdown list. "Sofia," I said into my mike, "has the bagpiper arrived? Over."

"Affirmative," my sister said. "I just took him to the main lodge. There's a crafts room between the kitchen and the housekeeper's room where he can tune up. Over."

"Roger. Steven, this is Avery. I need to change my clothes. Can you handle things while I take five? Over."

"Avery, that's a negative, we've got an issue with the dove release. Over."

I frowned. "Copy that, what's going on? Over."

"There's a hawk in the oak grove next to the wedding pavilion. The dove handler says he can't release his birds with a predator in the vicinity. Over."

"Tell him we'll pay extra if one of them gets eaten. Over."

Sofia broke in. "Avery, we can't have a dove snatched from the sky and killed in front of the guests. Over."

"We're at a South Texas ranch," I said. "We'll be lucky if half the guests don't start shooting the doves. Over."

"It's against state and federal law to capture, harm, or kill a hawk," Steven said. "How do you propose we deal with it? Over."

"Is it illegal to scare the damn thing off? Over."

"I don't think so. Over."

"Then have Tank figure it out. Over."

"Avery, stand by," Sofia interrupted urgently. After a pause, she said, "I'm with Val. She says the groom has cold feet. Over."

"Is this a joke?" I asked, stunned. "Over." All through the engagement and wedding planning, the groom, Charlie Amspacher, had been rock-solid. A nice guy. In the past, some couples had given me cause to wonder if they'd make it to the altar, but Charlie and Sloane seemed to be genuinely in love.

"No joke," Sofia said. "Charlie just told Val he wants to call it off. Over."

❦ Three ❧

O *ver.* The word seemed to echo in my head.

A million dollars, wasted.

All of our careers were on the line.

And Sloane Kendrick would be devastated.

I was filled with what felt like the equivalent of a hundred shots of adrenaline. *"No one is calling this wedding off,"* I said in a murderous tone. "I will handle this. Tell Val not to let Charlie talk to anyone until I get there. *Quarantine* him, understand? Over."

"Copy. Over."

"Out."

I stalked across the grounds to the guesthouse where the groom's family was getting ready for the ceremony. I fought to keep from breaking into a run. As soon as I entered the house, I blotted my sweating face with a handful of tissues. The sounds of laughter, conversation, and clinking glasses floated from the living room of the main floor.

Val was at my side instantly. She was dressed in a pale silver-gray skirt suit, her microbraids pulled back in a controlled low bun. High-pressure situations never seemed to fluster her; in fact, she usually became even calmer in the face of emergency. As I looked into her eyes, however, I saw the signs of panic. The ice in the drink she held was rattling slightly. Whatever was happening with the groom, it was serious.

"Avery," she whispered, "thank God you're here. Charlie's trying to call it off."

"Any idea why?"

"I'm sure the best man has something to do with it."

"Wyatt Vandale?"

"Uh-huh. He's been making comments all afternoon, like how marriage is nothing but a trap, and Sloane's going to turn into a fat baby machine, and how Charlie better make sure this isn't a mistake. I can't get him out of the upstairs parlor. He's stuck to Charlie like glue."

I cursed myself for not having anticipated something like this. Charlie's best friend, Wyatt, was a spoiled brat whose family's money had afforded him the luxury of delaying adulthood for as long as possible. He was crude and obnoxious and never wasted an opportunity to demean women. Sloane despised Wyatt, but she had told me that because he had been friends with Charlie since first grade, he would have to be tolerated. Whenever she complained about Wyatt's vileness, Charlie told her that Wyatt was good at heart but tended to express himself badly. The problem was, Wyatt expressed himself perfectly.

Val handed me the glass filled with ice and amber liquid. "This is for Charlie. I know about the no-booze rule, but trust me, it's time to break it."

I took the drink from her. "All right. I'll take it to him. Charlie and I are about to have a come-to-fiery-Jesus moment. Don't let any-one interrupt."

"What about Wyatt?"

"I'll get rid of him." I gave her my headset. "Keep in touch with Sofia and Steven."

"Should I tell them we're going to start late?"

"We are going to start precisely on time," I said grimly. "If we don't, we lose the best light for the ceremony, and we also lose the dove release. Those birds have to fly back to Clear Lake, and they can't do it in the dark."

Val nodded and put on the headset, adjusting the microphone. I ascended the stairs, went to the parlor, and tapped at the partially open door. "Charlie," I asked in the calmest tone I could manage, "may I come in? It's Avery."

"Look who's here," Wyatt exclaimed as I entered the room. His expensive tux was disheveled and his black tie was missing. He was full of swagger, certain that he'd ruined Sloane Kendrick's big day. "What did I tell you, Charlie? Now she's gonna try and talk you out of it." He shot me a triumphant glance. "Too late. His mind's made up."

I glanced at the ashen-faced groom, who sat slumped on a love seat. He didn't look at all like himself.

"Wyatt," I said, "I need a moment alone with Charlie."

"He can stay," Charlie said in a subdued voice. "He's got my back."

Yes, I was tempted to say, *that knife he stuck in it sure makes a nice handle.* But instead I murmured, "Wyatt needs to get ready for the ceremony."

The best man smiled at me. "Didn't you hear? Wedding's been canceled."

"That's not your decision," I said.

"What do you care?" Wyatt asked. "You'll get paid anyway."

"I care about Charlie and Sloane. And I care about the people who've worked hard to make this a special day for them."

"Well, I've known this guy here since first grade. And I'm not gonna let him be pushed around by you and your flunkies just because Sloane Kendrick decided it was time to put a noose around his neck."

I went to Charlie and handed him the drink. He took it gratefully.

I pulled out my cell phone. "Wyatt," I said in a matter-of-fact tone as I scrolled through my contacts list, "your opinions are not relevant. This wedding is not about you. I'd like you to leave, please."

Wyatt laughed. "Who's gonna make me?"

Having found Ray Kendrick's number on my contact list, I auto-dialed him. As a former rodeo rider, Sloane's father was a breed of man who, despite cracked ribs and bruised organs, willingly climbed atop an enraged two-thousand-pound animal for a ride that was the equivalent of being whacked repeatedly between the legs with a baseball bat.

Ray answered. "Kendrick."

"It's Avery," I said. "I'm next door with Charlie. We're having an issue with his friend Wyatt."

Ray, who had been visibly annoyed with Wyatt's behavior at the rehearsal dinner, asked, "That little sumbitch trying to stir up trouble?"

"He is," I said. "And I thought you'd be the one to explain to him how to behave on Sloane's big day."

"You got that right, honey," Ray said with untrammeled enthusiasm. As I had guessed, he was more than happy to have something to do rather than stand idly in his tuxedo and make small talk. "I'll be right over to give him a talkin'-to."

"Thank you, Ray."

As I ended the call and Charlie heard the name, his eyes bulged. "Shit. Did you just call Sloane's father?"

I turned a cool stare in Wyatt's direction. "I'd get lost, if I were you," I told him. "Or in a couple of minutes there won't be enough of you left to wad a shotgun."

"Bitch." Glaring at me, Wyatt stormed from the room.

I locked the door behind him and turned to Charlie, who had gulped down his drink.

He couldn't bring himself to look at me. "Wyatt's just trying to look out for me," he mumbled.

"By sabotaging your wedding?" I pulled up a nearby ottoman and sat to face Charlie, steeling myself not to look at my watch or think about how I needed to change my clothes. "Charlie, I've seen you with Sloane from the beginning of the engagement until right now. I believe you love her. But the fact is, nothing Wyatt said would have made a bit of difference unless something was going on. So tell me what the problem is."

Charlie's gaze met mine, and he gestured helplessly as he replied, "When you think about how many couples divorce, it's crazy that anyone wants to try it in the first place. A fifty-fifty chance. What guy in his right mind would go for those odds?"

"Those are the general odds," I said. "Those aren't your odds." Seeing his bewilderment, I said, "People get married for all kinds of wrong reasons: infatuation, fear of being alone, unplanned pregnancy. Does any of that apply to you or Sloane?"

"No."

"Then when you cut those people out of the equation, your statistics are a lot better than fifty-fifty."

Charlie rubbed his forehead with an unsteady hand. "I have to tell Sloane that I need more time to be sure about all of this."

"More time?" I echoed dazedly. "The wedding ceremony is going to start in forty-five minutes."

"I'm not canceling. I'm just postponing it."

I stared at him incredulously. "Postponement isn't an option, Charlie. Sloane has planned and dreamed about this wedding for months, and her family's spent a fortune. If you call it off at the last minute, you're not going to get another chance."

"We're talking about the rest of my life," he said in rising agitation. "I don't want to make a mistake."

"God help me," I burst out. "Do you think Sloane has no room for doubt? This wedding is an act of trust on her part too. It's a risk for her too! But she's willing to take a chance because she loves you. She's going to show up at that altar. And you're *seriously* telling me that you're going to humiliate her in front of everyone you both know and make her a laughingstock? Do you understand what that's going to do to her?"

"You don't know what this is like. You've never been married." As Charlie saw my face, he paused and said uncertainly, "Have you?"

My fury faded abruptly. In the process of planning and coordinating a wedding, especially one on this scale, it was easy to forget how terrifying the process was for the two people with the most at stake.

Taking off my glasses, I shook my head. "No, I've never been married," I said, cleaning the glasses with a tissue from my bag. "I was jilted on my wedding day. Which probably makes me the worst possible person to talk to you right now."

"Hell," I heard him mutter. "I'm sorry, Avery."

I replaced the glasses and balled the tissue in my fist.

Charlie was facing a life-altering decision, and he had the look of a five-month hog on butchering day. I had to make him aware of the consequences of what he was doing. For his sake, and especially for Sloane's.

I cast a longing glance at the empty glass in Charlie's hands, wishing I could have a drink, too. Hunkering down on the ottoman, I said, "Calling off this wedding isn't just canceling a social event, Charlie. It's going to change everything. And it's going to hurt Sloane in ways you haven't considered."

He stared at me alertly, his brow furrowed. "Sure, she'll be disappointed," he began. "But–"

"Disappointment is the least of what she's going to feel," I interrupted. "And even if she still loves you after this, she won't trust you. Why should she, when you've broken your promises?"

"I haven't made any promises yet," he said.

"You asked her to marry you," I said. "That means you promised to *be there* when she walks down the aisle."

As a heavy silence descended, I realized that I was going to have to tell Charlie Amspacher about the worst day of my life. The memory was a wound that had never fully healed, and I wasn't exactly eager to rip it open for the sake of a young man I didn't really know. However, I couldn't think of any other way to make the situation clear to him.

"My wedding was supposed to happen about three and a half years ago," I said. "I was living in New York at the time, working in bridal fashion. My fiancé, Brian, did equity research on Wall Street. We'd gone out for two years, and then we lived together for another two, and at some point we started talking about getting married. I planned a small, beautiful wedding. I even flew my deadbeat dad up to New York, so he could walk me down the aisle. Everything was going to be perfect. But on the morning of the wedding, Brian left the apartment before I woke up, and called to tell me that he couldn't go through with it. He'd made a mistake. He said he thought he'd loved me, but he didn't. He wasn't sure he ever had."

"Damn," Charlie said quietly.

"People are wrong when they say that time will mend a broken heart. It doesn't always. My heart stayed broken. I've had to learn to live with it that way. I'll never be able to trust anyone who says he loves me." I paused before forcing myself to say with stark honesty, "I'm so afraid of being dumped again that I'm always the first to leave. I've broken off potential relationships because I'd rather be lonely than hurt. I don't like it, but that's who I am now."

Charlie stared at me with concern and kindness. He looked like himself again, no longer spooked. "I'm surprised you stayed in the wedding business after being jilted."

"I thought about quitting," I admitted. "But somewhere inside, I still believe in the fairy tale. Not for myself, but for other people."

"For me and Sloane?" he asked, unsmiling.

"Yes. Why not?"

Charlie turned the empty glass around in his hands. "My parents divorced when I was eight," he said. "But they never stopped trying to use my brother and me against each other. Lying, backstabbing, arguing, ruining every birthday and holiday. That's why my mom and stepdad weren't on the guest list: I knew if they were here, they'd cause all kinds of problems. How am I supposed to have a good marriage when I've never seen it done right?" His gaze lifted to mine. "I'm not asking for a fairy tale. I just need to be sure that if I get married, it won't turn into a nightmare someday."

"I can't promise you'll never get divorced," I said. "Marriage doesn't come with guarantees. It's only going to work for as long as you and Sloane both want it to. For as long as you're both willing to keep your promises." I took a deep breath. "Let me see if I've got this straight, Charlie... You haven't gotten cold feet because you don't love Sloane... you have cold feet because you *do* love her. You want to call off the wedding because you don't want the marriage to fail. Is that right?"

Charlie's face changed. "Yeah," he said in a wondering tone. "That... kind of makes me sound like an idiot, doesn't it?"

"It makes you sound a little mixed up," I said gently. "Let me ask you something... has Sloane given you any reason to doubt her? Is there something about the relationship that's not working for you?"

"Hell, no. She's terrific. Sweet, smart... I'm the luckiest guy on earth."

I was quiet, letting him work it out for himself.

"The luckiest guy on earth," he repeated slowly. "Holy shit–I'm about to screw up the best thing that ever happened to me. To hell with being scared. To hell with my parents' sorry-ass marriage. I'm going to do this."

"Then... the wedding's on?" I asked cautiously.

"It's on."

"You're sure?"

"I'm positive." Charlie met my gaze directly. "Thanks for telling me about what you went through. I know it wasn't easy for you to talk about."

"If it helped, I'm glad." As we both stood, I discovered that my legs were shaky.

Charlie looked down at me with a slight grimace. "We don't have to mention this to anyone... do we?"

"I'm like a lawyer or doctor," I assured him. "Our conversations are confidential."

He nodded and heaved a sigh of relief.

"I'm going to go now," I told him. "In the meantime, I think you should keep your distance from Wyatt and his nonsense. I know he's your friend, but frankly, he's the worst best man I've ever seen."

Charlie grinned crookedly. "I won't argue with that."

As he walked me to the door, I reflected that it took courage for him to make the commitment he was most afraid of. A kind of courage I would never have. No man would ever again have the power to let me down the way Brian had . . . the way Charlie had nearly let Sloane down just now. Feeling relieved and wrung-out, I picked up my bag.

"See you soon," Charlie called after me as I left the room and went downstairs.

I supposed it was somewhat hypocritical, having urged someone to take a chance on getting married when I had no intention of ever doing the same. But my instincts told me that Charlie and Sloane would be happy together, or at least they had as good a chance as anyone.

Val was waiting downstairs by the front door. "Well?" she asked anxiously.

"Full steam ahead," I said.

"*Thank God.*" She handed me the radio headset. "I figured you had everything under control when I saw Wyatt trying to hightail it out of here. Ray Kendrick caught him at the front doorstep. Literally gripped him by the back of the neck like a dog with a rat."

"And?"

"Mr. Kendrick dragged him off somewhere, and no one's seen hide nor hair of either of them since."

"What's happening with the dove release?"

"Tank asked Steven to help him find some ABS pipe and a barbecue igniter, and he told me to rustle up a can of hair spray." She paused. "And he sent Ree-Ann to fetch some tennis balls."

"Tennis balls? What is he—"

I was interrupted by an earsplitting whistle followed by a violent blast. We both jumped and stared at each other with wide eyes. Another blast caused Val to cover her ears with her hands. *Boom . . . boom . . .* and in the distance I heard a masculine chorus of hoots and hollers.

"Steven," I said urgently into the headset, "what's happening? Over."

"Tank says the hawk's flown off. Over."

"What the hell was that noise? Over."

There was a distinct note of enjoyment in Steven's voice. "Tank rigged up a grenade launcher and made some exploding tennis balls. He emptied out some black powder from a handful of bullet cartridges, and . . . I'll tell you the rest later. We're about to start seating. Over."

"Seating?" I echoed, looking down at my dusty, sweat-stained outfit. "Now?"

Val practically shoved me outside. "You've got to change. Go straight to the main house. Don't stop to talk to anyone!"

I raced to the lodge and entered through a kitchen filled with busy caterers. As I proceeded to the nearby crafts room, I heard a strange musical bellow, fading into something like a moan. I saw Sofia standing at a large wooden table beside an elderly man dressed in a kilt. Both of them were looking at a tartan-covered bag bristling with black pipes.

Sofia, wearing a pink fit-and-flare dress, gave me an appalled glance. "You haven't changed yet?"

"What's going on?" I asked.

"The bagpipes are broken," she said. "Don't worry. I can get a couple of musicians from the reception orchestra to play for the ceremony–"

"What do you mean they're broken?"

"Bag's leaking," came the bagpiper's glum reply. "I'll refund your deposit like we agreed in the contract."

I shook my head wildly. Sloane's mother, Judy, had set her heart on a bagpipe processional. She would be deeply disappointed with a substitution. "I don't want a refund, I want bagpipes. Where are your backups?"

"I don't have backups. Not at two thousand dollars a set."

I pointed an unsteady finger at the plaid heap on the table. "Then fix that."

"There's not enough time, and no supplies. The seam of the inner bag's come loose. It has to be sealed with heat-sensitive tape, and cured with infrared light to–*Lady, what are you doin'?*"

I had gone to the table, seized the bag, and pulled out the Gore-Tex lining with a determined tug. The pipes moaned like an eviscerated beast. Digging into my handbag, I found a role of silver duct tape, pulled it out, and tossed it to Sofia. She caught it in midair. "Patch it," I said tersely. Ignoring the bagpiper's howls of protest, I raced off to the housekeeper's supply room, where I had hung a black top and midcalf skirt on a closet door. The top had slipped from the hanger to the dirty floor. Picking up the garment, I saw to my horror that a couple of ugly grease splotches had soaked into the front.

Swearing, I searched through my bag for antibacterial wipes and a fabric-cleaning pen. I tried to remove the stains, but the more I worked on them, the worse the top looked.

"Do you need help?" I heard Sofia ask in a couple of minutes.

"Come in," I said, my voice strung with frustration.

Sofia entered the supply room and took in the scene with a dis-believing gaze. "This is bad," she said.

"The skirt is fine," I said. "I'll wear it with the top I've got on now."

"You can't," Sofia said flatly. "You've been out in the heat for hours. That top is filthy, and there are sweat stains halfway down your sides."

"What do you suggest I do?" I snapped.

"Take the top I was wearing earlier. I've been in the air-conditioning for most of the day, and it still looks fine."

"That top won't fit me," I protested.

"Yes, it will. We're almost the same size, and it's a wrap top. *Hurry,* Avery."

Clumsy with haste, I took off my dusty pants and top and scoured myself with a handful of antibacterial towelettes. With Sofia's help, I changed into the black skirt and the borrowed top, a stretchy ivory blouse with three-quarter-length sleeves. Since my proportions were more generous than Sofia's, the V neckline that had been relatively modest on her was a definite plunge on me.

"I'm showing cleavage," I said indignantly, tugging the sides of the top closer together.

"Yes. And you look twenty pounds thinner." Busily, she yanked the pins from my hair.

"Hey, stop that—"

"Your updo was a mess. There's no time for a new one. Just leave it loose."

"I look like an alpaca in a lightning storm." I tried to flatten the wild mass of curls with my hands. "And this top is too tight, I'm all bound up—"

"You're just not used to wearing something that fits. You look fine."

I gave her a tortured glance and picked up my headset. "Have you checked in with Steven?"

"Yes. Everything's under control. The ushers are seating the guests, and the dove handler is ready with the birds. And Sloane and the bridesmaids are all set. Go. I'll bring the bagpiper as soon as you give me the okay."

By some miracle, the ceremony started on time. And the wedding unfolded more perfectly than Sofia or I could have imagined. Lavish arrangements of thistle, roses, and field flowers had been wrapped around every column of the pavilion. The bagpipe processional established a solemn but electrifying tone for the bridal party's entrance.

As Sloane proceeded along the flower-strewn aisle runner, she looked like a princess in her white lace gown. Charlie looked entirely happy as he stared at his bride. No one could have doubted that he was a man in love.

I doubted anyone even noticed the sullen scowl on the best man's face.

After the vows were exchanged, a flock of white pigeons burst into flight and soared through the coral-glazed sky in a moment so picturesque that the entire congregation let out a collective breath.

"Hallelujah," I heard Sofia whisper in the earpiece, and I grinned.

Much later, while the guests danced to orchestra music in the reception tent, I stood in a quiet corner and spoke to Steven on the headset. "I see a potential carry-off," I said quietly. "Over." On occasion, we had to perform a discreet assisted removal for guests who'd had too much to drink. The best way to avoid problems was to catch them early.

"I see him," Steven replied. "I'll have Ree-Ann handle it. Over."

Aware of a woman approaching, I turned and smiled automatically. She was whippet-thin and elegant in a beaded panel-construction dress. Her blond bob was perfectly highlighted with a bar code of platinum streaks.

"Can I help you?" I asked with a smile.

"You're the one who planned this wedding?"

"Yes, along with my sister. I'm Avery Crosslin."

She sipped from a glass of champagne, her hand weighted with an emerald the size of an ashtray. Noticing that my gaze had flickered to the beveled square-cut gem, she said, "My husband gave it to me for my forty-fifth birthday. A carat for each year."

"It's remarkable."

"They say emeralds bestow the power to predict the future."

"Does yours?" I asked.

"Let's say the future generally happens the way I want it to." She took another dainty sip. "This turned out nice," she murmured, surveying the scene. "Fancy, but not too formal. Imaginative. Most weddings I've been to this year have all looked the same." She paused. "People are already saying this was the best wedding they've been to in years. But it's only the second best."

"What's the best wedding?" I asked.

"The one you're going to do for my daughter, Bethany. The wedding of the decade. The governor and an ex-president will be attending." Her lips curved in a slender, catlike smile. "I'm Hollis Warner. And your career's just been made."

~ Four ~

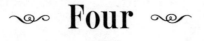

A s Hollis Warner sauntered away, Steven's voice came through my earpiece.

"Her husband is David Warner. He inherited a restaurant business and parlayed it into casino resorts. Their fortune is obscene even by Houston standards. Over."

"Do they–"

"Later. You've got company. Over."

Blinking, I turned to see Joe Travis approaching. The sight of him kicked my heart into a drumfire rhythm. He was dazzling in a classic tux, wearing it with unself-conscious ease. The white edge of his collar formed a crisp contrast to an amber tan that seemed to go several layers deep, as if he'd been steeped in sun.

He smiled at me. "I like your hair down like that."

Self-consciously, I reached up to try to flatten it. "It's too curly."

"For God's sake," I heard Steven's acid voice in the earpiece. "When a man gives you a compliment, don't argue with him. Over."

"Can you take a break for a few minutes?" Joe asked.

"I probably shouldn't–," I began, and I heard both Steven's and Sofia's voices at the same time.

"Yes, you should!"

"Tell him yes!"

I yanked off the earpiece and mike. "I don't usually take a break during the reception," I told Joe. "I need to keep an eye on things in case anyone has a problem."

"I have a problem," he said promptly. "I need a dance partner."

"There are a half-dozen bridesmaids here who would love to dance with you," I said. "Individually or collectively."

"None of them has red hair."

"Is that a requirement?"

"Let's call it a strong preference." Joe reached for my hand. "Come on. They can do without you for a few minutes."

I flushed and hesitated. "My bag..." I glanced at the bulk of it wedged beneath the chair. "I can't just–"

"I'll watch over it," came Sofia's cheerful voice. She had appeared out of nowhere. "Go have fun."

"Joe Travis," I said, "this is my sister Sofia. She's single. Maybe you should–"

"Take her away," Sofia told him, and they exchanged a grin.

Ignoring the dirty look I gave her, Sofia murmured something into her radio mike.

Joe kept possession of my hand, pulling me past tables and potted trees until we'd reached a semisecluded area at the other side of the reception tent. He signaled a waiter who was holding a tray of iced champagne.

"I'm supposed to be running things," I said. "I have to stay vigilant. Anything could happen. Someone could have a heart attack. The tent could catch on fire."

After taking two glasses of champagne from the waiter, Joe handed one to me and retained the other. "Even General Patton took a break sometimes," he said. "Relax, Avery."

"I'll try." I held the crystal flute by the stem, its contents shimmering with tiny bubbles.

"To your beautiful brown eyes," he said, lifting his glass

I flushed. "Thank you." We clinked glasses and drank. The champagne was dry and delicious, the chilled fizz like starlight on my tongue.

My view of the dance floor was obstructed by orchestra instruments, speakers, and ornamental trees. However, I thought I caught sight of Hollis Warner's distinctive white-blond bob in the milling crowd.

"Do you happen to know Hollis Warner?" I asked.

Joe nodded. "She's a friend of the family. And last year I took pictures of her house for a magazine feature. Why?"

"I just met her. She was interested in discussing ideas for her daughter's wedding."

He gave me an alert glance. "Who's Bethany engaged to?"

"I have no idea."

"Bethany's been going out with my cousin Ryan. But last time I saw him, he was planning to break up with her."

"Maybe his feelings went deeper than he thought."

"From what Ryan said, that doesn't seem likely."

"If I wanted to land Hollis as a client, what advice would you give me?"

"Wear garlic." He smiled at my expression. "But if you handle her right, she'd be a good client. What Hollis would spend on a wedding could probably buy Ecuador." He looked at my champagne glass. "Would you like another?"

"No, thanks."

He drained his own glass, took mine, and went to set them on a nearby busing tray.

"Why don't you do weddings?" I asked when he returned.

"It's the hardest job in photography, except for maybe working in a war zone." He smiled wryly. "When I was starting out, I managed to land a position as a staff photographer for a West Texas quarterly. *Modern Cattleman*. It's not easy trying to get an ornery bull to pose for a picture. But I'd still rather shoot livestock than weddings."

I laughed. "When did you first take up photography?"

"I was ten. My mom sneaked me off to a class every Saturday, and told my dad I was working out to get ready for Pop Warner football."

"He didn't approve of photography?"

Joe shook his head. "He had definite ideas about how his sons should spend their time. Football, 4-H, working outside, all that was fine. But art, music . . . that was taking it too far. And he thought of photography as a hobby, but nothing a man should try to make a career of."

"But you proved him wrong," I said.

His smile turned rueful. "It took a while. There were a couple of years we weren't exactly on speaking terms." He paused. "Later it worked out that I had to stay with Dad for a couple of months. That was when we finally made our peace with each other."

"When you stayed with him, was it . . ." I hesitated.

His head bent over mine. "Go on."

"Was it because of the boat accident?" Seeing his quizzical smile, I said uncomfortably, "My sister looked you up on the Internet."

"Yeah, it was after that. When I got out of the hospital, I had to stay with someone while I healed up. Dad was living by himself in River Oaks, so it made the most sense for me to go there."

"Is it hard for you to talk about the accident?"

"Not at all."

"Can I ask how it happened?"

"I was fishing with my brother Jack in the Gulf. We were heading back to the marina at Galveston, stopped near a seaweed mat, and managed to hook a dorado. While my brother was reeling it in, I started the engine so we could follow the fish. Next thing I knew, I was in the water and there was fire and debris everywhere."

"My God. What caused the explosion?"

"We're pretty sure the bilge blower malfunctioned, and fumes built up near the engine."

"That's awful," I said. "I'm so sorry."

"Yeah. That dorado was a five footer at least." He paused, his gaze flickering to my mouth as I smiled.

"What kind of injuries–" I broke off. "Never mind, it's not my business."

"Blast lung, it's called. When the shock waves from an explosion bruise the chest and lungs. For a while I couldn't work up enough air to fill a party balloon."

"You look pretty healthy now," I said.

"One hundred percent." A wicked glint entered his eyes as he observed my reaction. "Now that you're all sympathetic . . . come dance with me."

I shook my head. "I'm not *that* sympathetic." With an apologetic smile, I explained, "I never dance at an event I've planned. It's sort of like a waitress seating herself at a table she's supposed to be serving."

"I had two operations for internal bleeding while I was in the hospital," Joe informed me gravely. "For almost a week, I couldn't eat or talk because of the ventilator tube." He gave me a hopeful glance. "Now do you feel sorry enough to dance with me?"

I shook my head again.

"Also," Joe said, "the accident happened on my birthday."

"It did not."

"It did."

I lifted my gaze heavenward. "That's so sad. That's . . ." I paused, fighting my better instincts. "Okay," I found myself saying. "One dance."

"I knew the birthday would do it," he said in satisfaction.

"A *quick* dance. In the corner, where as few people as possible can see."

Joe took my hand in a warm grip. He led me past sparkling groves of potted trees and palms, back to a shadowy corner behind the orchestra. A sly, jazzy version of "They Can't Take That Away from Me" floated through the air. The female singer's voice had an appealing rough-sweet edge, like broken candy.

Joe turned me to face him and took me in a practiced hold, one hand at my waist. So this would be a real dance, not a side-to-side sway. Tentatively, I placed my left hand on his shoulder. He pulled me into a smooth pattern, his movements so assured that there could be no doubt about who was leading. As he lifted my hand to guide me into a twirl, I followed so easily that we didn't miss a step. I heard his low laugh, a sound of pleasure at discovering a well-matched partner.

"What else are you good at?" he asked near my ear. "Besides dancing and wedding planning."

"That's about it." After a moment, I volunteered, "I can tie balloon animals. And I can whistle with my fingers."

I felt the shape of his smile against my ear.

My glasses had slipped down my nose, and I briefly broke our hold to push them back up to the bridge. I made a mental note to have the earpieces adjusted as soon as I got back to Houston. "What about you?" I asked. "Do you have any hidden talents?"

"I can scissor dribble a basketball. And I know the entire NATO phonetic alphabet."

"You mean like Alfa, Bravo, Charlie?"

"Exactly."

"How did you learn it?"

"Scouting badge."

"Spell my name," I commanded, testing him.

"Alfa-Victor-Echo-Romeo-Yankee." He twirled me again.

It seemed the air had turned into champagne, every breath filled with free-floating giddiness.

My glasses slipped again, and I began to adjust them. "Avery," he said gently, "let me hold those for you. I'll keep them in my pocket until we're done."

"I won't be able to see where we're going."

"But I will." Carefully he drew the glasses from my face, folded them, and slipped them into the breast pocket of his tux. The room turned into a blur of glitter and shadow. I didn't understand myself, why I had surrendered control to him so easily. I stood there blind and exposed, my heart beating like a hummingbird's wings.

Joe's arms went around me. He took me in the same hold as before, except now we were closer, our steps intimately constrained. This time he no longer followed the orchestra rhythm, only settled into a slow, relaxed pace.

As I breathed in the scent of him, burnished with sun and salt, I was confounded by the yearning to press my mouth against his neck, taste him.

"You're nearsighted," I heard him say on a questioning note.

I nodded. "You're the only thing I can see."

He looked down at me, our noses nearly touching. "Good." The word was scratchy-soft, like a cat's tongue.

My breath caught. I turned my face away deliberately. I had to break the spell, or I was going to do something I would regret.

"Get ready," I heard him say. "I'm going to dip you."

I clutched at him. "Don't, you'll drop me."

"I'm not going to drop you." He sounded amused.

I stiffened as I felt his hand slide to the center of my back. "I'm serious. Joe–"

"Trust me."

"I don't think–"

"Here we go." He lowered me backward, supporting me securely. My head tipped back, my vision filled with the twinkling firefly lights entwined in the tree branches. I gasped as he pulled me upright with astonishing ease.

"Oh! You're strong."

"It has nothing to do with strength. It's knowing how to do it." Joe caught me against him, closer than before. Now we were matched front to front. The moment was charged with something I'd never felt before, a soft voltaic heat. I was quiet, unable to make a sound if my life had depended on it. I closed my eyes. My senses were busy gathering him in, the hard strength of his body, the caress of his breath against my ear.

All too soon, the song ended with a bittersweet flourish. Joe's arms tightened. "Not yet," he murmured. "One more."

"I shouldn't."

"Yes, you should." He kept me against him.

Another song started, the notes flaring softly. "What a Wonderful World" was a wedding staple. I'd heard it about a thousand times, interpreted every way imaginable. But every now and then an old song could pierce your heart as if you were hearing it for the first time.

As we danced, I tried to gather every passing second for safekeeping, like pennies in a Mason jar. But soon I lost track, and there was only the two of us, wrapped in music and dream-colored darkness. Joe's hand covered mine, and he pulled my arm around his neck. When I didn't resist, he reached for my other wrist and pulled that one up, too.

I had no idea what song played next. We stood locked in a subtle sway with my arms linked around his neck. I let my fingers drift over the nape of his neck, where the thick hair was tapered in close layers. A feeling of unreality swept over me, and my imagination kept veering in the wrong directions. . . . I wondered what he would be like in intimacy, the ways he might move and breathe and tremble.

His head lowered until his jaw grazed my cheek, the touch of shaven bristle delicious.

"I have to work," I managed to say. "What . . . what time is it?"

I felt him lift his arm behind me, but apparently it was too dark to read his watch. "Must be close to midnight," he said.

"I have to set up the after-party."

"Where?"

"The swimming pool patio."

"I'll go with you."

"No, you'll distract me." Realizing my arms were still linked around his neck, I began to pull free.

"Probably." Joe caught one of my wrists and turned his mouth to the inside of my wrist. A shock of sweetness went through me as I felt his lips touch the thin, tender skin, grazing the frantic thrum of a pulse. From inside his pocket, he withdrew my glasses and gave them back to me.

I couldn't stop staring at him. There was a crescent mark on the left side of his jaw, a thin white line amid the shadow of shaven bristle. And another mark near the outward corner of his left eye, a subtle parenthetical scar. Somehow the tiny imperfections made him even sexier.

I wanted to touch the marks with my fingertips. I wanted to kiss them. But the desire was hemmed by the instinctive knowledge that this wasn't a man I could ever be casual about. When you fell for a man like this, it would be an all-consuming bonfire. And afterward, your heart would resemble the contents of an ashtray.

"I'll meet you when you finish setting up," Joe told me.

"It may take a long time. I don't want you to wait."

"I've got all night." His voice was soft. "And you're how I want to spend it."

Desperately, I tried not to feel so flattered and overwhelmed. And I hurried away with the sense that I was running through a mine-field.

Five

W ell?" Sofia asked, removing her radio mike as I reached her. How could she look so relaxed? How could everything seem normal when it was the opposite of normal?

"We danced," I said distractedly. "Where's my bag? What time is it?"

"Eleven twenty-three. Your bag is right here. Steven and Val have already started the setup for the after-party. Tank helped the live band with all their speakers and power cords. Ree-Ann and the caterers are working on the pie buffet and the wine and coffee service. And the waitstaff is about to begin the reception cleanup."

"Everything's on schedule, then."

"You don't have to sound so surprised." Sofia smiled. "Where is Joe? Did you have a good time dancing?"

"Yes." I picked up my bag, which seemed to weigh a thousand pounds.

"Why do you look nervous?"

"He wants to meet me later."

"Tonight? That's wonderful." At my silence, Sofia asked, "Do you like him?"

"He's . . . well, he's . . ." I paused, floundering. "I can't figure out the angle."

"What angle?"

"Why he's pretending to be interested in me."

"Why do you think he's pretending?"

I scowled. "Come on, Sofia. Do I look like the kind of woman that a man like Joe Travis would go for? Does that even make sense?"

"*Ay, chinga.*" Sofia did a face palm. "A big, sexy man wants to spend time with you. This is not a problem, Avery. Stop worrying."

"People do stupid things at weddings–" I began.

"Yes. Go be one of them."

"My God. You give the worst advice."

"Then don't ask me for it."

"I didn't!"

Sofia regarded me with fond concern. A sisterly gaze. "*Mija.* You know how people always say 'You'll find someone when you stop looking'?"

"Yes."

"I think you've gotten too good at not looking. You've decided not to look even if the right man happens to be standing right in front of you." Taking my shoulders, she turned me around and gave me a little push. "Go on. Don't worry if it's a mistake. Most mistakes turn out okay."

"The *worst* advice," I repeated darkly, and left her.

I knew that Sofia was right: I had developed some bad habits since my catastrophic engagement. Solitude, avoidance, suspicion. But those coping mechanisms had warded off a hell of a lot of pain and damage. It wouldn't be easy to get rid of them, even if I wanted to.

By the time I reached the swimming pool patio, a couple of the bridesmaids had already changed into bikinis and were laughing and splashing in the pool. Noticing that no towels had been set out, I went to Val, who was arranging lounge furniture. "Towels?" I asked.

"Tank is assembling the towel stand."

"That should have been done earlier."

"I know. Sorry." Val made a little grimace. "He said he'll have it out here in ten minutes. We didn't expect anyone to be in the pool this early."

"It's fine. For now, go get a half-dozen towels and set them out on the lounge chairs."

She nodded and began to leave.

"Val," I said.

Pausing, she gave me an inquiring glance.

"It looks great out here," I said. "Terrific job."

A smile lit her face, and she went in search of the towels.

I went to the long table where the pie-and-coffee buffet had been artfully arranged, with a trio of white-jacketed servers lined up behind it. Three-level French wire stands held gold-crusted pies of every flavor imaginable...caramel apple, glazed peach, dense slabs of buttermilk custard, strawberries mounded over lofty cushions of cream cheese.

Nearby, Steven separated stacks of chairs and arranged them around cloth-draped tables in the adjoining courtyard. I approached him, raising my voice to be heard over the band. "What can I do?"

"Nothing." Steven smiled. "All under control."

"Any sign of scorpions?"

He shook his head. "We saturated the perimeter of the patio and courtyard with citrus oil." He gave me an intent glance. "How's it going with you?"

"Fine. Why?"

"Glad to see you took my advice. About getting back in the game."

I frowned. "I'm not back in the game. I danced with someone, that's all."

"It's progress," he said laconically, and went for another stack of chairs.

When the setup was complete and guests were lining up at the pie buffet, I caught sight of a man sitting at one of the tables near the pool. It was Joe, relaxed and casual, the black tie hanging on either side of his neck. Giving me an expectant glance, he lifted a plate invitingly.

I went to him. "What flavor is that?" I asked, looking at the perfect wedge of pie, topped with a thick layer of meringue.

"Lemon icebox," he said. "I have two forks. Want to share?"

"I suppose as long as we sit way back in the courtyard, off to the side—"

"Where no one can see," Joe finished for me, a sparkle of amusement in his eyes. "Are you trying to hide me, Avery? Because I'm starting to feel cheap."

I couldn't help laughing. "Of all the adjectives I might use for you, 'cheap' is not one of them."

He followed me, plate in hand, as I went into the courtyard and headed to a far-off table. "What adjectives would you use?" he asked from behind me.

"Are you fishing for compliments?"

"A little encouragement never hurts." He set down the plate and pulled out a chair to seat me.

"Since I'm not available," I said, "I have no intention of encouraging you. Although if I did . . . I'd say you were charming."

He handed me a fork, and we both dug into the slice of pie. The first bite was so good, I closed my eyes to focus on it. A foamy mantle of meringue collapsed on my tongue, followed by a rich filling infused with saliva-spiking tartness. "This pie," I said, "tastes like one lemon fell in love with another lemon."

"Or three lemons had a ménage." Joe grinned at my mock-reproving glance. "Usually it's never sour enough for my taste," he said, "but this is about right."

When there was one bite of pie left, Joe picked up my fork and fed me the last morsel. To my astonishment, I opened my mouth and let him. The gesture was at once casual and oddly intimate. I chewed and swallowed with difficulty, my cheeks turning hot.

"I need something to drink," I said, and at that very moment someone approached our table.

It was Sofia, carrying two wineglasses and a bottle of chilled white Bordeaux. Setting them on the table, she said brightly, "Steven said to tell you we've got everything covered, so you can take off now."

I frowned. "I'm the one who decides if I can take off, not Steven."

"You've had less sleep than any of us—"

"I'm not tired."

"—and there's nothing left except to manage the cleanup crew. We can do that without you. Have a drink and enjoy yourself." Sofia left before I could reply.

I shook my head as I watched her go. "I'm not as irrelevant as they seem to think." Relaxing back in my chair, I said, "However... they did well today. And they probably can manage the cleanup without me." I stared up at the sky, where the mottled white band of the Milky Way glowed against the plenitude of stars. "Look at that," I said. "You can't see that from a city."

Gesturing with his glass, Joe said, "See the dark lane running along the center?"

I shook my head.

He moved his chair closer and pointed with his free hand. "There, where it looks like someone scribbled through it with a Sharpie."

Following the line of his arm, I saw the ragged stripe. "Yes. What is that?"

"It's the Great Rift, a big cloud of molecular dust . . . a place where new stars are forming."

I stared in wonder. "Why haven't I seen it before?"

"You have to be in the right place at the right time."

We glanced at each other with a shared smile. The wash of star-light had turned the little crescent scar on his jaw a faint silver. I wanted to trace it with my fingertip. I wanted to touch his face and stroke the hard contours of his features.

I picked up my wineglass. "I'm going to turn in after I finish this," I said, drinking deeply. "I'm beat."

"Are you staying at the ranch, or at one of the hotels in town?"

"Here. There's a little cabin along the drive to the back pasture. The trapper's cabin, they call it." I made a face. "There's a stuffed coon on the mantel. Hideous. I had to put a pillowcase over it."

He smiled. "I'll walk you over."

I hesitated. "Okay."

The conversation turned quiet, halting, as I drank the rest of my wine. It seemed as if some secondary, unspoken dialogue were fill-ing up the space between the words.

Eventually, we stood and left the bottle and two empty glasses on the table.

As we walked on the side of the paved drive, Joe said, "I'd like to see you again, Avery."

"That's . . . well, I'm flattered. Thank you. But I can't."

"Why not?"

"I've enjoyed your company. Let's leave it at that."

Joe was silent the rest of the way to the cabin. Our pace was lei-surely, but my thoughts raced, my brain cataloging a jumble of ideas about how to keep him at a distance.

We stopped at the front door. While I fumbled in my bag for the key, Joe spoke quietly. "Avery . . . I don't mean to presume. But I know what it feels like to want someone who doesn't want me back." A long pause. "And I don't think that's the case here."

Shaken, I managed to say, "I'm sorry for whatever I've said or done to give you that impression."

"Then I'm wrong?" he asked gently.

"It's . . . no . . . but it's a matter of timing."

Joe didn't react, didn't appear to believe that, and Jesus, why should he? Why would anyone? He was like something from a dream as he stood there in a wash of moonlight, sexy in his rumpled tux, his eyes midnight dark.

"Can we talk about it for a minute?" he asked.

Reluctantly, I nodded and opened the door.

It was a one-room cabin, designery rustic with a handwoven rug and leather furniture and modern light fixtures that looked like crys-tal antlers. I flipped on a switch that illuminated a sconce in the cor-ner and set down my bag. Turning to face Joe, I saw him standing with his shoulder braced against the doorjamb. His lips parted as if he were about to say something, but he appeared to think better of it.

"What?" I asked in a hushed voice.

"I know there are rules for this. I know I'm supposed to play it cool." A rueful smile touched his lips. "But to hell with it. The fact is, I liked you the first moment I saw you. You are a beautiful, interesting woman, and I want to see you again." His tone softened. "You can say yes to that, can't you?" Seeing my uncertainty, he murmured, "Pick the time and place. I promise you won't regret it."

Pushing away from the door, Joe approached me without haste. My heart began to work in sharp jolts, and I went hot and cold with nerves. It had been too long since I had been alone with a man in a bedroom.

Studying me intently, Joe touched the side of my face, his hand curving beneath my jaw. I knew he could feel the way I was trembling.

"Should I leave?" he asked, and began to draw back.

"No." Before I could stop myself, I caught his wrist. A few minutes earlier, I'd been calculating how to push him away, and now the only thing I could think about was how to make him stay. My fingers curved around the thickness of bone and sinew, the strong rhythm of his pulse.

I wanted him. Every part of me wanted him. We were alone, and the rest of the world was far away, and I knew somehow that if I slept with him, it would be extraordinary.

To a woman who'd lived twenty-seven years of ordinary, one night with a man like this didn't seem too much to ask.

I pulled his hand to my waist, and I stood on my toes, deliberately molding my body against his, and he was warm and sturdy, his arms anchoring me firmly. He began to kiss me slow and deep, as if the world were about to end, as if it were the last minute of the last hour of the last day. The things he did with his mouth, his tongue . . . it was like a conversation, like sex, the way he found what I wanted and gave it to me. There was more pleasure in that kiss than in any act of physical intimacy I had ever known.

After drawing his mouth away, Joe cupped my head to his shoul-

der. We stayed like that for a hard-breathing minute. I was dismantled, everything inside me thrown into chaos. All I knew was that I
had to be close to him, I had to feel his skin. I grasped the lapels of
his tux jacket, pushing them back. He stripped off the garment and
dropped it to the floor. Without hesitation, he gripped my head back
and his mouth found mine again, ardent and intent, as if he were
feeding on something delicious. Somewhere in the midst of all those
kisses, he reached down to my bottom, cinching me closer against
a ridge of hard, impatient flesh. The need sharpened until it seemed
I would die of not having him. Nothing had ever felt like this. Nothing ever would again.

You had to run with a feeling like that, all the way to sunrise.

"Take me to bed," I whispered.

I heard a quick, rough-sawn breath, and I sensed the conflict of
desire and indecision.

"It's okay," I said anxiously. "I know what I'm doing, I want you
to stay—"

"You don't have to—" he began.

"Yes. I have to." I kissed him again, excitement pulsing through
me. "You have to," I whispered against his lips.

Joe responded voraciously, caught up in the heat just as I was, his
hold on me changing as he sought to make the fit between us even
closer, tighter. After a while he began to undress me, and himself,
clothes littering the floor in a trail to the bed. The light was switched
off, the darkness relieved only by the starlight sifting through the
mesh of the window blinds.

I pulled back the covers and lay on the mattress, shaking from
head to toe. He lowered over me, the feel of hair-roughened limbs
stimulating my skin into excruciating sensitivity. I felt the hot whisk
of his breath against my throat.

"Tell me if you want to stop," I heard him say hoarsely. "No matter what, I'll stop if you decide—"

"I know."

"I want you to understand—"

"I understand." I pulled him down to me.

Nothing was real in that quiet room. Things were being done to me, and by me, in an ecstasy of sexual greed that I knew I would be shamed by later. His mouth was at my breast, his tongue articulating delicate circles until the tip budded, and he began to lap and tug until the pleasure went singing to the quick of my body. I gripped his shoulders, the tough muscle of his back, massaging blindly.

Skilled and sure, his fingers teased along the insides of my thighs, coaxing them to part. The pad of his thumb brushed a place so tender that I cried out, my hips lifting. His finger slid inside me, caressing deep into a frantic wet pulse. My body tightened to hold the sensation, drawing the pleasure inward.

His weight slid over me, his legs spreading mine, and I gasped out a few words . . . we had no protection, we needed to use something . . . He reassured me with a hoarse murmur, reaching over to the bedside table for his wallet, which I hadn't even been aware of him setting there. I heard the rip of a plastic packet. Momentarily distracted, I wondered when that had happened, how he had managed—

My thoughts imploded as I felt the pressure of him working slowly, circling intimately. He entered me in a low, thick slide, sensation blooming within sensation, hot and sweet and maddening. A cry stirred in my throat.

Joe nuzzled at my ear. "Shhhh . . ." He slid an arm beneath my hips, pulling them high. Every thrust was a full-bodied caress, the hair on his chest teasing my breasts. I'd never felt so much at once, raw sensation eliding the spaces between every heartbeat and breath until I was blind and silent. The release wrung pleasure from every muscle, tightening until I shuddered in long, liquescent spasms. Joe held me tightly, breathing in rough gasps as he reached the pinnacle. He kissed my neck and shoulders, his hands moving over me gently. His fingers traversed my stomach, down between my legs to the verge of our joined flesh, and I felt him caressing intimately, teasing around the small centered ache. Moaning in astonishment, I sank into an erotic darkness where there was no thought, no past, no future, only pleasure that made me twist in helpless ecstasy.

∾

I awakened alone in the morning, aware of the slight aches left by another body's intrusion into mine, the faint whisker burns on skin that had been kissed and kissed, the tender pull of inner thighs.

I wasn't sure what to think about what I'd done.

Joe had said little when he'd left, other than the obligatory, "I'll call you." A promise that no one ever kept.

I reminded myself that I had the right to sleep with someone if I wanted to, even a stranger. No judgments were necessary. No one had to feel bad.

Still . . . I felt as if something had been taken from me, and I didn't know what it was or how to regain it. I felt as if I would never be the same again.

Letting out a shuddering sigh, I used the bedsheet to blot my eyes as tears threatened to well up.

I pressed hard against my eyes. "You're okay," I whispered aloud. "Everything's okay."

As I huddled back into the damp pillow, I remembered how, when

I was in grade school, we had studied butterflies for a science project. Samples of a butterfly's wing under a microscope had revealed that it was covered with tiny scales like feathers or roof shingles.

If you touched a butterfly's wing, the teacher had said, it would knock off some of the scales and they would never grow back. Some butterflies had clear patches on their wings where you could see right through the membrane. But even with some lost scales, a butterfly would still be able to fly after you let it go.

It would get along just fine.

Six

During the long drive home, Sofia and I talked about the wedding and rehashed every detail. I did my best to keep the mood light, forcing myself to laugh from time to time. When Sofia asked casually if anything had happened with Joe Travis, I replied, "No, but I gave him my number. He might call sometime." I could tell by her quick, speculative glance that she didn't entirely believe me.

After Sofia plugged her phone into the car audio and started a jaunty Tejano song, I let myself think about the previous night and tried to figure out why I felt so guilty and worried. Probably because having a one-night stand was so unlike me ... except that since I'd done it, it *was* like me.

The new me.

Feeling a stirring of panic, I pushed it back down.

I thought back to when I'd first met Brian, trying to remember how long I'd waited until sleeping with him. Two months, at least. I had been cautious about intimacy, having no desire to career from one man to the next the way my mother had. Sex would be on my terms, within the margins that I established. Brian had been fine with that, patient, willing to wait until I was ready.

We had been introduced by mutual friends at a cocktail party held in the outdoor sculpture garden at the Met. We had been instantly comfortable with each other, so naturally in tune that our friends had laughingly accused us of already knowing each other. We'd both been twenty-one at the time, full of ambition and energy, both of us having just moved from other places, me from Dallas, Brian from Boston.

It had been the happiest time of my life, that first year in New York, a city that had infused me with the perpetual feeling that something great, or at least interesting, was just around the corner. Having been accustomed to the lazy, sunstruck pace of Texas, where the heat forced everyone to ration their energy, I had been galvanized by Manhattan's cool autumn vitality. *You belong here,* the city seemed to say, with the honking of canary-colored taxicabs and the screeching and grinding of construction equipment, the sounds of street musicians and bars and rattling subways . . . all of it meant that I was in a place where things were happening.

It had been easy to find friends, a group of women who filled their spare time with volunteer work, clubs, lessons in things like foreign languages, dancing, tennis. The Manhattanite's passion for self-improvement had been contagious—soon I'd found myself signing up for clubs and lessons, trying to make every minute of the day purposeful.

In retrospect, I had to wonder how much of my falling in love with New York had been the adjuvant to falling in love with Brian. Had I met Brian in another place, I wasn't certain that we would have lasted as long as we had. He had been a good lover, considerate in bed, but his Wall Street job had entailed sixteen-hour workdays and preoccupations with things such as the upcoming nonfarm payroll numbers or what was happening on Bloomberg at one A.M. It had made him perpetually tired and distracted. He had used alcohol to relieve the stress, and that hadn't exactly helped our love life. But even at the beginning of our relationship, I had never experienced anything with Brian that even remotely resembled what had happened last night.

I had been like an entirely different person with Joe. But I wasn't ready to be someone new—I'd grown too accustomed to being the woman Brian Palomer had jilted at the altar. If I let go of that identity, I wasn't sure what would happen. I was afraid to imagine the possibilities. All I knew was that no man would ever hurt me the way Brian had, and I was the only one who could protect myself from that.

⌒ᕲ⌒

Later that night, as I sat in bed reading, my cell phone rang and vibrated on the nightstand.

I stopped breathing as I saw Joe's caller ID.

My God. He'd meant it when he'd said he would call.

My heart throbbed against a painful tightness, as if it had been wrapped in a million rubber bands. Covering my ears with my hands, closing my eyes, I didn't respond to the insistent ringtone. I waited it out. I couldn't talk to him—I wouldn't know what in the hell to say. I knew him in the most intimate way possible, yet I didn't know him at all.

As wildly pleasurable as it had been to sleep with Joe, I didn't want it to happen again. I didn't have to have a reason, did I? No. I didn't owe him any explanations. I didn't even have to explain it to myself.

The phone went silent. The tiny screen flashed a message that a voice mail had been left.

Ignore it, I told myself. I picked up the book I'd been reading and focused blindly on a page. After a couple of minutes, I realized that I'd read the same page three times without comprehending a word.

Exasperated, I tossed the book aside and grabbed the phone.

My toes curled beneath the covers as I heard his message, that unhurried drawl seeming to sink inside me and dissolve like hot sugar. "Avery, it's Joe. I wanted to find out how your drive back to Houston was." A pause. "I thought about you all day. Give me a call when you feel like it. Or I'll try you again later." Another pause. "Talk to you soon."

Blood heat had turned my cheeks red and prickly. I set the phone back on the nightstand.

The adult thing, I reflected, would be to call him back, talk to him in a calm and reasonable manner, and tell him that I wasn't interested in seeing him again. *It's just not going to click for me,* I could say.

But I wasn't going to do that. I was going to ignore Joe until he went away, because the thought of talking to him made me break out in a nervous sweat.

The phone rang again, and I stared at it in disbelief. Was he calling *again*? This was going to get annoying, fast. As I looked at the caller ID, however, I saw that it was my best friend from New York, Jasmine, who was the fashion director of a major women's magazine. She was a friend and a mentor, a woman of forty who seemed to do everything well and was never afraid to be opinionated. And her opinions were usually right.

Style was religion to Jasmine. She had the rare gift of translating street trends, shopping blogs, Internet chatter, and cultural influence into a clear-eyed assessment of what was happening in fashion and what was coming around the corner. From her friends, Jasmine demanded and gave absolute loyalty, friendship being the only thing she valued nearly as much as style. She had tried to stop me from leaving New York, promising to use her connections to secure me a job as a special fashion correspondent for a local entertainment show or possibly doing a retail collaboration with some bridal designer who wanted to tap into a more affordable market.

I had appreciated Jasmine's efforts to help, but I had refused. I'd felt defeated and tired, and I'd needed a break from fashion. Most of all, I had wanted to live with my newfound sister and form a relationship with her. I had wanted to have someone in my life whom I was related to. And part of me had liked the way Sofia looked up to me—I'd needed that. Jasmine hadn't necessarily understood, but she had relented and backed off, after telling me that someday she would find a way to lure me back to New York.

"Jazz," I exclaimed, delighted. "How are you?"

"Sweetie. Do you have time to talk?"

"Yes, I—"

"Great. Listen, I'm about to run to a party, but I have some news that can't wait. Here's the thing: You know who Trevor Stearns is."

"Of course."

I had been in awe of Trevor Stearns since I'd been in design school. The legendary celebrity wedding planner was also a megasuccessful bridal fashion designer, author, and host of a cable show titled *Rock the Wedding*. The show, based in L.A., was an effervescent mix of style, sentiment, and drama. Every episode featured Trevor and his team creating a dream wedding for a bride who didn't have the budget or the vision to do it on her own.

"Trevor and his producers," Jazz continued, "are planning to do a spin-off series based in Manhattan."

"Isn't that going to cause wedding show fatigue?" I asked. "I mean, how many people are willing to watch?"

"If there's a limit, they haven't found it yet. The cable channel is airing reruns of Trevor's show all the time, and the ratings are *huge*. So the thinking is, Trevor wants to mentor someone. Preferably a woman. He's going to create a star. Whoever he decides on will be the host of *Rock the Wedding: NYC,* and Trevor will make guest appearances on the show until it's established." Jazz paused. "Do you get where this is going, Avery?"

"You think *I* should give it a shot?" I asked in bewilderment.

"It's perfect for you. I still remember those interviews you did during Bridal Week–you looked amazing on camera, and you had so much personality–"

"Thanks, but Jazz . . . there's no way they would pick someone with so little experience. Besides–"

"You can't assume that. You don't know what they're looking for. They may not even know what they're looking for. I'm going to put together a video of various things you did on camera, and you're going to send me your résumé and a decent head shot, and I'll make sure Trevor Stearns's producers take a look at everything. If they're interested, they'll fly you up here to talk in person, so if nothing else, you'll get a free trip out of it and you can see me."

I smiled. "Okay. For that reason alone, I'll give it a try."

"Wonderful. Now, tell me quickly–everyone doing okay there? Your sister?"

"Yes, she's–"

"My ride's here. Let me call you later."

"Okay, Jazz. Take care of–"

The call ended. I looked down at my phone, still bemused by the rapid-fire conversation. "And Joe said *I* talked fast," I said aloud.

～2～

For the next week and a half, I received two more calls and several texts from Joe, the relaxed tone of his messages turning into perplexed impatience. Clearly he understood I was avoiding him, but he didn't give up. He even tried the event-planning studio's number and left a message that, although innocuous, provoked considerable interest from my employees. Sofia quieted them in a deliberately light, amused tone, telling them that whether or not I was going out with Joe Travis, it was no one's business but mine. After work, however, she cornered me in the kitchen and said, "You're not yourself, *mija*. You've been acting strange ever since the Kendrick wedding. Is everything okay?"

"Of course," I said quickly, "everything's fine."

"Then why have you been having an OCD meltdown?"

"I've been doing a little cleaning and reorganizing," I said defensively. "What's wrong with that?"

"You put all the takeout menus in color-coded folders, and stacked all the magazines in order of their dates. Even for you, that's too much."

"I just want everything to be under control." Uneasily, I opened a nearby drawer and began to rearrange the utensils. Sofia was silent, waiting patiently while I made certain that all the spatulas were in one compartment and slotted spoons were in another. "Actually," I said in a rush, fumbling with a set of measuring spoons, "I slept with Joe Travis the night of the wedding, and now he wants to go out with me, but I don't want to see him again and I can't make myself tell him, so I've been avoiding his calls and hoping he'll just go away."

"Why do you want him to go away?" she asked in concern. "Did you have a bad time with him?"

"No," I said, relieved at being able to talk about it. "Oh my God, it was so amazing that I think I lost brain cells, but I shouldn't have done it in the first place, and I *really* wish I hadn't, because now I feel weird, like I have emotional jet lag or something. I can't catch up to myself. And I'm embarrassed every time I think about how I jumped into bed with him like that."

"He's not embarrassed," Sofia pointed out. "Why should you be?"

I gave her a dark glance. "He's a man. Just because I don't agree with the double standard doesn't mean it's not there."

"In this situation," Sofia said gently, "I think the only person carrying around a double standard is you." Closing the utensil drawer, she turned me to face her. "Call him tonight," she said, "and tell him yes or no. Stop torturing yourself. And him."

I swallowed hard and nodded. "I'll text him."

"Talking is better."

"No, it has to be texting so there won't be any paraverbals."

"What are paraverbals?"

"All the things you communicate besides the words," I said. "Like the tone of your voice, or the pauses, or how fast or slow you talk."

"You mean the things that help to convey the truth."

"Exactly."

"You could just be honest with him," she suggested.

"I'd rather text."

～◎～

Before I went to sleep, I opened the messages on my phone and forced myself to read Joe's most recent text.

Why aren't you answering?

Gripping the phone tightly, I told myself that I was being ridiculous. I had to deal with the situation.

I've been busy, I texted back.

His reply appeared with startling immediacy. *Let's talk.*

I'd rather not. After a long silence, in which he was no doubt trying to figure out how to reply, I added, *No possibility of this going anywhere.*

Why not?

It was perfect for one night. No regrets. But I'm not interested in anything more.

After a few minutes had passed, it was clear that there would be no answer.

I spent the rest of the night struggling to fall asleep, battling my own thoughts.

Pillow's too flat. Covers are too hot. Maybe I need some herb tea . . . a glass of wine . . . melatonin . . . more reading . . . I should try deep breathing . . . I need to find a nature-sounds app . . . a late-night show . . . no, stop thinking, stop. Is three o'clock too early to get up? . . . maybe I should wait till four . . .

I finally started to doze just as the alarm sounded. Groaning, I crawled out of bed. After a long shower, I pulled on some leggings and a roomy knit tunic and went down to the kitchen.

Sofia and I lived in a partially renovated building, a former cigar factory in Montrose. We both loved the eccentric neighborhood, which was filled with art galleries, upmarket boutiques, and quirky restaurants. I had bought the warehouse at a steal, owing to its ramshackle condition. So far we had converted the ground floor into a spacious studio with exposed brick walls and endless rows of multi-paned factory windows. The main-floor plan included an open kitchen with granite countertops, a central seating area anchored by an electric-blue sectional sofa, and a design section with an idea wall and tables piled with books, swatches, trims, and samples. My bedroom was on the second floor, and Sofia's was on the third floor.

"Good morning," my sister said brightly. I flinched at her cheery tone.

"God. Please. Turn it down a notch."

"The light?" she asked, reaching for the dimmer.

"No, the perkiness."

Looking concerned, Sofia poured a cup of coffee and gave it to me. "You didn't sleep well?"

"No." I stirred sweetener and creamer into the coffee. "I finally texted Joe back last night."

"And?"

"I was blunt. I said I wasn't interested in seeing him again. He didn't reply." I shrugged and sighed. "I'm relieved. I should have done it a few days ago. Thank God I don't have to worry about it anymore."

"You're sure it was the right decision?"

"Without a doubt. Maybe I would have gotten another night of great sex, but I'm not interested in being some rich guy's cheap entertainment."

"Someday you'll run into him," Sofia said. "Another wedding, or some other event—"

"Yes, but by then it won't matter. He'll have moved on. And we'll both behave like grown-ups."

"Your paraverbals seem worried," Sofia said. "What can I do, *mija?*"

I didn't know what would have become of my life without Sofia in it. Smiling, I leaned sideways so our heads touched briefly. "If I ever get arrested," I said, "you will be my one phone call. Bail me out—that's what you can do."

"If you ever get arrested," Sofia said, "I'll already be in jail as your accomplice."

That morning, Val came to the studio at her usual time of nine o'clock. It was a mark of her innate tact that although she obviously noticed my unkempt condition, she said nothing, only went to take care of e-mails and answering machine messages. However, Steven showed no such reticence when he walked in a few minutes later.

"What's the matter?" he asked, giving me an appalled glance as I sat with Sofia on the blue sectional.

"Nothing," I said curtly.

"Then why are you wearing a Boy Scout tent?"

Before I could reply, Sofia retorted, "Don't you dare criticize how Avery looks!"

Steven inquired acidly, "So you *like* what she's wearing?"

"Of course not," Sofia said. "But if I didn't say anything about it, you shouldn't either."

"Thanks, Sofia," I said dryly. I sent Steven a warning glance. "I had a rough night. Today is not a good day to push me."

"Avery," Val called urgently from her desk in the design area, "we've gotten an e-mail from Hollis Warner's social secretary. You've been invited to a private party at the Warner mansion on Saturday. A black tie fund-raiser. It's their big annual contemporary art auction and dinner."

Sofia let out a little yelp of excitement.

The atmosphere in the studio seemed instantly diluted—my lungs had to work harder to obtain the necessary amount of oxygen. I strove to sound calm. "Did she mention a plus-one? Because I'd like for Sofia to come with me."

"There was no mention of that," Val said. "If you'd like me to call and ask—"

"No, don't," Sofia said instantly. "Let's not be pushy. Hollis may have a reason for inviting just you."

"She probably does," Steven said. "But that's irrelevant."

"Why?" Sofia, Val, and I all asked at the same time.

"Because the Warners are out of our league. If the wedding is scaled bigger than Amspacher-Kendrick, which Hollis told you it would be, we haven't developed our vendors and suppliers list enough to handle it. The big event planners in Houston and Dallas have the best professionals and venues all sewn up with exclusive contracts. We're still relatively new on the scene."

"Working for Hollis would put us on the fast track," I pointed out.

"It's a bargain with the devil. She'll expect you to cut our percentage to the bone in return for the prestige of having her as a client. This won't help the business, Avery. It's more than we can handle right now. We need to keep growing by focusing on smaller projects."

"I'm not going to let anyone take advantage of us," I said. "But I'm definitely going to the party. No matter what happens, it's an opportunity to make some great contacts."

He looked sardonic. "What are you planning to wear to this black-tie event?"

"My formal gown, of course."

"The black one you wore to the hospital fund-raiser? The one with the big shoulder pouf? No, you're not going to the Warner mansion in that." Steven stood and began to hunt for his keys and wallet.

"What are you doing?" I asked.

"I'm taking you to Neiman's. We have to find something decent off-the-rack and get it altered by Friday."

"I'm not spending money on a new dress when I've already got a perfectly good one," I protested.

"Look, if you want to dress like a parade float on your own time, it's your business. But when you're networking and trying to land a high-profile client, it becomes my business. Your appearance reflects on the studio. And your personal taste is a tragic misuse of some fine genetic endowments."

I directed my outraged gaze from him to Sofia and Val, silently commanding them to back me up. To my disgust, Sofia had suddenly become preoccupied with checking her text messages, and Val was intently straightening the piles of magazines on the coffee table.

"Okay," I muttered, "I'll get a new dress."

"And a new hairstyle. Because that one does you no favors."

"I think he's right," Sofia ventured before I could reply. "You wear it in an updo all the time."

"Every time I get my hair cut, it ends up looking like a Darth Vader helmet."

Ignoring my protests, Steven spoke to Sofia. "Call Salon One and ask them to squeeze in an appointment for Avery. If they give you any problems, remind them that they owe us a favor after we found a last-minute caterer for the owner's wedding. Also call Avery's optometrist for a contact lens fitting."

"No way," I said. "No contacts. I have a problem with touching my eyeballs."

"That's the least of your problems." Steven found his keys. "Come on."

"Wait," Sofia exclaimed, pulling something from a drawer. She hurried to hand it to Steven. "In case you need a backup," she said.

"Is that the studio credit card?" I asked indignantly. "That's only supposed to be used in case of emergency."

Steven gave me an assessing glance. "This qualifies."

As I picked up my bag and Steven ushered me to the front door, Sofia called out after us, "Don't let him in the dressing room, Avery. Remember, he's not gay."

✑

I hated trying on clothes, hated it, *hated* it.

More than anything, I despised the department store dressing room. The three-way mirror that magnified every little indulgence and unwanted pound. The fluorescent lighting that gave me the complexion of a bridge troll. The way the salesgirl trilled, "How's everything working out for you?" right at the moment I was tangled up in a garment that had turned into a straitjacket.

When trying on clothes was unavoidable, a dressing room at Neiman Marcus ranked above all others. From my perspective, however, deciding on a favorite department store dressing room was about as appealing as choosing my favorite way to be executed.

The Neiman Marcus dressing room was spacious and beautifully decorated, with lit columns on either side of the full-length mirrors and dimmable ceiling lights.

"Stop," Steven said, carrying in a half-dozen gowns he had pulled from the racks as we walked through the premier designer apparel.

"Stop what?" I hung up the two black dresses I had picked out in defiance of Steven's objections.

"Stop looking like one of those caged puppies on the SPCA commercials."

"I can't help it. That mirror with the pedestal in front of it makes me feel threatened and depressed, and I haven't even tried anything on yet."

Steven took a few garments from a helpful saleswoman, closed the door, and hung them on the double wall rack. "The person in that mirror is not your adversary."

"No, at the moment that would be you."

Steven grinned. "Start trying on dresses." He took the dresses I had chosen and began to walk out.

"Why are you taking those away?"

"Because you're not wearing black to Hollis Warner's party."

"Black is slimming. It's a power color."

"In New York. In Houston, color is a power color." The door closed behind him.

The saleswoman brought a long-line bustier bra and a pair of high heels and left me in privacy. I undressed as far as possible from the three-way mirror, hooked the placket at the back of the bra, and twisted it around to my front. The bra, with its boning and angled seaming, hoisted my breasts to shameless prominence.

I took the first dress from the hanger. It was a canary-yellow sheath with a beaded bodice and a stretch satin skirt. "Yellow, Steven? Please."

"Any woman can wear yellow if it's the right shade for her coloring," he said from the other side of the door.

I struggled into the gown and reached back to the zipper. It refused to budge. "Come in, I need help with the zipper."

Steven entered the room and gave me an assessing glance. "Not bad." Standing behind me, he closed the back of the dress with difficulty.

Tottering toward the mirror, I struggled to breathe. "Too tight." I was suffused with gloom as I saw the strained and distorted seams. "Could you get me the next size up?"

Steven lifted the tag dangling from one armhole and frowned as he read it. "This is the largest size it comes in."

"I'm leaving now," I informed him.

Steven unzipped me decisively. "We're not giving up."

"Yes, we are. I'm going to wear the dress I already have."

"It's gone."

"What do you mean, it's gone?"

"Right after we left, I texted Sofia and told her to get rid of it while you were out. You're at the point of no return."

I scowled. "I'm going to kill you with one of these stiletto heels. And I'm going to kill Sofia with the other one."

"Try another gown."

He left the dressing room while I fumed and reached for a floor-length aqua silk with an overlay of silver-beaded organza. The gown was sleeveless with a V neck. To my relief, it slid easily over my hips.

"I've always wanted to ask you this," I said. "Did Sofia really try on clothes in front of you?"

"Yes," Steven replied from the other side of the door. "But she wasn't naked, she was wearing underwear." After a pause, he added in a preoccupied tone, "A matched set. Black lace."

"Are you interested in her?" I asked, slipping my hands through the armholes and pulling up the rest of the dress. At his silence, I said, "Never mind, I know you are." I paused. "And it's not all one-sided."

His tone was decidedly less casual as he asked, "Is that opinion or confirmed fact?"

"Opinion."

"Even if I were interested in her, I never mix work with my personal life."

"But if you–"

"I'm not discussing Sofia with you. Are you almost done?"

"Yes, I think this one may actually fit." I wriggled to zip up the back. "You can come in."

Steven entered the dressing room and glanced over me approvingly. "This works."

The weight of the geometric-patterned beading made the gown pleasantly slinky. I had to admit that the modified Empire cut of the gown flattered my shape, the flared fullness of the skirt balancing my proportions.

"We'll have alterations cut it to knee-length," Steven said decisively. "Legs like yours should be flaunted."

"It's a nice dress," I admitted. "But the color is too bright. It competes with my hair."

"It's perfect with your hair."

"It's not me." I turned and gave him an apologetic glance. "I'm not comfortable in something that makes me look so . . ."

"Confident? Sexy? A dress that encourages people to look at you? Avery . . . nothing interesting ever happens to people who stay in their comfort zones all the time."

"Having gone outside my comfort zone in the past, I can say with authority that it's an overrated experience."

"All the same . . . you're never going to get what you want if you refuse to change. And we're not even talking big changes here. These are clothes, Avery. It's minor stuff."

"Then why are you making such a big deal out of it?"

"Because I'm tired of seeing you dressed like a Viking nanny. And so is everyone else. You're the last person on the planet who should be hiding her figure. Let's buy you a nice dress, and maybe some designer jeans and a couple of tops. And a jacket . . . ."

In no time at all, Steven had enlisted the help of two saleswomen who proceeded to fill the dressing room racks with a rainbow of garments. The three of them informed me that I had been buying bigger sizes than I needed, in styles that were the opposite of what someone with my body shape should wear. By the time Steven and I left Neiman Marcus, I had bought the aqua dress, a print blouse, a couple of silk-blend tees, designer jeans and slim-fitting black pants, silk shorts, a plum-colored leather jacket, an open peach cardigan, an eggshell-white skirt suit, and four pairs of shoes. The outfits were sleek and simple, with waist-defining silhouettes.

Aside from making a hefty down payment on the warehouse in Montrose, I had never dropped so much money at one time in my life.

"Your new wardrobe is smoking hot," Steven informed me as we left the store with bags in each hand.

"So is my credit card."

He checked his messages. "We're going to the optometrist now. After that, the salon."

"Just out of curiosity, Steven...is there anything about my personal style that you *do* like?"

"Your eyebrows aren't bad. And you have nice teeth." As we drove away from the Galleria, Steven asked casually, "Are you ever going to tell me what happened with Joe Travis at the Kendrick wedding?"

"Nothing happened."

"If that were true, you would have told me right away. But you haven't said anything for a week and a half, which means something happened."

"Okay," I admitted. "You're right. But I don't want to talk about it."

"Fine by me." Steven found a soft-rock station on the radio and adjusted the volume.

After a couple of minutes, I burst out, "I slept with him."

"Did you use protection?"

"Yes."

"Did you enjoy it?"

After an uncomfortable hesitation, I admitted, "Yes."

Steven lifted one hand from the wheel to high-five me.

"Wow," I muttered, returning the high five. "No lectures about one-night stands?"

"Of course not. As long as you use a condom, there's nothing wrong with commitment-free pleasure. That being said, I wouldn't advise using someone as a fuck-buddy. One of you always starts to have feelings. Expectations. Eventually someone gets hurt. So after the one-night stand, it's better to pull the plug right away."

"What if the other person asks to see you again?"

"I'm not a Magic Eight Ball."

"You're smart about these things," I insisted. "Tell me—is there any chance of a relationship after you've had a one-night stand?"

Steven gave me a wry sideways glance. "Most of the time, a one-night stand means you've both already decided it wasn't going to be serious in the first place."

✵

It was nine o'clock before Steven finally brought me back home. The stylist at Salon One had worked diligently on my hair for three hours, subjecting it to a regimen of relaxing chemicals, creams, and serums, heating and drying in between each step. She had proceeded to cut off eight inches, leaving me with a lob that fell to my shoulders in loose, silky waves. The salon's cosmetician had done a mani-pedi in pale taupe, and while the polish was drying, she had shown me how to apply makeup. I had subsequently bought a small bag of cosmetics that had cost as much as my monthly car payment.

As it turned out, the salon visit was worth every penny. Steven, who had decided to have a rejuvenating facial during the last hour of my treatments, emerged just as my makeup was finished. His reaction was priceless. His jaw dropped, and he let out a disbelieving laugh.

"My God. Who the hell are you?"

I rolled my eyes and blushed, but Steven persisted, walking a full circle around me, finally pulling me into his arms for a rare embrace. "You're gorgeous," he murmured. "Now *own it*."

Later, as we walked into the studio with a multitude of bags, Sofia came downstairs from her third-floor room. She was already dressed in pajamas and fuzzy slippers, her hair pulled up in a high ponytail. She gave me a questioning look and shook her head, as if she couldn't believe her eyes.

"We're bankrupt," I informed her with a grin. "I spent all our money on hair and clothes."

To my consternation, my sister's eyes welled up. Erupting into a stream of fluid Spanish, she embraced me so tightly that I could hardly breathe.

"Is it bad?" I asked.

She began to laugh through her tears. "No, no, you're so *beautiful*, Avery...."

Somehow, in the confusion of hugging and rejoicing, Sofia ended up kissing Steven on the cheek.

He went still at the innocent gesture, looking down at her with an odd, flummoxed expression. It lasted only a second before his face went carefully blank. Sofia didn't seem to notice.

If I'd had any doubts about whether Steven felt something for my sister, I knew what a Magic 8 Ball would have said:

Signs point to yes.

∽ Seven ∽

The night of Hollis Warner's art auction was humid and hot, the air pungent with wax myrtle and lantana. I pulled up to a valet stand beside a parking area filled with luxury vehicles, and a uniformed attendant helped me from the car. I was wearing the aqua beaded dress, its shortened hem now swirling around my knees. Thanks to Sofia's help with my hair and makeup, I knew I had never looked better.

Live jazz drifted through the air like smoke as I walked into the Warner mansion, a southern colonial built on a two-acre lot in River Oaks. The home had been one of the original residences back when River Oaks had been established in the twenties. Hollis had nearly doubled the size of the historic building by adding a modern glass extension at the back, a showy but jarring combination. The outline of a huge white tent loomed behind the roof line.

A rush of chilled air surrounded me as I entered a spacious foyer with antique parquet floors. The mansion was already crowded, and the evening had just started. Assistant hostesses handed out catalogs of the artwork that would be up for auction later. "They'll hold the dinner and auction in the tent," one of the hostesses told me, "but right now the house is open for viewing the artwork. The catalog describes the auction items, and lists where they're located."

"Avery!" Hollis appeared in a pink chiffon dress with a slim-fitting silhouette, the skirt a swirl of pale pink ostrich feathers. Her husband, David, a lean, attractive man with salt-and-pepper hair, accompanied her. Pressing an air kiss near my cheek, Hollis enthused, "We're going to have such fun tonight! My, don't you look gorgeous!" Glancing up at her husband, she prompted, "Sugar, tell Avery what you just said when you saw her."

He obliged without hesitation. "I said, 'That redheaded gal in the blue dress is proof that God's a man.'"

I smiled. "Thank you for inviting me. What an incredible house this is."

"I'll show you the new addition," Hollis told me. "All glass and granite. It took forever to get it right, but David supported me every step of the way." She stroked her husband's arm and beamed at him.

"Hollis loves to entertain more than anyone you'll ever meet," David Warner said. "She raises money for all kinds of charities. A woman like this deserves any kind of house she wants."

"Sugar," Hollis murmured, "Avery's the one who did that wedding for Judy and Ray's daughter. I'm going to introduce her to Ryan tonight, so she can help push things along with him and Bethany."

David looked at me with new interest. "Glad to hear it. That was some shindig, the Kendrick wedding. Lotta fun. Wouldn't mind doing something like that for Bethany."

Wondering exactly what Hollis had meant by the phrase *push things along*, I asked, "Has there been an official proposal yet?"

"No, Ryan's trying to figure out a special way to pop the question. I told him you'd be here tonight to give him some ideas."

"Whatever I can do to help."

"We couldn't have asked for a nicer young man for Bethany," Hollis said. "Ryan's an architect. Smart as a whip. His family, the Chases, are close kin to the Travises. Ryan's mama died young–so unfortunate–but his uncle Churchill looked after the family and made sure the kids got educations. And when Churchill passed on, the Chases were included in his will." Hollis gave me a significant glance as she continued. "Ryan could live off the interest of his trust fund and never work a day in his life." She grasped my wrist with a clatter of multiple cocktail rings. "David, I'm going to tour Avery around the house. You can do without me for a few minutes, can't you?"

"I'll try," her husband said, and she winked at him before pulling me away.

Hollis chatted with the ease of an accomplished hostess as she guided me through the house toward the modern addition. She stopped to show me some of the auction paintings displayed throughout the house, each lot numbered and accompanied by information about the artist. Along the way, Hollis texted Ryan to meet us in what she called "the skyroom."

"He's going to slip away from Bethany for a few minutes," Hollis explained, "so he can talk to you without her. He wants the proposal to be a surprise, of course."

"If he'd rather come to our Montrose studio," I said, "we could discuss it there. That might be easier and more private–"

"No, it's better to take care of it tonight," Hollis said. "Otherwise Ryan will drag his feet. You know how men are."

I smiled noncommittally, hoping that Hollis wasn't trying to push

Ryan into proposing. "Have he and Bethany been dating for a while?" I asked as we entered a small glass-sided elevator.

"Two or three months. When you meet the right one, you just know. David proposed to me just a couple of weeks after we met—and look at us now, twenty-five years later."

As the elevator ascended to the third floor, I had a perfect view of the tent in the back. It was connected to the house by a carpet runner of fresh flowers arranged in geometric swirls.

"Here's my skyroom," Hollis said with pride, showing me a spectacular gallery with steel-framed glass walls and a segmented glass ceiling. Sculptures perched on Lucite pedestals at various places in the room. The floor itself was made of clear glass with few visible supports. A tiled outdoor swimming pool glittered three stories directly below. "Isn't it fabulous? Come, I'll show you one of my favorite sculptures."

I hesitated, staring uneasily at the glass floor. Although I had never thought of myself as having a fear of heights, I didn't like the looks of it. The glass didn't look nearly substantial enough to support my weight.

"Oh, it's safe as could be," Hollis said as she saw my expression. "You get used to it right away." Her heels clinked like cocktail ice as she walked into the gallery. "This is the closest you'll ever get to walking on air."

Since I'd never had any desire to walk on air, that assurance wasn't exactly motivating. I reached the edge of the glass and my feet stopped, toes curling in my pumps. Every cell in my body warned that walking onto that expanse of clear glass would result in sudden and ignominious death.

Steeling myself not to glance at the sparkling swimming pool below, I ventured out onto the slick surface.

"What do you think?" I heard Hollis ask.

"Amazing," I managed to reply. I was tingling all over, not in a happy, excited way, but in an epic-freak-out way. Perspiration collected beneath my bra.

"This is one of my favorite pieces," Hollis said, guiding me to a sculpture on a pedestal. "It's only ten thousand. Such a bargain."

I found myself staring blankly at a cast polyurethane head that had been divided in half. A collection of found objects–things such as a broken dish, a plastic ball, a cell phone case–had been wedged between the two sides. "I'm not sure how to interpret postmodern sculpture," I admitted.

"This artist takes ordinary objects and changes their context–" Hollis was forced to pause as her phone vibrated. "Let me check this." Reading the message, she gave an exasperated sigh. "I can't slip away for ten minutes without someone needing me to do something. This is what I hired my secretary for. I swear, that girl is one twist short of a Slinky."

"If there's something you need to take care of, please go right ahead," I said, inwardly relieved at the prospect of being able to escape from the skyroom. "Don't worry about me."

Hollis patted my arm, her rings clattering like castanets. "I'll find someone for you to meet. I can't run off and leave you here alone."

"I'm fine, Hollis. Really–"

She pulled me even farther across the treacherous floor. We passed a trio of women chatting and laughing and an elderly couple examining a sculpture. Hollis tugged me toward a photographer who stood in the corner taking candid shots of the old couple. "Shutterbug," Hollis called out playfully, "look who I've got with me."

"Hollis," I protested faintly.

Before the man lowered his camera, I knew who he was. My whole body knew. I felt his presence instantly, even before I looked up into the eyes that had haunted me every night since we had met. Except that now they were as hard as onyx.

"Hi, Joe," I managed to whisper.

~ Eight ~

J oe's doing us a favor by taking some pictures for the website," Hollis said.

He set his camera by the sculpture, his gaze pinning me like a butterfly to a spreading board. "Avery. Nice to see you again."

"Would you mind keeping company with Avery while she waits here for your cousin Ryan?" Hollis asked.

"My pleasure," Joe said.

"There's no need–" I began uncomfortably, but Hollis had already disappeared in a flurry of ostrich feathers.

Silence.

I hadn't expected it would be this difficult to face Joe. The memories of everything we had done surrounded us like scorch marks in the air. "I didn't know you'd be here," I managed to say. Taking a deep breath, I let it out slowly. "I haven't handled this well," I said.

His face was unreadable. "No, you haven't."

"I'm sorry–" I stopped, having made the mistake of letting my gaze drop too far. A brief glimpse of the glass floor had given me a bizarre tilting sensation, as if the entire house had begun to rotate sideways.

"If you don't want to see me again," Joe said, "that's your decision. But I'd at least like to know–"

"Jesus." The room wouldn't stop moving. I wobbled and reached out to grasp the sleeve of Joe's jacket in a desperate bid for balance. My evening clutch dropped to the floor. I made the mistake of looking down at it and wobbled again.

Reflexively Joe reached out to steady me. "You okay?" I heard him ask.

"Yes. No." I gripped one of his wrists.

"Too much to drink?"

It was like standing on the deck of a ship in a rolling sea. "No, it's not that . . . the floor, it's giving me vertigo. Shit, *shit*–"

"Look at me." Joe gripped my wrist and reached for my other arm. I stared blindly at the dark blur of his face until my eyes refocused. The rocklike steadiness of his hold was the only thing that kept me from tipping over. "I've got you," he said.

A wave of nausea drained the color from my skin. Beads of cold sweat broke out on my forehead.

"The floor does this to at least half the people who try to walk on it," Joe continued. "The effect of the water below throws you off balance. Take a deep breath."

"I didn't want to walk out here," I said desperately. "I only did it because Hollis insisted, and I'm trying like hell to land her as a client." The sweat was going to ruin my makeup. I was going to dissolve like a chalk drawing in the rain.

"Would it help you to know that the floor is made out of layers of structural safety glass that's at least two inches thick?"

"No" came my woebegone reply.

The corner of his mouth twitched, and his expression softened. Carefully he released one of my arms and took my hand. "Close your eyes and let me lead you."

I gripped his hand and tried to follow as he moved us forward. After a couple of steps I stumbled, panic clamoring through my body. His arm locked around me immediately, hauling me against him, but the tumbling sensation persisted.

"Oh God," I said in dazed misery. "There's no way I'm getting off this stupid floor without falling."

"I'm not going to let you fall."

"I feel sick to my stomach–"

"Easy. Stay still and keep your eyes closed." Keeping his arm around me, Joe reached into his tux jacket and pulled out a hand-kerchief. I felt the soft folded cloth press gently against my forehead and cheeks, absorbing the film of sweat. "You just got yourself a little worked up, that's all," he murmured. "You'll feel better once your blood pressure goes down. Breathe." Pushing a lock of hair away from my face, he continued to hold me. "You're fine." His voice was quiet, soothing. "I won't let anything happen to you."

Feeling how solid he was, the strength of him all around me, I began to relax. One of my palms pressed against his chest, riding the steady rhythm of his breath.

"You look beautiful in that dress," Joe said quietly. His hand moved gently through the soft waves of my hair. "And I like this."

I kept my eyes closed, remembering the way he had gripped his hands in my hair that night, holding my head back while he'd kissed my throat–

I felt the movement of his arm as he gestured to someone.

"What are you doing?" I asked weakly.

"My brother Jack and his wife just got off the elevator."

"Don't call them over here," I begged.

"You'll get nothing but sympathy from Ella. She got stuck out on this floor when she was pregnant, and Jack ended up having to carry her off."

An affable voice entered the conversation. "Hey, bro. What's going on?"

"My friend has vertigo."

I opened my eyes cautiously. It was obvious that the striking man standing next to Joe was from the same supernally blessed Travis gene pool. Dark hair, alpha charisma, a raffish quality in his grin. "Jack Travis," he said. "Nice to meet you."

I began to turn to shake his hand, but Joe's arms tightened.

"No, keep still," he murmured. He told his brother, "She's trying to get her bearings."

"Fuckin' glass floor," Jack said ruefully. "I told Hollis to add a layer of smart glass, and then she could turn the whole thing opaque just by flipping a switch. People should listen to me."

"*I* listen to you," a woman said, approaching us with small, painstaking steps.

"Yeah," Jack replied, "but only so you can argue." He smiled down at her and slid an arm around her shoulders. She was slim and pretty, with chin-length blond hair, her eyes denim blue behind a delicate pair of cat's-eye glasses. "What are you doing, tiptoeing out here?" Jack asked her in a gently scolding tone. "You're going to get stuck again."

"I can handle it now that I'm not pregnant," she told him. "And I want to meet Joe's friend." She smiled at me. "I'm Ella Travis."

"This is Avery," Joe said. "Let's put off the rest of the introductions for now. The floor's making her dizzy."

Ella gave me a sympathetic look. "The same thing happened to me the first time I walked out on it. A see-through floor is such a ridiculous idea—do you realize that anyone in the swimming pool could look right up our skirts?"

I couldn't help glancing down in reflexive alarm, and the room lurched again.

"Whoa, there." Joe steadied me immediately. "Avery, *do not* look down. Ella—"

"Sorry, sorry, I'll shut up."

Laughter rustled through Jack's voice as he asked, "Anything I can do to help?"

"Yeah, see the rug they hung on that wall over there? Take it down, and we'll lay it across the floor like a bridge. That'll give Avery a fixed visual reference."

"Won't reach all the way," Jack pointed out.

"It'll be close enough."

I glanced at the rug on the distant wall. The artist had applied dozens of strips of colored duct tape to the surface of an antique Persian carpet and melted them onto the textile.

"You can't," I said. "That's an auction item."

"It's a rug," Joe replied. "It's supposed to go on the floor."

"It was a rug before. Now it's art."

"I was thinking about buying it," Ella volunteered. "The choice of materials represents a fusion of the past with the future."

Jack grinned at his wife. "Ella, you're the only one here who actually reads the catalog. You know I could duct-tape a rug and make it look just like that."

"Yes, but it wouldn't be worth a dime if you did it."

His eyes narrowed. "Why not?"

Ella's fingers walked playfully up the lapel of his tuxedo jacket. "Because, Jack Travis, you do not have the mind of an artist."

His face lowered until their noses nearly touched, and he said in a sexy purr, "Good thing you married me for my body."

Joe looked exasperated. "Cut it out, you two. Jack, go get the damn rug."

"Wait," I said desperately. "Let me try walking again. Please."

Joe didn't bother to hide his skepticism. "You think you can?"

I was feeling steadier now that my heart rate had returned to normal. "As long as I don't look down, I think I'll be okay."

Joe gave me an assessing glance, while his legs bracketed mine and his hands gripped my waist. "Take off your shoes."

I felt color flooding my face. Clinging to him, I slipped off my pumps.

"I'll get those," Jack said, retrieving the pumps and evening clutch.

"Close your eyes," Joe told me. After I complied, he slid an arm around my back. "Trust me," he murmured. "And keep breathing."

I obeyed the pressure of his hands and let him guide me.

"Why are you meeting with Ryan?" Joe asked as he steered me forward.

Grateful for the distraction, I said, "Hollis told me he needs help with ideas on how to propose to Bethany."

"Why would he need help with that? All he has to do is ask the question and give her a ring."

"Nowadays people make the proposal into an event." The soles of my feet were sweating. I hoped I wasn't leaving damp footprints on the glass. "You can take someone on a hot-air balloon ride and propose in midair, or go scuba diving and propose underwater, or even hire a flash mob to sing and dance."

"That's ridiculous," Joe said flatly.

"Being romantic is ridiculous?"

"No, turning a private moment into a Broadway musical is ridiculous." We stopped, and Joe turned me to face him. "You can open your eyes now."

"We're there?"

"We're there."

When I saw that we were safe on solid granite flooring, I let out a sigh of relief. Discovering that my fingers were still wrapped tightly around his wrist, I forced my grip to loosen. "Thank you," I whispered.

He leveled a steady gaze at me, and I writhed inwardly as I understood that before the evening was over, we were going to talk.

"I'll get my camera," he said, and went back to the skyroom.

"Here you go," Jack said, handing me the evening pumps and clutch bag.

"Thanks." I set the shoes on the floor and stepped into them. "I think that qualified as my first nervous breakdown," I said with chagrin.

"A little nervous breakdown never hurt anyone," Jack assured me. "I gave 'em to my mom all the time."

"You've given me one or two," Ella informed him.

"You knew what you were getting into, marrying a Travis."

"Yes, I knew." Ella smiled and reached over to adjust his tie. "After something this traumatic," she told me cheerfully, "you need to self-medicate. Let's go sit somewhere and have a drink."

"I would love to," I said, "but I can't. I have to wait here for Joe's cousin Ryan."

"Have you met him before?"

"No, and I have no idea what he looks like."

"I'll point him out to you," Ella said. "Although the family resemblance is unmistakable. Big, hairy, lots of attitude."

Jack bent to brush a casual kiss on her lips. "That's just how you like 'em," he said. "Want me to get you some champagne?"

"Yes, please."

Jack glanced at me. "Same for you, Avery?"

Although I would have loved some, I shook my head reluctantly. "Thank you, but I'd better stay as clearheaded as possible."

As he left, Ella turned a friendly gaze to me. "How long have you and Joe known each other?"

"We don't," I said quickly. "I mean . . . we met several days ago at a wedding I'd planned, but we're not . . . you know . . ."

"He's interested," she told me. "I could tell from the way he was looking at you."

"I'm too busy to even think about going out with someone."

She gave me a patently sympathetic look. "Avery, I'm an advice columnist. I write about this stuff all the time. No one is ever too busy for a relationship. Katy Perry's busy, but she dates, right? A-Rod's busy, but he has a new girlfriend every month. So I'm guessing you were burned in your last relationship. You've lost faith in the entire male half of our species."

There was something so perky and engaging about her that I couldn't help smiling. "That about sums it up."

"Then you need to–" She broke off as Joe returned with his camera.

"Ryan's heading over here," he said. "I just saw him get off the elevator."

A tall, well-dressed man approached us. His thick hair had been clipped conservatively short, the locks the color of dark chocolate. With his high cheekbones and icehouse-blue eyes, he was remarkably handsome, more austere and polished than the Travis brothers. He possessed a self-contained quality, with no hint of the Travises' consummate charm or easy humor, but rather a sense that he was a man who would let his guard down only reluctantly, if at all.

"Hi, Ella," he said as he reached us, leaning down to kiss her cheek. "Joe."

"How's it going, Rye?" Joe asked as they shook hands.

"I've been better." Ryan turned to me, his expression masked with politeness. "You're the wedding planner?"

"Avery Crosslin."

His grip was firm but careful as we shook hands. "We'll have to make this quick," Ryan said. "I only have a few minutes before Bethany tracks me down."

"Of course. Would you like to talk in private? I'm not familiar with the house–"

"Not necessary," Ryan said. "Joe and Ella are family." His gaze was cool. "What has Hollis told you about my situation?"

I answered readily. "She said that you're going to propose to her daughter, Bethany, and you wanted to talk to me about ideas for the proposal."

"I don't need proposal ideas," Ryan said flatly. "Hollis only said that because she's afraid I won't go through with it. She and David are trying to hold my feet to the fire."

"Why's that?" Joe asked.

Ryan hesitated for a long moment. "Bethany's pregnant." The battened-down tension in his reply made it clear that the news had been neither expected nor welcome.

A sober silence descended.

"She said she wants to have the baby," Ryan continued. "I told her I'd stand by her, of course."

"Ryan," Ella ventured, "I know you're traditional about these things. But if that's the only reason you're proposing to Bethany, the marriage doesn't have a great chance of working out."

"We'll make it work."

"You can be part of your child's life without having to get married," I said quietly.

"I'm not here to discuss the pros and cons. The wedding is going to happen. All I want is a say in how it turns out."

"So you want to take an active part in the planning?" I asked.

"No, I just want to set some reasonable parameters and have them enforced. Otherwise, Hollis will have the entire wedding party riding on elephants dressed in gold chain mail, or worse."

I was troubled by the prospect of planning a wedding for a reluctant groom. It seemed doubtful that he and Bethany would make it to the altar, but even if they did, the process would likely be miserable for everyone involved. "Ryan," I said, "there are several very experienced and well-established event planners in Houston who could do a wonderful job—"

"They're all in the Warners' pocket. I've already made it clear to Hollis that I won't put up with any event planner who's worked for her in the past. I want someone she doesn't own. It doesn't matter to me about how good you are, or what kind of flowers you pick, or any of that. All I want to know is if you can stand up to Hollis when she tries to take over."

"Of course I can," I said. "I'm a pathological control freak. And I happen to be great at my job. But before we discuss this any further, why don't you come to my studio and—"

"You're hired," he said abruptly.

I responded with a startled laugh. "I'm sure you'll want to run it by Bethany first."

Ryan shook his head. "I'll stipulate that hiring you is a requirement for the engagement. She won't say a word about it."

"Usually the procedure for this starts with a studio visit. We look at a portfolio and discuss ideas and possibilities—"

"I don't want to drag this out any longer than necessary. I've already decided to give the job to you."

Before I could reply, Joe intervened with a flicker of amusement in his eyes. "Rye, I don't think the question is whether you want to hire Avery. I think she's trying to figure out if she wants to take you on."

"Why wouldn't she?" Ryan's perplexed gaze arrowed to mine.

While I was busy trying to come up with a diplomatic reply, we were interrupted by Jack's return. "Hey, Rye." He had arrived with Ella's champagne in time to overhear the last of the conversation. "What are you hiring Avery for?"

"Wedding planning," Ryan said. "Bethany's pregnant."

Jack stared at him blankly. "Damn, son," he said after a moment. "There are precautions for that."

Ryan's eyes narrowed. "No method's a hundred percent except abstinence. Explain that word to him, Ella—God knows he's never heard it before."

Jack grinned briefly. "She knows me well enough not to bother."

Privately, I reflected that beneath Ryan's high-handed manner, he had to be feeling what any man would in this situation: anxiety, frustration, and a tremendous need to obtain control over *something*. "Ryan," I said gently, "I understand your desire to start making decisions right away, but this isn't the way to pick a wedding planner. If you're interested in hiring me, come to my studio at your earliest convenience and we'll talk." As I spoke, I fished a business card from my clutch and gave it to him.

Frowning, Ryan tucked the card into his pocket. "Monday morning?"

"That works fine for me."

"Avery," Ella said, "may I have a card too? I need your help."

Jack gave her a quizzical glance. "We're already married."

"Not for *that*, it's for Haven's baby shower." Ella took the card I gave her and gave me an imploring look. "How good are you at salvaging a disaster in the making? I had to arrange a baby shower for my sister-in-law Haven, because our other sister-in-law is swamped with a salon opening—she's starting her own business—and I'm a terrible procrastinator, so I put it off for way too long. And Haven just told me that she'd rather not have a traditional girly shower, she'd rather it be appropriate for families. The whole thing is only half-planned, and it's a mess."

"When is it?" I asked.

"Next weekend," Ella said sheepishly.

"I'll do the best I can. I can't promise miracles, but—"

"Thank you, what a relief! Anything you can do will be great. If you want to—"

"Wait a minute," Ryan interrupted. "Why does Ella get an instant 'yes' and I don't?"

"She needs the help more," Joe said, perfectly deadpan. "Have you been to one of Ella's parties?"

Ella gave him a warning glance, although her eyes sparkled with laughter. "Careful, you."

Joe grinned at her before turning his attention to Ryan. "Let's catch a game on Sunday," he said.

"Sounds good." Ryan paused before asking with a subtle smile, "Does Jack have to come along this time?"

"You'd better hope I do," Jack said. "I'm the only one who ever pays for the damn beer."

Joe took my elbow. "We'll see y'all in a bit," he said easily. "I want Avery's opinion on some paintings I might bid on."

Ella winked at me as Joe drew me away.

"Do you think your cousin is really going to go through with it?" I asked Joe in a low tone. "If he takes some time to think it through–"

"Rye won't change his mind," Joe said. "His dad died when he was ten. Trust me, he'd never let a kid of his grow up fatherless."

We stepped into the elevator. "But it doesn't sound as if he's considered all his options."

"There are no options. If I were in his place, I'd do the same thing."

"You'd propose to a woman you'd accidentally gotten pregnant, even if you didn't love her?"

"Of course I would. Why do you look surprised?"

"It's just . . . an old-fashioned notion, that's all."

"It's the right thing to do."

"I don't necessarily agree. The chances of divorce are very high when a marriage starts out that way."

"In my family, if you get a woman pregnant, you take responsibility."

"What about what Bethany wants?"

"She wants to marry a man with money. And she's not too particular about who it is, as long as he can afford her."

"You have no way of knowing that."

"Honey, everybody knows it." Joe cast a grim glance at the scenery on the other side of the elevator glass. "Ryan's spent most of his life with his nose to the grindstone, and then when he finally decides to take a break and have some fun, he hooks up with Bethany

Warner. A party girl. A professional socialite. You don't get caught by a girl like that. I don't know what the hell he was thinking."

The doors opened, and we were on the main floor again. Joe took my free hand and began to tow me through the crowd.

"What are we doing?" I asked.

"I'm finding us a place to talk."

I blanched, knowing exactly what he wanted to discuss. "*Here? Now?* There's no privacy."

Joe sounded sardonic. "We could have had plenty of privacy, if you'd picked up your phone when I called."

We proceeded through one packed room after another, pausing occasionally for brief conversations. Even in this exalted gathering of insiders, it was clear that he was something special. The combination of his name, money, and looks was all a man needed to unlock the world. But he adroitly deflected people's eager interest, turning it around to focus on them as if they were infinitely more worthy of attention.

Eventually, we entered a room lined with dark paneled wood and bookshelves, the ceiling low and coffered, the floor covered with a thick Persian rug. Joe closed the door, muffling the sounds of conversation, laughter, and music. His polite social mask disappeared as he turned to face me. In the silence, my heartbeat gathered momentum, rolling into a hard repeated wallop.

"Why did you say there was no chance of this going anywhere?" he asked.

"Isn't it obvious?"

Joe gave me a caustic glance. "I'm a guy, Avery. Nothing about relationships is obvious to me."

No matter how I tried to explain, I knew I would end up sounding self-pitying or pathetic. *I don't want to end up being hurt the way you're going to hurt me. I know how these things work. You want sex and fun, and when it's over you'll move on, but I won't be able to, because you'll have broken what's left of my heart.*

"Joe . . . one night with you was all I expected, and it was wonderful. But I . . . I need something different." I paused, trying to think of how to explain.

His eyes widened, and he said my name on a quiet breath. Confused by the change in his demeanor, I backed up reflexively as he came to me. One of his arms slid around me, while his free hand lifted to cradle the side of my face. "Avery, sweetheart . . ." There was a slight rasp in his voice, something concerned . . . raw . . . sexual. "If I didn't give you what you needed . . . if I didn't satisfy you . . . all you had to do was tell me."

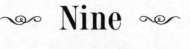

Nine

Realizing that Joe had misunderstood, I stammered, "No, that– that's not–I didn't mean–"

"I'll make it up to you." He caressed my cheek with his thumb, and his mouth grazed mine with an erotic gentleness that left me gasping. "Let me have another night with you. You can ask me for anything. Anything. I'll make it so good for you, honey ... there are so many ways ... All you have to do is come to bed with me, and I'll take care of you."

Dazed, I tried to explain that he'd gotten it all wrong, but as I opened my mouth, Joe kissed me again and again, murmuring promises about the pleasure he would give me, the things he would do for me. He was so remorseful, so determined ... and to my shame, I found it sexy as hell to be caught in the grasp of a big, aroused male who wouldn't stop apologizing and kissing me. Gradually, it seemed less important to break free. His mouth ravished mine, all silk and hunger, draining me of strength. The insane chemistry between us didn't just feel good, it felt necessary, as if I needed him to breathe,

as though my body would stop functioning if I couldn't keep touching him.

He reached down to anchor my hips against his, aggressive hard-
ness nudging into a lush, intimate ache. I quivered and began to
breathe in long sighs. Remembering what it had been like—the way
he had filled me—I was overcome with disorienting heat, and all I
wanted to do was sink to the floor with him and have him take me
right there. I welcomed the stroke of his tongue, opened for it, and
a groan resonated in his throat. His hand slid to my breast.

Dimly realizing that the situation was about to blaze out of control, I struggled and pushed at him until his arms loosened. Panting,
I wrenched free. Just as he reached for me again, I held up a staying
hand, my fingers trembling.

"Wait . . . Wait . . ." I was breathing as if I'd sprinted a hundred
yards. So was Joe. I made my way to a big upholstered chair and sat
on the arm of it. My legs were weak. Every nerve shrilled in protest.
"I don't think we can talk without a buffer zone. Please, just . . . stay
over there and let me say a couple of things, okay?"

Sliding his hands in his pockets, Joe gave me a nod of assent. He
began to pace slowly.

"Just to be clear," I said, my face throbbing hotly, "I was more than
satisfied that night. You're great in bed, as I'm sure a lot of women
have told you. But I want an ordinary guy, someone I can be sure of,
and you . . . you are not that guy."

The pacing stopped. Joe gave me a confounded glance.

I licked at my dry lips and tried to think over the clamor of my
pulse. "You see, it's like . . . a long time ago, my mother wanted a
Chanel bag for her birthday. She taped a magazine picture of it to
the fridge and never stopped talking about it. My stepfather bought
it for her. She kept it on the top shelf of her closet in the special pro-

tective cover it came with. But she never carried the bag. So a few years later I asked her why the Chanel bag had always stayed in the closet, and why she'd never taken it out. She said it was too nice for every day. Too fancy. She didn't want to worry about it getting damaged or lost, and besides that, it didn't go with any of her clothes. It didn't fit who she was." I paused. "Do you understand what I'm trying to say?"

Joe shook his head with baffled annoyance.

"You're the Chanel bag," I said.

His scowl deepened. "Let's drop the metaphors, Avery. Especially ones where I'm in a damn closet."

"Yes, but do you get what I—"

"I want a real reason for why you won't go out with me. Something I can understand. Like you don't like the way I smell, or you think I'm an asshole."

Looking down at the fabric of the chair, I traced the geometric pattern with the tip of my fingernail. "I love the way you smell," I said, "and you're not at all an asshole. But . . . you are a player."

An unaccountably long pause followed before I heard his bewildered reply.

"Me?"

I lifted my head. I hadn't expected him to look so stunned.

"Where did you get that idea?" he asked.

"I've *been* with you, Joe. I'm a personal witness to your hookup skills. The conversation, the dancing, the way you knew exactly how to play it so I'd feel comfortable with you. And when we were in bed, you had a condom conveniently ready, right there on the nightstand, so there was no pause in the action. Obviously you'd figured out every step beforehand."

He shot me an affronted glance, color heightening his tan to a shade of rosewood. "You're mad because I had a condom? You'd rather have done it without one?"

"No! It's just that the whole thing was so . . . so practiced. So smooth. A routine you've perfected."

His voice was quiet but biting. "There's a difference between having experience and being a player. I don't score women. I don't have a routine. And setting my wallet on the nightstand doesn't make me fuckin' Casanova."

"You've been with a lot of women," I insisted.

"How are you defining 'a lot'? Is there a number I'm not supposed to go over?"

Stung by the note of scorn, I asked, "Before last weekend, had you ever slept with a woman the first time you met her?"

"Once. In college. The rules were understood beforehand. Why does that matter?"

"I'm trying to make the point that sex doesn't mean the same thing to you that it does to me. This was the only one-night stand I've ever had, not to mention the first time I've slept with someone since Brian. You and I have never even been out on a date. Maybe you don't think of yourself as a player, but compared to–"

"Brian?" He looked at me alertly.

Regretting my slip of the tongue, I said curtly, "My fiancé. I was engaged, and we broke it off. That's not important. My point is–"

"When did that happen?"

"It doesn't matter." I stiffened as Joe began to approach me.

"When?" he insisted.

"A while ago." I stood from the chair and took a step back. "Joe, the buffer zone–"

"When was the last time you slept with him? With anyone?" He reached me, taking hold of my arms as I shrank back. I ended up against the bookshelves, crowded by his big frame.

"Let go," I said faintly. My gaze ricocheted as I tried to look anywhere but directly at him. "Please."

Joe was ruthless. "One year?" A pause. "Two?" As I kept silent, he stroked my upper arms, his warm hands bringing up gooseflesh. His voice turned gentle. "More than two years?"

I had never felt more vulnerable or mortified. Too much of my past had just been revealed, along with an avalanche of self-doubt and naïveté. As I wilted in the heat of exposure, it occurred to me that I may have judged him differently from how a more emotionally secure woman would have.

I threw a longing glance at the door, desperate to leave. "We have to get back to the party—"

Joe pulled me against him. I writhed in protest, but his arms tightened, restraining me easily. "I understand now," I heard him say after a moment. Although I wanted to ask what, exactly, he thought he understood, I could only stand there in a trance. A minute passed, and another. I began to say something, but he hushed me and kept holding me. Clasped securely against the rise and fall of his chest, steeped in his body heat, I felt myself relaxing.

I was filled with the bittersweet knowledge that this was the last time he would ever hold me. After this we would cut our losses. We would put the memory of that night behind us for good. But I was going to remember this embrace, because it was the best, safest, warmest feeling I'd ever had in my life.

"We slept together too soon," he said eventually. "My fault."

"No, it wasn't—"

"It was. I could tell you didn't have much experience, but you were willing, and . . . hell, it felt too good to stop. I wasn't trying to play you. I'm—"

"Don't apologize for having sex with me!"

"Easy." Joe began to smooth my hair. "I'm not sorry that it happened. Only that it happened too soon for you to feel comfortable with it." He bent his head and kissed the soft skin around my ear, making me shiver. "It wasn't casual," he murmured. "Not for me. But I would never have let it go so far if I'd known it would scare you."

"It didn't scare me," I said, nettled by the implication that I was behaving like some terrified virgin.

"I think it did." His hand went to the back of my neck, kneading the small muscles gently, easing the ache into pleasure. It was all I could do not to arch and purr like a cat.

I tried to summon more indignation. "And what do you mean, you could tell I didn't have experience? Did I do something wrong? Was I a disappointment? Was I—"

"Yeah," Joe said, "it's a hell of a disappointment when I come so hard, I see stars. It was such a downer that I've been chasing after you ever since." He braced his hands on either side of me, gripping the edges of the bookshelf.

"It's over now," I managed to say. "I think we should chalk it up to—to a spontaneous moment—" I broke off with an incoherent sound as he leaned forward to kiss my neck.

"It can't be over when it never even started," he said against my skin. "I'll tell you what's going to happen, brown-eyed girl: You're going to answer the phone when I call. You're going to let me take you out, and we're going to do some talking. There's too much we don't know about each other." He found a pulse, and his lips lingered on the tiny, rampant rhythm. "So we're going to take it slow. I'll get to know you. You'll get to know me. And then it's up to you."

"It's too late," I managed to say in between shivering breaths. "Sleeping together ruined the getting-to-know-you part."

"It's not ruined. It's just a little more complicated."

If I agreed to go out with him again, I was asking for heartbreak. *Begging* for it. "Joe, I don't think–"

"No decisions right now," he said, his head lifting. "We'll talk later. For now . . ." He retreated a step and held out his hand. "Let's go back out there and have dinner. I want a chance to prove that I can behave around you." His hot gaze chased over me. "But I swear, Avery Crosslin . . . you don't make it easy."

∽

Dinner was an elaborate six-course affair, with a piano-and-violin duet playing in the background. The tent had been decorated in black and white, with white phalaenopsis orchid centerpieces, all of it a perfect setting for the art auction. I sat with Joe at a table for ten, along with Jack, Ella, and a few assorted friends.

Joe was in a relaxed good mood, at times casually resting his arm at the back of my chair. The group was chatty and animated, making small talk with the ease of people who did it often, who knew exactly how to keep the conversation fluid. As the Travis brothers exchanged quips and good-natured jabs, it was obvious that they genuinely enjoyed each other's company.

Joe recounted a recent road trip he'd taken to do photos for a Texas magazine's "bucket list" issue, featuring activities and places that no Texan should miss during his life, among them to go two-stepping at Billy Bob's in Fort Worth, eat chicken-fried steak topped with white gravy at a particular diner in San Antonio, and visit Buddy Holly's grave in Lubbock. Ella volunteered that she didn't like white gravy on her chicken-fried steak, at which point Jack half covered his face. "She eats it dry," he confessed, as if it were blasphemy.

"It's not dry," Ella protested, "it's fried. And if you ask me, battering and deep-frying cube steak *and* drowning it in biscuit gravy is the worst–"

Gently, Jack laid his fingers over her mouth. "Not in public," he cautioned. As he felt the shape of her grin, he promptly removed his hand and kissed her.

"I've eaten chicken-fried steak for breakfast," Joe volunteered. "With two fried eggs on the side."

Jack gave him an approving glance. "That there's a real man," he told Ella.

"That there is a cardiovascular tragedy waiting to happen," she retorted, making her husband grin.

Later, as Ella and I walked to the restroom together, I remarked, "There is no shortage of testosterone at that table."

Ella smiled. "It's the way they were raised. The oldest brother, Gage, is just the same. But don't worry: Despite all the brawn and bluster, Travis men are pretty enlightened." With a rueful grin, she added, "By Texas standards."

"So Jack helps with things like household chores and changing the diapers?"

"Oh, absolutely. But there are certain man-rules, like opening the door, or holding your chair, that are never going to change. And since Joe is obviously interested in you, I'll tell you right now, don't bother trying to split the check when he takes you out. He'd sooner commit hari-kari with a steak knife."

"I don't know if Joe and I will go out," I said cautiously. "It's probably better if we don't."

"I hope you do. He's a terrific guy."

We exited the tent and walked along the flowered pathway to the house. "Would you say he's a player?" I asked. "A heartbreaker?"

"I wouldn't put it that way." After a pause, Ella said frankly, "Women like Joe, and Joe likes women, so . . . yes, there have been one or two who wanted more of a commitment than he was willing to give. Let's face it, a lot of women would snap him up right away just because of the Travis name."

"I'm not one of them."

"I'm sure that's one of the reasons Joe likes you." We stopped beside an outdoor steel sculpture made of thick plates almost fifteen feet high, its edges curved and shaped in organic lines. Ella's voice lowered. "The Travises set quite a store by normalcy. They want to be part of the real world, experience it like everyone else, which is practically impossible at their level. Most of all they want to be treated like regular people."

"Ella . . . they're not regular people. I don't care how much chicken-fried steak they eat, they're just not. The money, the name, the looks . . . nothing about them is normal, no matter how they pretend otherwise."

"They're not pretending," Ella said thoughtfully, "it's more like . . . a value they want to live by. Trying to erase the distance between themselves and other people. They keep their egos in check, and they try to be honest with themselves." She shrugged and smiled. "I figure they deserve some credit for making the effort . . . don't you?"

⤟ Ten ⤞

At nine o'clock on Monday morning, Ryan Chase arrived at the Crosslin Event Design studio, determined to do or say whatever was necessary to "solve the problem" and move on. Except that a wedding wasn't supposed be a problem, it was supposed to be joyful. A union of two people who wanted to spend their lives together.

However, at this point in my career, I had learned that some weddings didn't match the fairy-tale template. So the goal in this case was to figure out what *was* possible. What might be appropriate for a bridegroom who viewed his wedding as an obligation.

I welcomed Ryan into the studio and introduced him to Sofia, who would be the only other person present at the meeting. I had told everyone else, including Steven, not to come in until noon. As we showed Ryan around, he seemed pleasantly surprised by the studio, looking closely at our renovations, the rows of factory windows left intact. "I like this place," he said. "I thought everything was going to be pink."

Sofia and I laughed.

"We have to live here," I said, "so it had to be comfortable and not too fussy. And on occasion, we do plan events other than weddings."

"It's nice that you kept some of the industrial elements." Ryan glanced up at a couple of exposed pipes overhead. "I do a lot of restoration projects. Old courthouses, theaters, and museums. I like buildings with character."

We sat on the blue sofa, while a video monitor played a photo stream from past weddings that the studio had planned and coordinated. "Ryan," I began carefully, "I've given a lot of thought to your circumstances. Every wedding comes with a certain amount of built-in stress. But when you add the stress of Bethany's pregnancy, and the drama Hollis brings to the table, it's going to be . . ."

"A nightmare?" he supplied.

"I was going to say 'challenging,'" I said wryly. "Have you considered talking Bethany into an elopement? Because we could arrange something simple and romantic, and I think it would be much easier on you."

Sofia shot me a startled glance. I knew she was wondering why I would risk the loss of a huge opportunity for our business. But I had to bring up the idea of eloping—I couldn't have lived with myself otherwise.

Ryan shook his head. "There's no way Bethany would ever go for that. She told me she's been dreaming her whole life about a big wedding." He relaxed a little, his blue eyes warming several degrees. "But it was nice of you to mention it. Thanks for taking my feelings into consideration." This was said without a trace of self-pity, only a matter-of-fact friendliness.

"Your feelings are important," I said. "And so are your opinions. I'm trying to get a sense of how much involvement you'll want in the wedding-planning process. Some men prefer to take part in every decision, whereas others—"

"Not me," he said flatly. "I'll leave all that to Bethany and Hollis. Not that I'd have a choice, anyway. But what I don't want is for the wedding to turn into something . . ." He paused, trying to think of the right word.

"*Una paletada hortera,*" Sofia supplied. At our questioning glances, she said, "There's not really a phrase for it in English . . . the best translation is 'a shovelful of tacky.'"

Ryan laughed, the flash of humor and warmth transforming his face. "That's exactly what I meant."

"All right, then," I said. "During the planning process, I'll give you updates as things are decided. If there's something you don't like, I'll shut it down. There may be a couple of things we'll have to compromise on, but overall, the wedding will be elegant. And it will not turn into *The Hollis Warner Show.*"

"Thank you," Ryan said feelingly. He looked at his watch. "If that's it for now—"

"Wait, what about the proposal?" I asked.

A slight frown crossed his brow. "I'll probably propose to Bethany next weekend."

"Yes, but do you know how you're going to do it?"

"I'll get a ring and take her out to dinner." His frown deepened as he saw my expression. "What's wrong with that?"

"Nothing at all. But you could do it in a more imaginative way. We could come up with something cute and fairly easy."

"I'm not good at cute," Ryan said.

"Take her to Padre Island," Sofia suggested. "Stay at a beachside villa for a night. The next morning, the two of you could go for a walk on the beach . . ."

"And you'll pretend to find a message in a bottle," I said, brainstorming.

"No, no," Sofia interrupted, "not a bottle ... a sand castle. We'll hire some professional sand sculptors to do it—"

"Based off a sketch that Ryan's provided," I said. "He's an architect—he can design a special sand castle for Bethany."

"Perfect," Sofia exclaimed, and we high-fived each other.

Ryan had been glancing back and forth between us as if he were attending a tennis match.

"Then you'll get down on one knee and propose," I continued, "and—"

"Do I have to take a knee when I ask her?" Ryan asked.

"No, but it's traditional."

Ryan rubbed the lower half of his jaw, clearly not liking the idea.

"Men used to kneel when they were being knighted," Sofia pointed out.

"Or beheaded," Ryan said darkly.

"Kneeling will look nicer for the pictures," I said.

"Pictures?" Ryan's brows lifted. "You want me to propose to Bethany with camera guys there?"

"One photographer," I said hastily. "You'll hardly notice him. We'll camouflage him."

"We'll hide him in a sand dune," Sofia added.

Frowning, Ryan raked his hand through the close-cut layers of his brown hair, the light picking out glints of mahogany.

I looked at Sofia. "Never mind. A camera at the proposal sounds like a shovelful of tacky to me."

Ryan lowered his head, but not before I saw a reluctant smile emerge. "Damn it," I heard him mutter.

"What?"

"Suggesting you as the wedding planner is turning out to be the first nice thing Hollis has ever done for me. Which means I might have to thank her."

∽

"You answered," Joe said later that night in a tone of mild surprise.

I smiled, leaning back against the pillows with my cell phone in hand. "You told me to."

"Where are you right now?"

"In bed."

"Should I call another time?"

"No, I'm not sleeping, I always sit in bed and do some reading at the end of the day."

"What do you like to read?"

I glanced at the pile of candy-colored novels on the nightstand and replied with self-conscious amusement, "Love stories. The kind with the happy endings."

"Do you ever get tired of knowing how the book's going to end?"

"No, that's the best part. Happily-ever-afters are hard to come by in real life, even in the wedding business. But at least I can count on one in a book."

"I've seen some great marriages in real life."

"They don't stay that way, though. Every marriage starts as a happy ending, and then it turns into a marriage."

"How did someone who doesn't believe in happily-ever-after end up as a wedding planner?"

I told him about my first job after graduating in fashion design, how I'd apprenticed under a New York designer for a bridal fashion label, managing the sample room, learning to analyze sales reports, developing relationships with buyers. I had worked on a few of my own designs and had even won a prize as an emerging designer. But when I'd tried to start my own label, it had never gotten off the ground. No one had shown any enthusiasm for backing me.

"I was honestly stunned," I told Joe. "The collection I'd designed was beautiful. I had a great reputation, and I'd built up all these amazing contacts. I couldn't figure out what was wrong. So I called Jasmine, and she said–"

"Who's Jasmine?"

"Oh, I forgot I hadn't told you about her. Jasmine's my best friend in New York. A mentor. She's the head fashion director at *Glimmer* magazine. She knows everything about style, and she can always tell which trends will be huge, and which ones will never get off the ground–" I paused. "Is this boring?"

"Not at all. Tell me what she said."

"Jasmine said there was nothing wrong with my collection. It was competently designed. Everything was in perfect taste."

"Then what was the problem?"

"That was the problem. I didn't take any risks. I didn't push my ideas enough. The extra *something*, that spark of originality . . . it wasn't there. But she said I was a fantastic businesswoman. I was good at networking and promoting; I got the business side of fashion like no one else she knew. I didn't like hearing any of this; I wanted to be a creative genius. But I had to admit that the business was what I'd really enjoyed, way more than the design work."

"Nothing wrong with that."

"I know that now. At the time, though, it was hard to let go of something I'd worked so hard for. Not long after that, my father had a stroke. So I flew down to visit him in the hospital, and I met Sofia, and my whole life changed."

"And the broken engagement?" Joe surprised me by asking. "When did that happen?"

The question made me tense and uncomfortable. "I hate talking about that."

"We don't have to." The gentleness of his voice eased the tightness in my chest. I settled back deeper into the pillows. "Do you miss New York?" he asked.

"Sometimes." I paused and said ruefully, "A lot. But there are some days when I don't think about it as much as others."

"What do you miss most about it?"

"My friends most of all. And . . . it's hard to put it into words, but . . . New York is the only place where I could be the person I want to be. It speeds me up and makes me think bigger. God, what a city. I still dream about going back someday."

"Why did you leave in the first place?"

"I was sort of . . . not myself . . . after the broken engagement, and my father passing away. I needed a change. And I especially needed to be with Sofia. We had just found each other. It was the right decision to move down here. But someday, when Sofia is ready to take over, I'm going to go back to New York and give it another shot."

"I think you'll do fine wherever you live. In the meantime, you can go visit, can't you?"

"Yes, but I've been too busy the past three years. Soon, though. I want to see my friends in person. I want to go to a couple of plays, and some of my favorite restaurants, and find a street fair with five-dollar pashminas, and have a slice of really good pizza, and there's this rooftop bar on Fifth where you get the most perfect view of the Empire State Building . . ."

"I know that bar."

"You do?"

"Sure. The one with the garden."

"Yes! I can't believe you've been there."

Joe sounded amused. "I've been outside the state of Texas, despite appearances to the contrary."

He told me about a couple of his past trips to New York. We exchanged stories about places where we'd traveled, about ones we'd want to go back to and the ones we wouldn't. About the freedom of traveling alone, but also the loneliness.

When I realized how late it was, I couldn't believe the conversation had lasted for over two hours. We agreed it was time to call it a night. But I had no desire to stop. I could have gone on talking.

"This was fun," I said, feeling warm and even a little giddy. "I wish we could do it again." In the short silence that followed, I covered my eyes with my free hand, wishing I could take back the impulsive words.

There was a smile in Joe's voice. "I'll keep calling," he said, "if you'll keep answering."

Eleven

As it turned out, we talked every night for a week, including the night Joe was driving back late from a photo shoot in Brownwood. He'd done a session for a young congressman who'd just been elected to the U.S. House in a special runoff. The congressman had been a difficult subject, controlling and awkward, posing like a politician, roosterlike, despite Joe's efforts to catch him in a relaxed moment. And the guy was a braggart, a name-dropper, qualities that were nearly intolerable to a Travis.

While we talked during Joe's long drive to Houston, he told me about the photo shoot, and I filled him in on the planning for Haven's baby shower. It was going to be held at the Travis River Oaks mansion, which had gone unoccupied ever since Churchill's passing, mostly because no one knew what to do with it. None of the Travises particularly wanted to sell the place—it was where they'd grown up—but neither did any of them want to live in it. Too big. Too reminiscent of their parents, who were both gone now. However, the pool and patio on the mansion's three-acre lot would provide the perfect setting for a party.

"I went to the River Oaks house today," I said. "Ella showed me around."

"What did you think?"

"Very impressive." The massive stone house had been designed to look like a château, surrounded by vast tracts of mowed green lawn, precisely trimmed hedges, and elaborate flower beds. After seeing walls sponged with a Tuscan faux finish and windows smothered with swag draperies, I had agreed with Ella's assessment that someone needed to "de-eighties" the place.

"Ella said that Jack had asked if she wanted to move there," I continued, "since they have two kids and the apartment's getting cramped."

"What did she say?"

"She told him the house is too big for a family of four. And Jack said they should move there anyway and just keep having children."

Joe laughed. "Good luck to him. I doubt he'll ever talk Ella into moving there, no matter how many kids they end up with. It's not her kind of place. Or his, for that matter."

"What about Gage and Liberty?"

"They've built their own house in Tanglewood. And I don't think Haven and Hardy have any more interest in living in River Oaks than I do."

"Would your father have wanted one of you to keep it?"

"He didn't say anything specific." A pause. "But he was proud of that place. It was a measure of what he'd achieved."

Joe had previously told me about his father, a tough bantam of a man who'd come from nothing. The deprivation of Churchill's childhood had instilled a fierce drive to succeed, almost a rage, that had never fully left him. His first wife, Joanna, had died soon after giving birth to a son, Gage. A few years later, Churchill had married Ava Chase, a glamorous, cultured, supremely elegant woman whose ambition was equal to Churchill's, and that was saying something. She had smoothed some of his rough edges, taught him about subtlety and diplomacy. And she had given him two sons, Jack and Joe, and a petite dark-haired daughter, Haven.

Churchill had insisted on raising the boys with responsibility and a sense of obligation, to become the kind of men he approved of. To be like him. He had been a man of absolutes: A thing was either good or bad, right or wrong. Having seen how the children of some of his well-to-do peers had turned out—spoiled and soft—Churchill had been determined not to raise his offspring with a sense of entitlement. His boys had been required to excel in school, especially math, a subject that Gage had mastered and at which Jack had been proficient and Joe, on his best days, had never been more than adequate. Joe's talents had been in reading and writing, pursuits Churchill considered somewhat unmanly, especially because Ava had liked them.

His youngest son's lack of interest in Churchill's private equity investments and financial management consulting business had finally resulted in a huge blowup. When Joe turned eighteen, Churchill had wanted to put him on the board of his holding company, as he'd done with Gage and Jack. He'd always planned on having all three sons on the board. But Joe had flat-out refused. He hadn't even accepted a nominal position. The mushroom cloud had been visible for miles. Ava had passed away from cancer two years earlier, and there had been no one to mediate or intervene. Joe's relationship with his father had been ice cold for a couple of years after that and hadn't entirely recovered until Joe had stayed with him after the boat accident.

"I had to learn patience fast," Joe had told me. "My lungs were shot, and it was hard to argue with Dad when I was breathing like a Pekingese."

"How did you two manage to reconcile?"

"We went out to play golf. I hated golf. Old-man sport. But Dad insisted on dragging me to the driving range. He taught me how to swing a club. We played a couple of times after that." A grin emerged. "He was so old, and I was so busted up, neither of us could break one thirty on eighteen holes."

"But you had a good time?"

"We did. And after that, everything was fine."

"But . . . it couldn't have been. If you didn't talk about the issues . . ."

"That's one of the great things about being a guy: Sometimes we fix things by deciding it was bullshit and ignoring the hell out of it."

"That's not fixing," I had protested.

"Sure it is. Like Civil War medicine: Amputate and move on." Joe had paused. "Usually you can't do that with a woman."

"Not usually," I had agreed dryly. "We like to solve problems by actually facing them and working out compromises."

"Golf's easier."

～◎～

In less than a week, my team had put together a vintage-boardwalk-themed party for Haven Travis's baby shower. Tank had enlisted a local theater set crew to help him construct and paint a dessert station that resembled a boardwalk game arcade. Steven hired a landscaper to install a temporary mini golf course on the grounds of the Travis mansion. Together Sofia and I met with caterers and agreed on an outdoor party menu featuring gourmet burgers, grilled shrimp kebabs, and lobster rolls.

The forecast for the day of the party was ninety degrees and humid. The event team arrived at the Travis mansion at ten A.M. After helping the tent company reps to set up a row of open-sided cabana tents by the pool, Steven returned to the kitchen, where the rest of us were unboxing decorations.

"Tank," he said, "I need you and your guys to assemble the board-walk arcade, and after that—" Steven broke off as he saw Sofia. His gaze traveled over the sleek length of her legs. "That's what you're wearing?" he asked, as if she were half-naked.

Sofia gave him a perplexed glance, a large bleached starfish in her hand. "What do you mean?"

"Your outfit." Scowling, Steven turned his attention to me. "Are you actually going to let her wear that?"

I was dumbfounded. Sofia was dressed like a forties pinup girl in red-and-white polka-dotted shorts with a matching halter top. The outfit showed off her curvy figure, but there was nothing immodest about it. I couldn't fathom why Steven would object.

"What's wrong with it?" I asked.

"It's too short."

"It's ninety degrees outside," Sofia snapped at Steven, "and I'm going to be working all day. Do you expect me to wear an outfit like Avery's?"

I sent her an irritated glance.

Before getting dressed that morning, I had considered wear-ing some of my new clothes, most of which had hung in my closet untouched. However, old habits were hard to break. Rather than choose something silky and colorful, I had reverted to one of my old standbys: a relaxed-fit white cotton tunic. It was loose and sleeve-less, worn over a pair of billowy gathered-hem pants that–despite their charming name of "poet pants"–were admittedly unflattering. But the outfit was comfortable, and I felt safe wearing it.

Steven gave Sofia a caustic glance. "Of course not. But it's still better than dressing like the featured performer at a strip club."

"Steven, that's enough," I said sharply.

"I'm going to fire you for sexual harassment," Sofia cried.

"You can't fire me," Steven informed her. "Only Avery can fire me."

"She won't have to if I kill you first!" She leapt toward him, hold-ing the starfish like a weapon.

"Sofia," I yelped, grabbing her from behind. "Take it easy! Put that down. Jesus, have you both lost your minds?"

"Someone around here has," I heard Steven say. "Unless the plan is to flaunt Sofia as millionaire bait."

That did it. *No one* insulted my sister that way. "Tank," I said in a murderous tone, "get him out of here. Throw him into the pool to cool him off."

"Literally?" Tank asked.

"Yes, literally throw him into the pool."

"Not the pool" came Steven's muffled voice. Tank already had him in a headlock. "I'm wearing linen!"

One of the qualities I appreciated most about Tank was his un-qualified allegiance to me. He hauled Steven out of the kitchen, lum-bering like a small bear. No amount of struggling and swearing would dissuade him.

"If I let go of you," I said to Sofia, who was straining to break free, "promise not to follow them outside."

"I want to watch Tank throw him into the pool."

"I understand. So do I. But this is our *business,* Sofia. We have work to do. Don't let Steven's lapse of sanity interfere with it." When I felt her relax, I dropped my arms from around her.

My sister turned to face me, looking furious and crestfallen. "He hates me. I don't know why."

"He doesn't hate you," I said.

"But why–"

"Sofia," I said, "he's an asshole. We'll talk about it later. For now, let's get to work."

When I saw Steven two hours later, he was mostly dry. He worked on the finishing touches of the mini golf course, positioning an old-fashioned diver's helmet so a golf ball could roll up a ramp into the front porthole.

As I approached, he spoke tersely while adjusting the ramp. "Dolce and Gabbana shorts. Dry-clean only. You owe me three hundred bucks."

"You owe me an apology," I said. "This is the first time you've ever been less than professional during a job."

"I apologize."

"You owe an apology to Sofia."

Steven remained mutinously silent.

"Care to explain what's going on?" I asked.

"I've already explained. Her outfit is inappropriate."

"Because she looks cute and sexy? It's not a problem for anyone else. Why does it bother *you* so much?"

Another stony silence.

"The caterers are here," I finally said. "The band is arriving at eleven. Val and Sofia have almost finished decorating the indoor areas, and then I'll have them start on the patio tables."

"I need Ree-Ann to help with the cabanas."

"I'll send her out." I paused. "One more thing. From now on, I insist that you treat Sofia with respect. Even though I'm technically in charge of hiring and firing, Sofia and I are equal partners. And if she wants you gone, you're gone. Understood?"

"Understood," he muttered.

As I headed back to the house, I passed Tank, who was carrying two huge bunches of helium-filled balloons for the dessert arcade. "Thanks for helping me with Steven," I said.

"You mean tossing him into the pool? No problem. I'll throw him in again if you want."

"Thank you," I said with grim amusement, "but if he steps out of line again, I'll throw him in myself."

I returned to the kitchen, where Ree-Ann and the caterers were uncrating sets of plates and glassware for the indoor dining area.

"Where's Sofia?" I asked.

"She went to say hi to some of the Travises. They just arrived."

"When you're done with the plates, Steven needs you to help him with the cabanas."

"Sure thing."

I went to the main living room to find the group standing at the row of long windows with Sofia. They looked out at the pool and patio area, exclaiming and talking and laughing. A small dark-haired boy jumped up and down and tugged on the hem of Jack's shirt. "Daddy, take me outside! I wanna go see! Daddy! Daddy–"

"Hold your horses, son." Jack ruffled the boy's hair gently. "They're not ready for us yet."

"Avery," Ella exclaimed as she saw me, "what an amazing job you've done. I was just telling Sofia that it looks like Disneyland out there."

"I'm so glad you're happy with it."

"I'm never having a party without the two of you again. Can I keep you on retainer like lawyers?"

"Yes," Sofia said immediately.

Laughing, I turned my attention to the baby in Ella's arms. The infant was adorably chubby and pink-cheeked, with big blue eyes and curly blond hair pulled up in a topknot.

"Who is this?" I asked.

"That's my sister, Mia," the little boy answered before Ella could reply, "and I'm Luke, and I want to go to the party!"

"It'll be ready soon," I promised. "You can be the first one to go outside."

Deciding that it had fallen to him to make introductions, Luke pointed to the couple nearby. "That's my aunt Haven. She's got a big tummy. There's a baby in there."

"Luke—" Ella began, but he continued earnestly.

"She eats more than Uncle Hardy, and he could eat a whole *dinosaur.*"

Ella clapped a hand to her forehead. "Luke—"

"I did once," Hardy Cates said, lowering to his haunches. He was big and ruggedly built, a good-looking man with the bluest eyes I had ever seen. "Back when I was a boy camping in the Piney Woods. My friends and I were chasing armadillos across a dry river bottom, and we saw a big shape moving through the trees . . ."

The child listened, enraptured, as Hardy told him a tall tale about a dinosaur being pursued, lassoed, and eventually barbecued.

No doubt the prospect of marrying the only daughter in the Travis family would have deterred more than a few men. But Hardy Cates didn't seem like the type who was capable of being intimidated. He was a former roughneck who had started his own oil recovery company, going into spent fields to extract leftover reserves that bigger companies had left behind. Ella had described him as hardworking and wily, covering up his outsize ambition with plenty of laid-back charm. Hardy seemed so affable, Ella had said, that people were fooled into thinking they'd gotten to know him, even though they hadn't. But the Travises all agreed on one thing: Hardy loved Haven intensely, would have died for her. According to Ella, Jack had facetiously claimed he almost felt sorry for the guy, being wrapped around his little sister's finger like that.

I reached out to shake Haven's hand. She was delicately pretty, with dark winged brows. A Travis, unmistakably, although she was so much slighter and smaller than her towering brothers that she seemed to be a half-scale version. She was far along in her pregnancy, her ankles swollen and her stomach so heavy that it made me want to wince in sympathy.

"Avery," she said, "it's so nice to meet you. Thanks for doing this."

"We had a lot of fun," I said. "If there's anything we can do to make the party more enjoyable, just tell me. Can I get you some lemonade? Ice water?"

"No, I'm fine."

"She should be drinking something continuously," Hardy said, coming to his wife's side. "She's dehydrated and retaining water."

"At the same time?" I asked.

Haven smiled ruefully. "Apparently so. Who knew it was possible? We just came from my weekly checkup." She leaned against Hardy, and her smile widened. "We also found out that we're having a girl."

Luke received this announcement with a look of disgust. *"Awwww . . ."*

Amid the general congratulations, I heard a familiar deep voice. "That's good news—we need more girls in the family." My heart kicked into a faster pace as Joe entered the room, lean and athletic in a pair of board shorts and a blue T-shirt.

He went straight to Haven, gathering her in a careful hug. Keeping her at his side, he reached out to shake Hardy's hand. "Let's just hope she has her mama's looks."

Hardy chuckled. "No one's hoping for that more than me." They prolonged the handshake for a couple of extra seconds, in the way of good friends.

Joe looked down at Haven affectionately. "How are you, sis?"

She looked up at him with chagrin. "When I'm not throwing up, I'm starving. I have aches and pains, mood swings and hair loss, and this past week I sent poor Hardy out for chicken nuggets at least a half-dozen times. Other than that, I'm great."

"I don't mind going out to get you the chicken nuggets," Hardy told her. "The hard part is watching you eat them with grape jelly."

Joe laughed and grimaced.

While Ella engaged the parents-to-be in a conversation about the doctor's visit, Joe came to me and bent to kiss my forehead. The touch of his mouth, the soft rush of his breath, sent a ripple of excitement down my spine. After the long talks we'd had, I should have felt comfortable with him. Instead I was nervous and oddly shy.

"You been busy today?" he asked.

I nodded. "Since six."

His fingers tangled gently with mine. "Can I help with something?"

Before I could reply, more of the family arrived. Gage, the oldest Travis sibling, was tall and athletic like his brothers, but his manner was quieter, composed, in comparison with their rough-and-tumble charm. His eyes were a striking pale gray, the light irises contained in darker rims.

Gage's wife, Liberty, was an attractive brunette with a warm, open smile. She introduced me to her son, Matthew, a boy of about five or six, and his big sister, Carrington, a pretty blond girl in her early teens. Everyone was laughing and talking at once, at least a half-dozen conversations happening simultaneously.

Even without prior knowledge of the Travises, I would have perceived instantly that they were a close-knit bunch. You could see and feel it in the way they interacted, with the familiarity of people who knew one another's schedules and habits. The genuine liking between them was unmistakable. These were not relationships that would be set aside lightly or taken for granted. Having never been part of such a group, or anything remotely similar, I was fascinated but leery. I wondered how you could become part of a family like that and not be subsumed.

I stood on my toes to murmur near Joe's ear, "I have to carry some things out to the mini golf course."

"I'll come with you."

Although I began to tug my hand free, Joe's grip tightened. Amusement sparkled in his eyes as he murmured, "It's okay."

But I pulled away, reluctant to make any kind of demonstration in front of his family.

"Uncle Joe," I heard Luke ask, "is that your girlfriend?"

I turned crimson, while someone choked back a laugh.

"Not yet," Joe said easily, holding one of the French doors for me. "You have to work a little harder to get one of the good ones." He accompanied me out to the patio and reached down for a bag of miniature golf clubs and a bucket of balls. "I'll carry these," he said. "You lead the way."

As we walked across the patio and past the row of poolside cabanas, I debated inwardly about saying something to him, about giving his family the wrong impression. I didn't want them to think there was anything going on between us other than friendship. However, this didn't seem to be the right time or place to discuss it.

"Everything looks great," Joe said, taking in the arcade dessert buffet, the band setting up near the house.

"Considering how little time we had, it's not bad."

"Everyone appreciates the effort you put into it."

"I'm glad to help." I paused. "Your family seems really close. Even a bit clannish."

Joe considered that and shook his head. "I wouldn't say we're clannish. We all have outside friends and interests." As we walked over a section of mowed green lawn, he said, "I'll admit, we've seen a lot of each other since Dad died. We decided to start a charity foundation, with the four of us as the board of trustees. It's taken some time to get it up and running."

"When you were growing up," I asked, "did you have the usual fights and sibling rivalries?"

Joe's mouth twitched as if he were amused by a distant memory. "You could say that. Jack and I nearly killed each other a couple of times. But whenever we got too rough, Gage would come and beat on us until we settled down. The way to earn a surefire killing was to do something mean to Haven—kidnap one of her dolls or scare her with a spider—Gage would come after us like the wrath of God."

"Where were your parents when all of that was happening?"

Joe shrugged. "We were left on our own a lot. Mom was always cochair of one charity or another, or busy with her friends. Dad was usually gone doing TV appearances or flying overseas."

"That must have been difficult."

"The problem wasn't Dad being gone. The problem was when he tried to make up for lost time. He was afraid we were being raised soft." Joe gestured with the bag of clubs. "See that retaining wall over there? One summer Dad had a truck unload three tons of stone in the backyard, and he told us to build a wall. He wanted us to learn the value of hard work."

I blinked at the sight of the dry-stacked wall, three feet high, extending approximately twenty feet before tapering to the ground. "*Just* the three of you?"

Joe nodded. "We cut rock with chisels and hand sledges, and stacked it, all in hundred-degree heat."

"How old were you?"

"Ten."

"I can't believe your mother allowed that."

"She wasn't happy about it. But once Dad put his foot down, there was no changing his mind. I think when he'd had a chance to think about it, he was sorry about having made the job that big. But he couldn't back down. To him, changing his mind was a weakness."

After setting down the clubs, Joe went to pour the golf balls into a painted wooden container. He glanced at the wall, squinting against the sun. "It took the three of us a month. But when we finished building the son of a bitch, we knew we could rely on each other. We'd made it through hell together. From then on we never raised a fist against each other again. No matter what. And we never took Dad's side against each other."

I reflected that while the family's wealth had conferred many advantages, none of the Travis offspring had escaped the pressures of expectation and obligation. No wonder they were close—who else would understand what their lives had been like?

Pensively, I wandered to the first hole of the mini golf course. The ramp on the diver's helmet didn't look quite straight, and I went to fiddle with it. I rolled a ball up the ramp and frowned as it bounced off the edge of the helmet's porthole. "I hope this is going to work."

Joe pulled a club from the bag, dropped a ball to the green, and putted. The ball rolled neatly across the green, up the ramp, and into the porthole. "Seems fine." He handed me the club. "You want to give it a try?"

Gamely, I placed a ball on the green and took a swing. The ball careened up the ramp, bounced off the helmet, and rolled back to me.

"You've never played golf before."

"How can you tell?" I asked dryly.

"Mostly because you're holding the club like a flyswatter."

"I hate sports," I confessed. "I always have. In school, I avoided gym class whenever possible. I faked sprains and stomachaches. On three different occasions, I told them my parakeet died."

His brows lifted. "That got you out of gym class?"

"The death of a parakeet is not an easy thing to get over, pal."

"Did you even have a parakeet?" he asked gravely.

"He was a metaphorical parakeet."

Laughter danced in his eyes. "Here, I'll show you how to hold the club." He reached around me. "Wrap your fingers around the handle... No, left hand. Rest your thumb farther down the shaft... Perfect. Now take hold below with your right. Like this." He shaped my fingers around the grip. I took an extra breath to make up for the one that had stuck in my throat. I could feel the rise and fall of his chest, the solid, vital strength of him. His mouth was close to my ear. "Feet apart. Bend your knees a little and lean forward." Releasing me, he stood back and said, "Swing easy and follow through."

I swung, connected gently, and the ball rolled into the porthole with a satisfying *plunk*. "I did it!" I exclaimed, whirling to face him.

Joe smiled and caught me close, his hands at my waist. I looked up at him and time stopped, everything stopped. It seemed as if an electric current had locked up every muscle, and all I could do was wait helplessly with the awareness of him flooding me.

His dark head lowered, and his mouth came to mine.

In the privacy of my imagination, I had relived his kisses, I had tasted them in my dreams. But nothing was close to the reality of him, the heat and soft, searching pressure, the intense sensuality of the way he brought up the desire slowly.

Gasping, I managed to pull back. "Joe, I . . . I'm not comfortable with this, especially in front of your family. And my employees. Someone might get the wrong impression."

"What impression would that be?"

"That there's something going on between us."

A series of expressions crossed his face: puzzlement, annoyance, mockery. "There's not?"

"No. We're friends. That's all it is for now, and that's all it's ever going to be, and . . . I have to work."

With that, I turned and strode toward the house in a subdued panic, feeling more relieved with every footstep I could put between us.

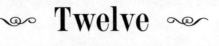

Twelve

The band played jaunty surfer-pop as guests began to arrive. In no time at all, the house and patio were packed. People swarmed around the buffet and went out to the boardwalk arcade for dessert. A bartender served tropical drinks at a grass hut near the pool, while waitstaff walked around with trays of ice water and glasses of non-alcoholic punch.

"The mini golf course is a hit," Sofia said as we passed each other on the patio. "So is the dessert station. In fact, everything is a hit."

"Any problems with Steven?" I asked.

She shook her head. "Did you say anything to him?"

"I made it clear that anyone who disrespects you will be out on his ass."

"We couldn't afford to lose Steven."

"Out on his ass," I repeated firmly. "No one talks to you like that."

Sofia smiled at me. *"Te amo."*

For the rest of the afternoon, I stayed busy, taking care not to cross paths with Joe. A couple of times, when I passed by him, I could feel him trying to catch my gaze, but I ignored him, afraid that he would pull me into a conversation. Afraid that my face would reveal too much or that I would say something foolish.

Seeing Joe in person forced me to contend with him not as a friendly voice on the phone, but as a robust male who made no secret of the fact that he wanted me. Any notion I might have had of trying for a platonic friendship with Joe was gone. He wasn't going to settle for that. Neither would he let me slip away without a confrontation. My mind buzzed with ideas about how to handle him, what to say.

After lunch had been cleared and the caterers were washing dishes, I found Sofia and Ree-Ann standing just outside the kitchen door, drinking glasses of iced tea. They stared intently in the direction of the pool, neither of them sparing me a glance.

"What are you two looking at?" I asked.

Sofia made a shushing motion with her hand.

Following their gazes, I saw Joe emerging from the pool, shirtless and dripping. The sight of his athletic body, bronzed and taut, all those wet muscles gleaming in the sun, was spectacular. He shook his head like a dog, sending water drops flying.

"That is the hottest guy I've ever seen," Ree-Ann said reverently.

"A *papi chulo*," Sofia agreed.

Joe lowered to sit beside the pool as his nephew Luke came to him with an orange plastic water wing, the kind that slid over the upper arms. Joe pried open the valve on the plastic wing and blew air into it. I noticed a neat diagonal surgical scar on his side, parallel to his ribs, extending upward almost to his back. The line was nearly invisible, only a shade or two darker than the surrounding skin, but I could tell from the way the light hit it that the scar was slightly raised. After turning Luke around, Joe repeated the procedure on the other water wing.

"I wish he'd inflate my flotation devices," Ree-Ann said wistfully.

"Can't either of you find something productive to do?" I asked in annoyance.

"We're taking our ten-minute break," Sofia said.

Ree-Ann shook her head in admiration as Joe stood, his board shorts riding low on his hips. "Mmmn. Look at that rear view."

Scowling, I muttered, "It's not right to objectify men any more than it is for them to do it to us."

"I'm not objectifying him," Ree-Ann protested. "I'm just saying his ass is cute."

Before I could respond, Sofia said, "I think our break is over, Ree-Ann." She was struggling to hold back a laugh.

The three of us went to work in the kitchen with the catering staff as they boxed up untouched food to be taken to a women's shelter directly afterward. Glassware, dishes, and table accessories were washed and dried, table linens were put into laundry bags, the garbage was bagged, and the kitchen was scrubbed until it was spotless.

As the last of the party guests went inside to mingle with the family in the main room, Steven and Tank supervised the breakdown of the cabana tents and the dessert station, while the rest of the crew cleaned the pool and patio. After the caterers and cleanup staff had left, I walked around to make certain we had left everything exactly as we'd found it.

"Avery . . ." Sofia came out to the patio, looking satisfied but tired. "I just went through the house—it's perfect. The Travises are relaxing in the living room. Ree-Ann can drop me off at home, or I can stay here with you."

"Go with Ree-Ann. I'll ask Ella if there's anything else they'd like me to do."

"You sure?"

"Absolutely."

Sofia smiled. "I probably won't be home when you get back. I'm going to the gym."

"Tonight?" I asked incredulously.

"There's a new combo class with spinning and core training."

I gave her an arch glance. "What's his name?"

Sofia smiled sheepishly. "I don't know yet. He always takes bike twenty-two. Last spin class, he challenged me to a race."

"Who won?"

"He did. But only because I was distracted by his glutes."

I laughed. "Have a good workout."

After Sophia left, I continued to walk around the pool. Sunset wouldn't occur for another couple of hours, but the low-slung light was already braised with the last red fire of day. I was hot and sticky, and my feet were sore from walking back and forth across the patio. Sighing, I slipped off my sandals and flexed my toes and arches.

As I glanced into the water, I noticed a small, brightly colored object at the bottom of the pool. It looked like a child's toy. The cleanup crew had left by then; I was the only one outside. I walked to the shed where pool supplies were kept and found a long-handled net hung on a wall rack. It was the kind of net used for skimming debris. After fumbling to extend the telescoping handle to its fullest length, I crouched at the edge of the pool and sank the net as deep as I could. Unfortunately, it wasn't long enough.

One of the patio doors opened and closed. Somehow I knew it was Joe, even before I heard him ask casually, "Need a hand?"

I felt a thrill of worry, shrinking inwardly as I wondered if he would want to talk.

"I'm trying to get something out of the pool," I replied. "It looks like a kid's toy." Standing, I offered the pool net to Joe. "Do you want to give it a try?"

"That won't reach. It's about fourteen feet deep. We used to have a diving board at that end." Joe stripped off his shirt and dropped it to the sun-warmed tile.

"You don't have to—" I began, but he had already dived cleanly into the water, heading straight to the bottom with powerful, efficient strokes.

He emerged with a red-and-yellow toy car. "It's Luke's," he said, setting it on the side. "I'll take it in to him."

"Thank you."

Joe seemed in no hurry to get out of the pool. After pushing back his wet hair, he braced his folded arms on the tiled edge. Feeling that it would seem rude to just walk away, I lowered myself to sit on my heels, bringing our gazes closer to the same level.

"Did Haven enjoy the party?" I asked.

Joe nodded. "It was a good day for her. For all of us. The family doesn't want to clear out yet—they're talking about sending out for Chinese." A brief hesitation. "Why don't you stay and have dinner?"

"I should probably go home," I said. "I'm tired and sweaty. I wouldn't be good company."

"You don't need to be good company. That's the point of family: They have to tolerate you anyway."

I smiled. "It's your family, not mine. Technically they don't have to tolerate me."

"They will if I want them to."

Hearing a mockingbird's raggedy cry, I glanced at the distant tangle of trumpet vines and wax myrtle that bordered the bayou. Another mockingbird responded. Back and forth, one aggressive shriek after another.

"Are they fighting?" I asked.

"Could be a boundary dispute. But this time of year, there's still a chance they're courting."

"So it's a serenade?" The birds shrieked with all the musicality of torn sheet metal. "God, how romantic."

"It gets better when they reach the chorus."

I laughed and made the mistake of looking into his eyes. We were too close. I could smell his skin, sun and salt and chlorine. His hair was disheveled, and I wanted to smooth the wet locks, play with them.

"Hey," Joe said gently. "Why don't you come in here with me?"

The look in his eyes sent a rush of hot color over my face. "I don't have a swimsuit."

"Jump in with your clothes on. They'll dry out."

I shook my head with a flustered laugh. "I can't do that."

"Then take them off and swim in your underwear." His tone was practical, but I saw the mischief in his eyes.

"You," I informed him, "are out of your mind."

"Come on. It'll feel good."

"I'm not going to do something stupid with you just because it feels good." After a pause, I added with chagrin, "Again."

Joe laughed in that soft way he had, smoky and deep in his throat. "Come in here." He caught my wrist lightly with one hand.

"There's no way I'm . . . *Hey*." My eyes widened as I felt him exerting tension on my wrist. "Joe, I swear I'll kill you—"

One gentle tug was all it required to pull me off balance. I toppled forward with a little scream, into the water, readily enclosed in his waiting arms.

"Damn you!" I began to splash him furiously, flailing. "I can't believe you did that . . . . Stop laughing, you idiot! This is not funny!"

Snorting and chuckling, Joe grabbed me and pressed kisses wherever he could, on my head and neck and ear. I struggled indignantly, but his arms were too strong and his hands were everywhere. It was like wrestling an octopus.

"You are so damn cute," he gasped. "Like a little wet cat. Sweetheart, don't wear yourself out, you can't kick someone underwater."

As he played and I struggled, we slid to deeper water, and my feet left the bottom. Instinctively I clutched at him. "It's too deep."

"I've got you." Joe was still standing, one arm locking low on my hips. Some of his playfulness melted into concern. "Can you swim?"

"It would have been nice to ask before pulling me in," I said testily. "Yes, I can swim. But not well. And I don't like deep water."

"You're safe." He pulled me closer. "I'd never let anything happen to you. Now that you're in here, you might as well stay for a few minutes. Feels good, doesn't it?"

It did, although I wasn't about to give him the satisfaction of admitting it.

My clothes turned virtually transparent, the wet cotton billowing and undulating like the fins of exotic sea creatures. One of my hands encountered the diagonal scar at the side of Joe's chest. Hesitantly, I let my fingertips follow the slight ridge.

"This is from the boat accident?"

"Uh-huh. Surgery for a blood clot and a partially collapsed lung." One of his hands ventured beneath the drifting hem of my tunic to find the bare skin of my waist. "You know what that whole damn experience taught me?" he asked softly.

I shook my head, staring into his eyes, seeing reflected glimmers of sunset like tiny rushlights.

"Don't waste a minute of your life," he said. "Look for every reason you can to be happy. Don't hold back, thinking you'll have more time later . . . none of us can ever be sure about that."

"That's what makes life so scary," I said soberly.

Joe shook his head, smiling. "That's what makes it great." He lifted me higher, closer, and my hands crept around his neck.

Just before his lips met mine, a sound attracted his attention. He glanced over his shoulder as someone approached. "What do you want?" he asked irritably.

I started as I heard his brother Jack's laconic reply. "Heard someone holler."

Mortified to be caught in the pool with nowhere to hide, I shrank against Joe's chest.

"Did Avery fall in?" I heard Jack ask.

"No, I dunked her."

"Nice move" came the deadpan reply. "Want me to bring y'all a couple of towels?"

"Yeah, later. For now, I'd like some privacy."

"Sure thing."

After Jack left, I wriggled free from Joe and swam toward the shallow end. He kept pace with me, surging through the water with the ease of a dolphin. When I could stand with the water at chest level, I stopped and turned to face him with a scowl. "I don't like to be embarrassed. And I don't like to be pulled into swimming pools!"

"Sorry." He tried to look and sound contrite, with only limited success. "I wanted to get your attention."

"My *attention*?"

"Yeah." He moved around me slowly, his gaze holding mine. "You've been ignoring me all day."

"I was working."

"And ignoring me."

"All right," I admitted, "I was ignoring you. I don't know how we're supposed to behave in front of people. I'm not even sure what we're doing, and–" I broke off uneasily. "Joe, stop circling like that. I feel like I'm in the pool with a bull shark."

He reached for me, pulling me forward until I was lifted off my feet, the momentum floating me against him. Pressing a scorching kiss to my neck, he murmured, "I'd like to take a bite out of you."

As I tried to wriggle out of his arms, he gathered me up, deliberately keeping me off balance. "Come back here."

"What are you doing?"

"I want to talk to you." He took me to deeper water, where I was forced to cling to the hard slopes of his shoulders.

"About what?" I asked anxiously.

"About the problem we're having."

"Just because I don't want to have a relationship with you doesn't mean I have a problem."

"I agree. But if you wanted to have a relationship and you couldn't because you were afraid of something . . . then you would have a problem. And it'd be my problem, too."

The skin of my face tightened until I could feel my cheeks pulsing. "I want to get out of the pool."

"Let me say something–just give me a couple of minutes–and then I'll let you go. Deal?"

I responded with a quick nod.

There was something spare and focused in the way he spoke.

"Everyone has secrets they don't want anyone to know. When you reckon all of it up . . . all those things we did or were done to us . . . all our sins and mistakes and guilty pleasures . . . those secrets are the sum of who we are. Sometimes you have to take a chance on letting someone in, because your gut tells you that person's worth it. But then all bets are off. You have to trust them, and hope they won't rip your heart out, and fuck it, sometimes you make the wrong call." He paused. "But you have to keep taking chances on the wrong people till you find the right one. You quit too damn early, Avery."

I felt suffocated and miserable. It didn't matter that he was right; I wasn't ready for this. For him. "I'd like to get out now." My voice came out thin and rickety.

Joe began to tow me to the shallow end. "Have you ever looked yourself up online, honey?"

Bewildered, I shook my head. "Steven handles most of the Internet stuff—"

"I don't mean your business. I mean your own name. The first results page is all related to your work: some blogs that mention you, a link to a Pinterest board, that kind of stuff. But on the second page, there's a link to an older article in a New York paper . . . about a bride who was jilted on her wedding day."

I felt myself turn bleach white.

Sometimes when I thought about that day, I could will myself into a state of detachment and view it as if it had happened to someone else. I tried to do that right now, but I couldn't manage to put any distance between me and that memory. I couldn't be detached about anything when Joe was holding me. And he was going to force me to explain how, on what should have been the happiest day of my life, I'd been rejected, abandoned, and humiliated in front of everyone whose opinion mattered to me. For a woman with normal self-esteem, that day would have been devastating. For a woman whose self-esteem hadn't been all that robust to begin with, it had been annihilating.

I closed my eyes as shame scalded every vein like poison. People who had experienced true shame didn't fear death the way regular people did . . . we knew that death would be a lot easier to tolerate. "I can't talk about it," I whispered.

Joe guided my wet head to his shoulder. "The groom called it off that morning," he continued evenly. "No one would have blamed the bride for falling apart. But instead she started making calls. She changed all the plans she'd made, so she could donate the wedding reception—which she'd paid for—to a local charity. And she spent the rest of the day with two hundred homeless people, treating them to a five-course dinner with live music. She was a fine, generous woman, and well rid of the asshole."

It was a long time before I could speak. Joe's fingers shaped to my skull and he kept his hand there, as if he were protecting me from something. I needed this more than I would have believed, latched so securely against him that his body formed the necessary margin, the boundary between me and the rest of the world.

It was more intimate than sex, to have someone hold the broken pieces of you together like that.

Gradually, I felt warmth coming back into my body, sensation returning until I was aware of his bare shoulder against my cheek, how hot and smooth the skin was. "I didn't want it in the paper," I said. "I asked the shelter not to say anything."

"It's hard to keep a gesture like that secret." Turning his mouth to my ear, he kissed it gently. "Can you tell me just a little, sweetheart? About what he said that morning?"

I swallowed hard. "Brian called and told me he wouldn't be at the ceremony. I thought he meant he was going to be late, so I asked if he was caught in traffic, and he said no, he wasn't coming at all. I was so shocked, I couldn't say anything. I couldn't even ask why. He said he was sorry, but he wasn't sure if he'd ever loved me ... or maybe he'd loved me but it had just gone away."

"If it's real," Joe said quietly, "it doesn't go away."

"How do you know?"

"Because that's what real is."

We moved slowly through the water, turning, floating in a lazy push and pull. I had no connection to anything except Joe, no contact with solid ground. He was in absolute control, leading me in a languid glide, and I was lulled by the peculiar sensuality of it.

"Brian didn't cheat on me, or anything like that," I found myself saying. "He had a terrible lifestyle—no one who works on Wall Street should even try to have a relationship until they're at least thirty. The schedule was insane. Eighty-hour workweeks, heavy drinking, no exercise, no spare time ... Brian could never stop long enough to figure out what he really wanted."

As Joe turned in a slow circle, I found myself wrapping around him like a mermaid. "Sometimes you think you love someone," I said, "but it's really just that they've become a habit. At the last minute, Brian realized that was how he felt about me."

Joe pulled my arms around his neck, locking my fingers together at his nape. I brought myself to look into his eyes, lost in the dark, steady heat. Our progress around the pool resumed, and I held on to him, drifting easily. Whatever Joe's opinions were about Brian— and no doubt he had some strong ones—he kept to himself for now. He was quiet, waiting patiently for whatever I might want to tell him. Somehow that made it easier to confide the rest, the part that only Sofia knew.

"I went to my father after Brian called," I said. "I'd paid for him to fly up from Texas, so he could walk me down the aisle. My mother was livid when she found out. She and I were never all that close—I think we were both relieved when I left home to go to school. I love her, but I've always known that something wasn't right between us. She got married and divorced twice after Dad left us, but of all the men in her past, he was the one she hated the most. She always said that getting involved with him was the worst mistake she ever made. I don't think she can ever look at me without thinking of me as the daughter of the mistake."

We were in deep water now. I tightened my arms around Joe's neck.

"I've got you," he said, his tone reassuring. "Go on."

"My mother said she wouldn't come if Eli was there. She said I had to choose between them. And I chose him. That was pretty much the end of our relationship—she and I have hardly talked since then. I've invited her to come to Houston and meet Sofia, but she always refuses." I relaxed as Joe eased us to shallower water. "I don't know why I wanted Eli there so badly. He'd never done any of the things fathers were supposed to do. I guess I thought having him walk me down the aisle would make up for some of that. It felt like it would make everything right."

Joe's face was unreadable as he looked down at me. "What happened when you told him that Brian had called off the wedding?"

"He gave me a tissue, and hugged me, and I remember thinking, *This is my dad, and he's here for me, and I can lean on him when I'm in trouble, and it might even be worth losing Brian to find that out.* But then he said . . ."

"What?" Joe prompted when I fell silent.

"He said, 'Avery, it was never going to last anyway.' He told me that men weren't cut out for monogamy—you know, the biological thing—and he said most men ended up disappointed with their wives. He said he wished someone had told him a long time ago that no matter how much in love you were—no matter how convinced you were that you'd found 'the one'—you would always find out when it was too late that you'd been lying to yourself." I smiled bleakly. "It was my father's way of being kind. He was trying to help me by telling me the truth."

"His truth. Not everyone else's."

"It's my truth too."

"The hell it is." Joe's voice had changed, no longer quite so patient. "You spend most of your time planning one wedding after another. You started a business doing that. Some part of you believes in it."

"I believe in marriage for some people."

"But not for yourself?" When it became clear that I wasn't going to reply, he said, " 'Course you don't. The two most important men in your life gave you a hell of a one-two punch, at a time when you couldn't protect yourself." Fervently he added, "I'd like to go back and kick both their asses."

"You can't. My father's gone, and Brian's not worth it."

"I still might kick his ass someday." Joe's hold on me altered, his hands becoming bolder, more intimate. The sky had turned blood orange, the hot evening air pungent with lantana. "When do you think you'll be ready to try another relationship?"

In the electric silence that followed, I didn't dare tell him what I really thought . . . that rehashing the sad, bitter memories had reminded me how much I wanted to avoid becoming involved with him. "When I find the right kind of man," I said eventually.

"What kind is that?"

I tensed as I felt his fingers sliding beneath the back placket of my bra. "Independent," I said. "Someone who agrees that we don't have to experience everything together. A guy who doesn't mind if we have separate interests and separate friends, and separate households. Because I like a lot of alone time–"

"What you just described isn't a relationship, Avery. It's friends with benefits."

"No, I wouldn't mind being part of a couple. I just don't want a relationship to take over everything."

We had stopped at the side of the pool, my back to the wall. My toes wouldn't quite touch the bottom, obliging me to cling to the hard slopes of his shoulders. I dropped my gaze and found myself staring at his chest, mesmerized by the way the water had darkened and flattened the coarse hair.

"That sounds like the same setup you had with Brian," I heard him say.

"Not exactly the same," I said defensively. "But yes, something like that. I know what's right for me."

I felt a deft tug at the back of my bra, the heavy padded cups loosening. I gasped, my legs churning in a search for traction. His hands slid to my breasts, caressing me under the water, teasing the hardening tips. He pressed me back against the wall, his thigh intruding between mine. "Joe–" I protested.

"Now it's my turn to talk." The sound of his voice in my ear was pure sin. "I'm the guy who's right for you. I may not be what you're looking for, but I'm what you want. You've been alone long enough, honey. It's time for you to wake up with a man in your bed. Time for the kind of sex that lays you out, owns you, leaves you too shaky to pour your morning coffee." He pulled me more fully against his thigh, the intimate pressure making me weak with desire. "You're going to have it every night, any way you want it. I have the time for you, and I sure as hell have the energy. I'll make you forget every man you ever knew before me. The catch is, you have to trust me first. That's the hard part, isn't it? You can't let anyone get too close. Because someone who knows you like that, he could hurt you—"

"That's enough." I floundered and pushed at him clumsily, dying to make him shut up.

His head lowered, and he kissed the side of my neck, using his tongue, making me squirm. In the middle of the twisting and splashing, he wedged both legs between mine and slid a hand over my bottom. I whimpered as he pulled me up against him, *there*, making me feel how big he was, how ready, and all my senses focused on that stiff, tantalizing pressure.

Gripping his hand in my hair, Joe brought my mouth to his and kissed me, deep and hungry. His other hand kept urging my hips closer, forcing me to ride him in an erotic protean rhythm, and I couldn't believe how damned shameless he was, and how good he felt, his body so hot and hard against mine. He was deliberate, doing exactly as he pleased, feeding every sensation with raw lust.

As the pleasure climbed, I couldn't stand it anymore, I had to wrap my legs around him, my nerves screaming, *yes, yes, now,* and nothing mattered except his hands and mouth and body, the way he was taking me over, bringing more and more pleasure to my dazzled senses. All I wanted was to kiss him and writhe against that relentless heat. I needed this so badly, the feeling that had begun to roll up to me with visceral force—

"Baby, no," Joe said hoarsely, pulling away with a shiver. "Not here. Wait. This isn't . . . no."

Clinging to the side of the pool, I stared at him with bewildered fury. I couldn't think straight. I was throbbing in every limb. My brain was slow to process that we weren't going to finish.

"You . . . you . . ."

"I know. I'm sorry. Hell." Breathing heavily, he turned away, the muscles of his back bunched and sharply delineated. "I didn't mean to take it that far."

I was temporarily incoherent with rage. Somehow this man had gotten me to confide in him until I was more vulnerable than I'd ever been with anyone, and then after driving me half-crazy with sexual frustration, he'd called a halt at the last minute. *Sadist.* I made my way toward the shallowest part of the pool and tried to fasten the back of my bra. But I was shaking and unsteady, and my wet shirt clung obstinately to my skin. I struggled with the sopping mess.

Joe came up behind me and rummaged beneath the back of my shirt. "I promised we'd take it slow," he muttered, hooking up my bra. "But I can't seem to keep my hands off you."

"You don't have to worry about that now," I said vehemently. "Because I wouldn't touch you with a ten-foot pole, unless you were dangling off the edge of a cliff, and then I would use that pole to *clobber* you."

"I'm sorry—" Joe began to put his arms around me from behind, but I shrugged him off and sloshed away in high dudgeon. He followed, continuing apologetically, "After our first time turning out like it did, I couldn't let the second time happen in a swimming pool."

"There's not going to be a second time." With effort, I hauled myself out of the pool. The wet clothes felt as heavy as chain mail. "I'm not going into the house like this. I need a towel. And my purse, which is on one of the kitchen counters." I sat on a lounge chair, trying to look as dignified as possible while water streamed off me.

"I'll get it." Joe paused. "About dinner . . ."

I gave him a withering glance.

"Forget dinner," he said hastily. "I'll be right back."

After he had brought the towels and I had dried off as much as possible, I walked to my car, with Joe at my heels. My hair was stringy and my clothes were clammy. The evening air was still warm, and I was overheated, almost steaming. As I sat in my car seat, I could feel the upholstery soaking up the water from my clothes. *If my car interior turns moldy,* I thought furiously, *I am going to make him pay to have the seats re-covered.*

"Wait." Joe held the edge of the car door before I could close it. To my outrage, he didn't look at all remorseful. "Are you going to answer when I call?" he asked.

"No."

That didn't seem to surprise him. "Then I'll show up at your place."

"Don't even think about it. I've had enough of your manhandling."

I could tell from the way he chewed on his lip that he was trying to hold back a smart-ass comment. Losing the battle, he said, "If I'd manhandled you just a little longer, honey, you'd be a hell of a lot happier right now."

I reached for the car door and slammed it shut. Extending my middle finger, I flipped him off through the window. As I started the car, Joe turned away . . . but not before I saw the flash of his grin.

Thirteen

Sunday night went by without a word from Joe. So did Monday night. I waited with growing impatience for him to call. I kept my cell phone with me at all times, pouncing on every call or text.

Nothing.

"I don't give a damn if you call or not," I muttered, glaring at the silent phone on its charger. "I couldn't be less interested, as a matter of fact."

Which was a lie, of course, but it felt good to say it.

The truth was, I couldn't stop reliving those weightless floating moments with Joe in the swimming pool, the memory cringe-inducing and haunting and wildly pleasurable. The way he had talked to me . . . unsparing, sexual . . . I'd felt his words sinking in-side me, right through my skin. And the promises he'd made . . . was any of that even possible?

The idea of letting go, with him, was terrifying. Feeling that much. Flying that high. I didn't know what would happen afterward, what internal mechanisms might be shattered by the altitude, how much oxygen would be robbed from my blood. Or if a safe landing was even an option.

On Tuesday morning, I had to turn my full focus on Hollis Warner and her daughter, Bethany, who were visiting the studio for the first time. Ryan had proposed over the weekend, and from what Hollis had told me on the phone, Bethany had been delighted with the sand-castle proposal. The weekend had been romantic and relaxing, and the newly engaged couple had discussed possible wedding dates.

To my consternation—and Sofia's—the Warners wanted the ceremony to be held in four months.

"We're on a time limit," Bethany told me, her hand sliding to her flat stomach. "Four months is all we've got before I show too much for the kind of wedding dress I want."

"I understand," I said, keeping my expression impassive. I didn't dare look at Sofia, who was seated nearby with her sketch pad, but I knew she had to be thinking the same thing: No one could pull off a megawedding that fast. Every decent location would be booked up, and the same could be said for all the good vendors and musicians. "However," I continued, "a time frame that narrow is going to limit our options. Have you thought about having the baby first? That way—"

"No." Bethany gave me a chilling blue-eyed glare. In the next moment her face relaxed, and she smiled sweetly. "I'm an old-fashioned girl. To me, the wedding has to come before the baby. If that means the wedding has to be a little smaller, Ryan and I are fine with that."

"I'm not fine with a smaller wedding," Hollis said. "Anything less than four hundred guests is not possible. This occasion is going to show the old guard that we're a family to be reckoned with." She gave me a small smile that didn't quite coordinate with her fierce, fixed stare. "This is Bethany's wedding, but it's my show. I just want everyone to remember that."

This was not the first time I'd planned a wedding in which people had brought different agendas to the table. But it was the first time the mother of the bride had been so blunt about wanting the occasion to be her show.

It couldn't have been easy to grow up in the shadow of such a mother. Some children of dominating parents turned out to be timid and insecure, desperate not to attract attention. Bethany, however, seemed to be have been made in the same tough, diamond-hard mold. Although Bethany wanted a stylish wedding, it was clear that above all she desired expediency. I couldn't help wondering if she was worried about Ryan wriggling off the hook.

The pair sat side by side on the blue sectional, their legs crossed identically on the diagonal. Bethany was a gorgeous young woman, lean and lanky, her hair long, white blond, and stick straight. A large engagement solitaire glittered on her left hand as she draped her arm gracefully along the back of the sofa.

"Mother," she said to Hollis, "Ryan and I have already agreed that we're only going to invite guests that we have personal connections to."

"What about *my* personal connections? An ex-president and first lady–"

"We're not going to invite them."

Hollis stared at her daughter as if she had just spoken in tongues. "Of course we are."

"I've been to weddings with Secret Service, Mother. Bomb-sniffing dogs, the magnetometers, everything in lockdown for a five-mile radius . . . Ryan wouldn't stand for it. There's only so far I can push him."

"Why isn't anyone worried about pushing *me*?" Hollis asked, and laughed angrily. "Everyone knows the mother is in charge of the wedding. It's all going to reflect on *me*."

"That doesn't mean you can bully everyone into doing what you want."

"I'm the one being bullied. I'm the one everyone's trying to sideline!"

"Whose wedding is this?" Bethany asked. "You had your own. Do you have to take mine too?"

"Mine was *nothing* compared to this." Hollis shot me an incredulous glance as if to convey how impossible her daughter was. "Bethany, do you know how much you have in your life that I didn't get?"

"Of course I do. You never stop talking about it."

"No one is being sidelined," I interceded hastily. "We all have the same goal, for Bethany to have the wedding she deserves. Let's get the contractual obligations out of the way, and then we can start working on a master guest list. I'm sure we can find some ways to pare it down. We'll consult with Ryan, of course."

"Isn't it up to me to decide–" Hollis began.

"I'm positive we can have Bethany featured as bride of the month in *Southern Weddings* and *Modern Bride*," I interrupted, trying to distract her.

"And *Texas Bride*," Sofia added.

"Not to mention some local media coverage leading up to the wedding," I continued. "First we'll come up with a compelling narrative–"

"I know all that," Hollis said irritably. "I've been interviewed dozens of times about my galas and fund-raisers."

"Mother knows everything," Bethany said in a saccharine tone.

"One of the most appealing angles to this story," I said, "is about a mother's and daughter's joy in planning a wedding together while the daughter is expecting her own child. That could be a great hook for–"

"We're not going to mention the pregnancy," Hollis said decisively.

"Why not?" Bethany asked.

"The old guard won't approve. It used to be that these situations were covered up and kept quiet, which is still the best way, if you ask me."

"I didn't ask you," Bethany retorted. "I haven't done anything to be ashamed of, and I'm not going into hiding. I'm marrying the father of my child. If the old bitches don't like it, they should try living in the twenty-first century. Besides, my bump is going to be obvious by the time the wedding takes place."

"You'll have to watch your weight, sweetheart. Eating for two is a myth. During my entire pregnancy, I only gained fifteen pounds. You're already looking puffy."

"Bethany," Sofia broke in with artificial cheer, "you and I need to arrange a time to brainstorm ideas and color palettes."

"I'll come too," Hollis said. "You'll want my ideas."

∽ᘿᔓ

After the Warners had left the studio, Sofia and I collapsed on the sectional and groaned in unison.

"I feel like roadkill," I said.

"Are they going to act like this the whole time?"

"This is only the beginning." I stared up at the ceiling. "By the time we make it to the seating plan, blood will have been shed."

"Who is the old guard?" Sofia asked. "And why does Hollis keep talking about him?"

"It's not a him, it's a them. An older, established group that wants everything to stay the same. There can be an old guard in a society, in politics, a sports organization, pretty much any group you can come up with."

"Oh. I thought she meant someone in the army."

It was probably because of the contentious meeting we'd just been through, and the sudden release from tension, but Sofia's innocent remark struck me as irresistibly funny. I began to laugh.

A throw pillow came flying out of nowhere, hitting me in the face.

"What was that for?" I demanded.

"You're laughing at me."

"I'm not laughing at you, I'm laughing at what you said."

Another pillow struck me. I sat up and fired it back at her. Giggling wildly, Sofia leapt over the back of the sofa. I leaned over and whacked her with a pillow and ducked as she popped up to swat me again.

We were so busy that neither of us noticed the front door opening and closing.

"Uh . . . Avery?" came Val's voice. "I brought sandwiches for lunch, and–"

"Just set it on the counter," I called, leaning over the back of the sofa to wallop Sofia. "We're having an executive meeting." *Thwack.*

Sofia launched a counterattack, while I flung myself to the sofa cushions. *Thwack. Thwack.*

"Avery." A note in Val's voice caused my sister to stop. "We have a visitor."

I lifted my head and peeked over the sofa back. My eyes widened as I saw Joe Travis standing there.

Mortified, I dropped back out of sight. I lay back on the sofa, my heart thundering. He was here. He had shown up, as he'd said he would. I felt light-headed. Why hadn't he chosen a moment when

I'd been composed and professional, instead of finding me in the middle of a pillow fight with my sister like a couple of twelve-year-olds?

"We were letting off steam," I heard Sofia say, still breathless.

"Can I watch?" Joe asked, making her laugh.

"I think we're done now."

Joe walked around the sectional and came to stand over me as I lay on my back. His gaze skimmed briefly over the length of my body. I was wearing another one of my shapeless but expensive dresses, black and sleeveless. Although the hem usually reached to midcalf, it had ridden above my knees when I'd flopped onto the sofa.

I couldn't look at him without remembering the last time we'd been together, the way I'd writhed and kissed him and told him everything. Mortified color blanketed me head to toe. What made it worse was that Joe smiled as if he understood exactly what was causing my distress.

"You have great legs," he said as he reached down for me, his fingers closing around mine. I was hauled to my feet with easy strength. "I told you I'd show up," he murmured.

"A little more advance notice would have been nice." Hastily I pulled my hand away from his and tugged my dress into place.

"And give you a chance to run?" He pushed back a wave of hair that had fallen over my eyes and tucked another behind my ear with unmistakable familiarity.

Conscious of Sofia's and Val's interested regard, I cleared my throat and said in a professional voice, "What can I help you with?"

"I came by to see if you wanted to go out to lunch. There's a Cajun diner downtown—it's not fancy, but the food is good."

"Thank you, but Val already brought sandwiches."

"I didn't bring anything for you, Avery," Val called from the kitchen. "Just for me and Sofia."

Like hell. I looked around Joe's shoulder, ready to call Val on it, but she ignored me, staying busy in the kitchen.

Sofia smiled at me, her eyes mischievous. "Go have lunch, *mi hermana.*" Deliberately she added, "Take as long as you want–your schedule is clear for the rest of the afternoon."

"I had plans," I said. "I was going to look over everyone's expense accounts."

Sofia gave Joe an imploring glance. "Keep her away as long as possible," she said, and he laughed.

"I'll do that."

~ຂ໌~

The Cajun diner was lined with a counter and steel-framed stools on one side and a row of booths on the other. The atmosphere was agreeably boisterous, the air filled with brisk conversation, the scrape of flatware on melamine plates, and the rattling of ice cubes in tall glasses of sweet tea. Waitresses carried plates filled with steaming food... étouffée thick with plump crawfish tails, ladled over patties of grits fried in butter... po'boy rolls stuffed with lobster and shrimp.

To my relief, our conversation stayed in safe territory, with no mention of our last encounter. As I described the meeting with the Warners, Joe was amused and sympathetic.

The waitress brought out our order, two plates of pompano that had been stuffed with shrimp and crabmeat and baked in foil pouches with a butter-and-wine velouté sauce. Every bite was creamy and tender, melting luxuriously on my tongue.

"I have an ulterior motive for asking you out today," Joe said as we ate. "I need to stop by an animal shelter and take some pictures of a couple of new dogs. Want to come and help?"

"I'll try... but I don't think I'm good with dogs."

"Are you afraid of them?"

"No, I've just never been around them."

"It'll be fine. I'll tell you what to do."

After lunch, we drove to the shelter, a small brick building with abundant windows and crisp white trim. A sign featuring cartoon cats and dogs read "Happy Tails Rescue Society." Joe pulled a camera bag and a duffel bag from the back of his Jeep, and we walked into the shelter. The lobby was bright and cheerful, featuring an interactive screen where visitors could browse through photos and descriptions of available animals.

An elderly man with a shock of white hair came from behind the counter to greet us, his blue eyes twinkling as he shook hands with Joe. "Millie called you about the latest group?"

"Yes, sir. She said four had been sent by a city shelter."

"Another one arrived this morning." The man's friendly gaze turned to me.

"Avery, this is Dan," Joe said. "He and his wife, Millie, built this place five years ago."

"How many dogs do you keep here?" I asked.

"We average about a hundred. We try to take the ones that other places have trouble adopting out."

"We'll go to the back and set up," Joe said. "Bring out the first one whenever you're ready, Dan."

"You bet."

Joe led me to an exercise area in the back of the building. The room was spacious, the rubber floor designed like a black-and-white checkerboard. One wall was lined with a low-slung red vinyl sofa. There was a basket of dog toys and a plastic children's playhouse with a ramp.

After taking a Nikon from a camera bag, Joe attached a lens and adjusted the exposure and scene modes. All of it was accomplished with the quickness and ease of someone who'd done it a million times before. "First I take a couple of minutes to get to know the dog a little," he said. "Some of them are nervous, especially if they've been neglected or abused. The important thing to remember is not to approach a dog directly and step into his space. He'll see that as a threat. You're the pack leader—the follower is supposed to come to you. No eye contact at first, just stay calm and ignore him until he gets used to you."

The door opened, and Dan led in a large black dog with raggedy ears. "This here's Ivy," he said. "A Lab-retriever mix. Blinded in one eye after she got caught into a bobwire fence. No one can get a good picture because of the coloring."

"Solid black is tricky for lighting," Joe said. "Do you think she can handle it if I bounce a flash from the ceiling?"

"Sure, Ivy was a gun dog. A flash won't bother her a bit."

Setting aside the camera, Joe waited as Ivy came to sniff his hand. He petted her and scratched her neck. Her one good eye closed in ecstasy, and she panted happily. "Who's a good girl?" Joe asked, lowering to his haunches, rubbing her chest and neck.

Ivy padded over to the basket of toys, pulled out a stuffed gator, and brought it to Joe. He tossed the toy into the air, and Ivy caught it deftly. She brought the toy back, her tail wagging enthusiastically, and the process was repeated a few more times. Eventually Ivy dropped the toy and wandered toward me, sniffing curiously.

"She wants to meet you," Joe said.

"What should I do?"

"Stand still and let her smell your hand. Then you can rub under her chin."

Ivy sniffed a fold of my skirt, and then her cold nose touched against my hand. "Hello, Ivy," I murmured, stroking her beneath the chin and on her chest. The dog's jaw relaxed and she sat promptly, her tail thumping the floor. Her one good eye closed as I continued to pet her.

At Joe's direction, I held a reflector board while he took some shots of Ivy. She turned out to be a willing photography subject, lounging on the red sofa with a toy between her paws.

Three more dogs were brought out in turn, a beagle mix, a Yorkshire terrier, and a short-haired Chihuahua that Dan said would be the most difficult to adopt out. She was beige and white, with an adorable face with big, soft eyes, but she had two things going against her: She was ten years old, and toothless.

"Her owner had to go into assisted living," Dan explained, carrying the tiny creature into the room. "Dog's teeth went bad and every last one had to be pulled."

"Can she survive with no teeth?" I asked.

"As long as she gets soft food." Carefully, Dan set the Chihuahua on the floor. "Here you go, Coco."

The dog looked so fragile that I felt a pang of concern. "How long do they usually live?"

"This one might could last five years, maybe more. We've got a friend whose Chi lived to be eighteen."

Coco surveyed the three of us uncertainly. Her tail wagged once, twice, in a hopeful gesture that caused a sharp twinge in my heart. To my surprise, she came to me in a fit of bravery, miniature feet pattering on the floor. I leaned down to pick her up. She weighed nothing; it was like holding a bird. I could feel her heart beating against my fingers. As she strained to lick my chin, I could see hairline cracks at the tip of her tongue.

"Why is her tongue so dry?" I asked.

"She can't hold it in because of the missing teeth." Dan left the room, saying over his shoulder, "I'll let y'all get to work."

I carried the Chihuahua to the sofa and placed her on it carefully. Her ears drooped and her tail tucked between her legs. Staring up at me, she began to pant in distress.

"Everything's okay," I encouraged, backing away. "Stay still."

But Coco looked increasingly worried, creeping to the edge of the sofa as if preparing to jump and follow me. I returned and sat on the sofa. As I petted her, she crawled into my lap and tried to curl up. "What a love sponge," I said, laughing. "How do I make her sit by herself?"

"I have no idea," Joe said.

"I thought you knew how to handle dogs."

"Honey, there's no way I could convince her that a cold vinyl seat is better than your lap. If you'll keep holding her, I'll zoom the shots and make the depth of field as shallow as possible."

"So the background will be blurry?"

"Yes. See if you can get her to relax. With her ears flattened like that, she looks scared."

"What do you want her ears to do?"

"See if you can get them perked up and facing forward."

I held Coco in different poses, calling her a sweetheart, an angel, a sugar-pie, saying if she behaved, I would give her all the treats she wanted. "Are her ears perked up now?" I asked.

His mouth twitched. "Mine sure as hell are." Lowering to his haunches, he took multiple shots, the camera shutter clicking nonstop.

"Do you think someone will adopt her?"

"I hope so. It's not easy to get someone to take a senior dog. Not much time left, and health problems on the horizon."

Coco looked up at me with shining eyes and a gummy grin. I felt a sinking sensation as I thought of what would probably happen to this vulnerable, not-pretty creature.

"If life were simpler . . . ," I heard myself say, "if I were another kind of person . . . I'd take her home with me."

The shutter clicks stopped. "Do you want to?"

"It doesn't matter. I can't." I was surprised by the plangent sound of my own voice.

"That's okay."

"I have no experience with pets."

"I understand."

I held Coco up and looked at her. She regarded me earnestly with that little-old-lady face, paws dangling, tail wagging in midair. "You have too many problems," I told her.

Joe approached, looking amused. "You don't have to take her."

"I know. It's just . . ." I let out a tight, disbelieving laugh. "Somehow I can't stand the idea of walking away from her."

"Leave her here and think about it overnight," Joe said. "You can always come back tomorrow."

"If I don't take her now, I won't come back." I held her in my lap, smoothing her fur, wondering what to do. She curled up into a little donut and closed her eyes.

Joe sat next to me, sliding an arm around my shoulders. He stayed silent, letting me think it through.

"Joe?" I asked after a couple of minutes.

"Mmm-hmm?"

"Can you give me a practical reason for taking this dog home with me? Anything at all? Because she's not big enough to protect me, and I don't need her as a service dog or to herd sheep. So give me a reason. Please."

"I'll give you three. One, a dog will give you unconditional love. Two, having a dog reduces stress. Three . . ." His arm slid away, and he turned my face toward his, his thumb stroking the edge of my jaw. He looked into my eyes and smiled. "Hell, do it because you want to," he said.

～ठ～

On the way back home, we stopped at a pet store for some basic supplies. Along with the basics, I bought a tote with mesh panels on the sides and a soft padded interior. As soon as I put Coco inside, she poked her head through an opening at the top and looked around. I was now a woman with a purse-dog, except that instead of a fluffy Pomeranian or a teacup poodle, mine was a toothless Chihuahua.

The studio was empty and silent when we arrived. Joe carried my purchases in from the car, including a pet crate and a case of premium canned dog food. I arranged a foam mat and a soft blanket in the crate. Coco crawled in eagerly.

"I'd like to give her a bath," I said, "but she's had enough excitement for now. I'll let her adjust to her new surroundings."

Joe set the dog food on the counter. "You sound like an expert already."

"Ha." I began to stack cans in the pantry. "Sofia's going to kill me. I should have asked her before doing this. Except that she would have said no, and I would have brought Coco home anyway."

"Tell her I pressured you."

"No, she knows I wouldn't do this unless it was something I really wanted. But thanks for offering to take the rap."

"Anytime." Joe paused. "I'll head out now."

I turned to face him, my nerves humming with anticipation as he approached. "Thanks for lunch," I said.

His warm gaze swept over me. "Thanks for helping at the shelter." He reached around me, bringing me against a wealth of hard muscle. My hands crept up his back. The clean, earthy scent of him was becoming familiar, and it was a thousand times better than cologne. Finishing the hug, he let go.

"Bye, Avery," he said huskily.

I watched with wide eyes as he headed to the door. "Joe . . ."

He paused with his hand on the knob, glancing over his shoulder.

"Aren't you . . ." I blushed before continuing, "Aren't you going to kiss me?"

A slow grin crossed his face. "Nope." And he left, closing the door gently behind him.

While I stared at the door with astonished indignation, Coco ventured cautiously out of her crate.

"What is this?" I asked aloud, pacing in a tight circle. "He takes me out for lunch and brings me back with a secondhand Chihuahua, and on top of that, no kiss good-bye or any mention of when or if he's going to call . . . . What kind of game is he playing? Was this even a date?"

Coco watched me expectantly.

"Are you hungry? Thirsty?" I pointed to a corner of the kitchen. "Your bowls are over there."

She didn't move.

"Want to watch some TV?" I asked.

Her spindly tail wagged.

After scrolling through channels on the flat-screen TV, I found an episode of a telenovela that Sofia and I had been following. Despite the eye-rolling theatrics and the eighties-style hair and makeup, the story was as addictive as crack. I had to find out how it ended.

"Telenovelas teach important life lessons," Sofia had once told me. "For example, if you're in a love triangle with two handsome men who never wear shirts, remember that the one you reject will become a villain and plot to destroy you. And if you're beautiful but poor and mistreated, you were probably switched at birth with another baby who has taken your rightful place in a powerful family."

I entertained myself by reading the English subtitles to Coco, infusing high emotion in the dialogue: "I swear you will pay dearly for this outrage!" and "Now you must fight for your love!" While misting Coco's tongue with Evian spray during the commercial, I said, "Wait a minute, you don't need translation. You're a Chihuahua. You already speak Spanish."

Hearing the front door open and close, I glanced over the back of the sofa. Sofia came in, looking demoralized.

"How's it going?" I asked.

"Remember the guy in spin class?"

"Bike twenty-two?"

"Uh-huh. We went out for drinks." She heaved a sigh. "It was *awful*. The conversation kept stalling. It was more boring than watching bananas ripen. All he does is exercise. He doesn't like to travel because it interferes with his workout schedule. He doesn't read books or keep up with the news. But the worst thing was that he kept looking at his phone for an entire hour. What kind of guy reads his phone and texts during a date? Finally I put a twenty-dollar bill on the table to pay for my share of the drinks, and said, 'I don't want to interfere with your phone time,' and I left."

"I'm so sorry."

"Now I can't even enjoy watching his glutes during spin class." Sofia plugged her phone into a charger on the counter. "How did your lunch go?"

"Great food."

"What about Joe? Did you have a good time? Was he charming?"

"It was fun," I said. "But I have something to confess."

She gave me an expectant glance. "Yes?"

"After lunch, we went shopping."

"For what?"

"A bed and a dog collar."

Her brows lifted. "That's a little kinky for a first date."

"The bed and dog collar are for an actual dog," I said.

Sofia's face went blank. "Whose?"

"Ours."

My sister walked around the sofa. Her incredulous gaze dropped to the Chihuahua in my lap. Coco shrank back against me, trembling.

"This is Coco," I said.

"Where's the dog? All I see is a mole rat with bulging eyes. And I can smell her from here."

"Don't listen to her," I told Coco. "You just need a better stylist."

"I asked you once if I could get a dog and you said it was a terrible idea!"

"I was right. It's a terrible idea if we're talking about a regular-sized dog. But this one is perfect."

"I *hate* Chihuahuas. Three of my aunts have them. They need special food and special collars and special stairs to get on the couch, and they pee five hundred times a day. If we get a dog, I want one that can go running with me."

"You don't run."

"Because I don't have a dog."

"Now we do."

"I can't run with a Chihuahua! She would drop dead after a half mile."

"So would you. I've seen you run."

Sofia looked infuriated. "I'm going to go out and buy a dog too. A *real* dog."

"Fine, go get one. Bring home a half dozen."

"Maybe I will." She scowled. "Why is her tongue hanging out like that?"

"She has no teeth."

Our gazes clashed in the charged silence.

"She can't keep her tongue in," I continued, "so it's chronically dry. But a lady at the pet store suggested massaging it with some organic coconut oil every night, and misting it with water through-out the day– Why is that funny?"

Sofia had started to choke with laughter. In fact, she could barely talk, she was snorting and wheezing so hard. "You have such high standards. You love beautiful, tasteful things. And this dog is so ugly and scraggly, and . . . *Dios mío,* she's a lemon." Sitting beside me, she reached out to let Coco smell her hand. Coco sniffed daintily and let Sofia pet her.

"She's not a lemon," I said, "she's *jolie laide.*"

"What does that mean?"

"It's a term for a woman who's not conventionally beautiful, but she's beautiful in a unique way. Like Cate Blanchett or Meryl Streep."

"Did Joe talk you into this? Are you doing it to make him think you're compassionate?"

I gave her a haughty glance. "You know that I've never wanted anyone to think of me as compassionate."

Sofia shook her head in resignation. "Come here, Meryl Streep," she said to Coco, trying to coax her out of my lap. *"Ven aquí, niña."*

Coco shrank back, panting anxiously.

"An asthmatic lemon," Sofia said, settling back in the corner of the couch with a sigh. "My mother's coming to visit tomorrow," she said after a moment.

"God, is it that time again?" I made a face. "Already?"

Every two or three months, Sofia's mother, Alameda, drove from San Antonio to visit for a night. These occasions always consisted of hours of relentless interrogation about Sofia's friends, her health, her work, and her sexual activities. Alameda had never forgiven her daughter for moving so far away from the family and for ending a relationship with a young man named Luis Orizaga.

Sofia's entire family had tried to pressure her to marry Luis, whose parents were respectable and had money. According to Sofia, Luis had been overbearing and egotistical, and terrible in bed, besides. Alameda blamed me for helping Sofia to leave Luis and start a new life in Houston. As a result, Sofia's mother could barely bring herself to be civil in my presence.

For Sofia's sake, I tried to be nice to Alameda. On one level I felt sympathy for her, as I would for anyone whom my father had hurt. However, the way she treated Sofia was hard to tolerate. Since Alameda couldn't vent her anger on her ex-husband, she had made their daughter the scapegoat. I knew all too well how that felt. Sofia was always depressed for a day or two after her mother visited.

"Is she staying here?" I asked Sofia.

"No, she doesn't like sleeping on our pullout. It hurts her back. She's checking into the hotel tomorrow afternoon, and coming here for dinner at five."

"Why don't you take her out to eat?"

Sofia rested her head on the back of the couch and rolled it in a slow negative shake. "She wants me to cook so she can tell me everything I'm doing wrong."

"Do you want me to leave while she's here?"

"It would be better if you stayed." With a halfhearted smile, Sofia said, "You're good at deflecting some of the arrows."

"As many as I can," I said, feeling a rush of love for her. "Always, Sofia."

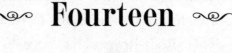

Fourteen

After brainstorming and mulling over ideas, Sofia had come up with two concepts for the Warner wedding. The first was a traditional formal wedding, perfectly feasible and impressive. Following a grand ceremony at Memorial Drive Methodist, a fleet of pearl-white limos would transport the guests to a crystal-and-roses ballroom reception at the River Oaks Country Club. It would be tasteful and elegant, the kind of affair that everyone would expect. But not the one we wanted the Warners to choose.

The second wedding plan was a knockout. The location was the Filter Building at White Rock Lake, near Dallas. The historic building was a spectacular lakefront industrial design, with corbeled brick and exposed iron trusses and big windows overlooking the lake. It was almost a guarantee that Ryan would love the location, which would appeal to his architectural taste.

Inspired by the Depression-era building, Sofia had conceived of a lavish Gatsbyesque wedding in creams, tans, and gold, with bridesmaids wearing drop-waist dresses and ropes of beads and the men in dinner suits. The tables would be covered in beaded fabric, and the flower arrangements would feature orchids and plumes. Guests would be transported from a hotel in Dallas to White Rock Lake in a succession of vintage Rolls-Royces and Pierce-Arrows.

"We'll make it fresh," Sofia said. "Fancy but modern. We want it to be inspired by the Jazz Age without making it too accurate, or it will look like a costume party." The team at the studio all loved the Gatsbyesque concept.

Everyone except Steven.

"You all know that Gatsby is a tragic story, right?" he asked. "Personally I wouldn't care for a wedding based on themes of power, greed, and betrayal."

"What a shame," Sofia said. "It would be so perfect for you."

Val interrupted before they could start bickering. "*The Great Gatsby* is one of those books that everyone's heard of but no one reads."

"I did," Steven said.

"Required high school reading?" Sofia asked disdainfully.

"No, for my own enjoyment. It's called literature. You should try it sometime, if you ever manage to tear yourself away from those Spanish soap operas."

Sofia's brows lowered. "You're a fine one to judge, with all the silly sports games you watch."

"That's enough, you two," I interceded, giving Steven a blistering glance.

He ignored me, picking up his phone. "I'm going to make a couple of calls. I'll be outside. I can't hear with all of you yammering."

"Go easy on him today," Tank suggested as soon as Steven wandered out of earshot. "He and his girlfriend broke up over the weekend."

Sofia's eyes widened. "He has a girlfriend?"

"They just started going out a couple of weeks ago. But on Sunday, they were watching football at his place, and all of a sudden she turned down the volume and told Steven she didn't think they should see each other again, because he was emotionally unavailable."

"What did he say?"

"He asked if they could wait to talk about it until half-time." At our looks of disgust, Tank said defensively, "We were playing the Cowboys."

The doorbell rang.

"It's *Mamá*," Sofia muttered.

"All hands to their battle stations," I said, only half kidding. Since everyone at the studio had encountered Alameda on previous occasions, they wasted no time in collecting their belongings quickly. No one had any desire to make small talk with a woman who was so utterly humorless. Every conversation with her was the same, a litany of complaints concealed within complaints, like a set of toxic Russian nesting dolls.

Sofia stood, tugged at the hem of her turquoise top, and went reluctantly to welcome her mother. She squared her shoulders before opening the door and saying brightly, "*Mamá!* How was the drive? How was—"

Breaking off abruptly, Sofia backed up as if confronted with a rearing cobra. Without thinking, I leapt from the sofa and went to her. My sister's face was leached of color except for bright pink streaks across the crest of each cheek, like signal flags sent up for a panic alert.

Alameda Cantera was at the threshold, looking the same as always, her eyes stony and her mouth set with the bitterness of someone who had been defrauded by life. Alameda was an attractive woman, her figure small and trim in a suit jacket and hot-pink blouse and trouser jeans. The wealth of jet-black hair was pulled tightly back from her face and pinned into a controlled bun at her nape. It was an unfortunate style for someone whose hard features could have used some softening around the edges. But when Alameda had been young, before Eli had soured her, she must have been beautiful.

She had brought someone with her, a young man still in his twenties. He was black-haired, a bit heavyset, his short but muscular frame clad in pressed khakis and a crisp button-down shirt. Although he was handsome, his expression conveyed an impression of smug, sly machismo that I instinctively disliked.

"Avery," Sofia said, "this is Luis Orizaga."

Holy shit, I thought.

Even knowing Alameda, I couldn't believe she had brought her daughter's ex-boyfriend here, uninvited and *very* unwelcome. Although Luis had never been physically abusive, he had dominated Sofia in every other way, determined to extinguish every spark of independence.

Apparently, it had never occurred to Luis that Sofia might not have been happy in the relationship. It had been a shock to him when she had ended their engagement and moved to Houston to start a business with me. Luis had gone into a monthlong rage that had involved heavy drinking, multiple bar fights, and broken furniture. Less than a year later, he'd married a seventeen-year-old girl. They'd had a child, Alameda had informed Sofia peevishly, and had gone on to say that it should have been her grandchild, and Sofia should be having babies.

"Why are you here?" Sofia asked Luis. She sounded so young and vulnerable that I was tempted to push her behind me and snap at the pair in the doorway to leave her alone.

"I invited Luis to come with me," Alameda replied, aggressively cheerful, her eyes birdlike. "It's lonely to drive all that way by myself, which I have to do since *you* never come to visit *me*, Sofia. I told Luis that he never left your heart–that's why you've stayed single."

"But you're married," Sofia said, giving Luis a bewildered glance.

"We're divorced now," he said. "I gave my wife too much. I was too good to her. All that spoiling made her want to leave me."

"Of course it did," I couldn't resist saying acidly.

My comment was roundly ignored.

"I have a son named Bernardo–" Luis told Sofia.

"The most beautiful child," Alameda chimed in.

"He's almost two years old," Luis continued. "I have him every other weekend. I need help to raise him."

"You are the luckiest girl in the world, *mija,*" Alameda said to Sofia. "Luis has decided to give you another chance."

I turned to Sofia. "You've hit the jackpot," I said dryly.

She was too shaken to smile. "You should have asked me first, Luis," she said. "I told you when I left Houston that I didn't want to see you again."

"Alameda explained everything," he replied. "Your sister talked you into moving away when you were grieving your father's death. You didn't know what you were doing."

I opened my mouth to protest, but Sofia made a shushing motion without even looking at me. "Luis," she said, "you know why I left. I'll never go back to you."

"Things are different. I've changed, Sofia. I know how to make you happy now."

"She's already happy," I burst out.

Alameda gave me a dismissive glance. "Avery, this does not concern you. It's a family matter."

"Don't be rude to Avery," Sofia said, flushing angrily. "She is my family."

A rapid volley of Spanish ensued, all three of them speaking at once. I couldn't follow more than a few words. In the background, Ree-Ann, Val, and Tank waited with their bags and laptops.

"Need help?" Tank asked meaningfully.

Grateful for his presence, I murmured, "Not sure yet."

Sofia looked increasingly distressed as she tried to defend herself. I inched closer, longing to intervene on her behalf. "Could we do this in English, please?" I asked crisply. No one appeared to have heard. "The fact is," I tried again, "Sofia has a great life here. A successful career. She's an independent woman." When none of that had any discernible effect, I added, "She has a new man."

To my satisfaction, an abrupt silence descended.

"That's right," Sofia said, seizing on the excuse. "I have a man, and we're engaged."

Alameda's eyes narrowed into spider-lashed slits. "You never said anything about him before. Who is he? What is his name?"

Sofia's lips parted. "He's—"

"Excuse me," Steven said, shouldering his way back into the studio through the half-open door. He paused with a quizzical frown, glancing at our blank faces in the fraught silence. "What's going on?"

"*Querido,*" Sofia exclaimed, and flung herself at him.

Before Steven could react, she wrapped her arms around his neck, tugged his head down, and pressed her mouth against his.

Fifteen

Taken by surprise, Steven froze as Sofia kissed him. I held my breath, silently willing him not to shove her away. His hands, suspended in the air as if by marionette strings, descended by slow degrees to her shoulders. *Take pity on her, Steven,* I thought desperately. *Just this once.*

But Steven's reaction had nothing to do with pity. His arms slid around her, and he began to kiss her as if he never wanted to stop. As if she were a dangerously addictive substance that had to be handled with care, rationed slowly, or he might die from a fatal overdose. The concentrated hunger of that blind, impassioned kiss seemed to radiate outward and heat up the entire room.

Somewhere behind me, I heard a thud on the floor. Tank had dropped his laptop. He and the two interns stared at the entwined couple with slack-jawed astonishment.

Bending to retrieve the laptop, Tank reported, "It's okay. Fell on the carpet. Not even dinged."

"Nobody cares," Ree-Ann said, her dumbfounded gaze still locked on Steven and Sofia.

"You can all go now," I told them, pointing in the direction of the back door.

"I forgot to clean the coffeemaker," Val said.

"I'll help," Ree-Ann added.

"Out," I commanded.

Reluctantly, they all shuffled through the kitchen and out the back entrance, glancing repeatedly over their shoulders.

Abruptly, Steven broke the kiss and shook his head as if to clear it. His gaze went from Sofia's flushed face to the pair at the door. "What the—"

"Mamá is here to visit," Sofia told him hastily. "She brought my old boyfriend Luis."

My hands clenched as I waited for Steven's reaction. He knew enough about Sofia's past to understand how devastating the situation was. If he'd ever wished for an opportunity to humiliate Sofia... no, *decimate* her, it had just been handed to him.

"There's been a misunderstanding," Sofia continued, her desperate gaze locked on his. *"Mamá* thought there was a chance that I would go back to Luis, so she talked him into coming here with her. But I was just starting to explain that it's not possible, because... because..."

"You and I are together," Steven said, the last word tipped with a faint questioning note.

Sofia nodded vigorously.

"I've seen him before," Alameda said to Sofia in an accusatory tone. "He works here. You don't even like him!"

I couldn't see Steven's face, but as he spoke, his voice was warm and wry. "It wasn't love at first sight," he conceded, keeping his arm around Sofia. "But the attraction was there from the beginning."

"For me too," Sofia said immediately.

"Sometimes when the feelings run deep," Steven said, "it's hard to know how to deal with them. And it's not like Sofia was the kind of woman I ever thought I would fall in love with."

Sofia looked up at him with a frown. "Why not?"

Staring into Sofia's eyes, Steven began to play with a lock of her hair. "Let me count the ways: You're an insufferable optimist, you start decorating for Christmas three months early, and you put glitter on anything that can't run away from you." His fingertips ran over the curve of her ear and caressed the side of her face. "When you get excited about a project, you start rubbing your hands together like a villain with an evil plan. You routinely eat peppers hot enough to make a normal person pass out. There are some words you never pronounce right. Salmon. Pajamas. Every time you hear a phone ring, you think it's yours, except when it actually is yours. The other day I watched you park in front of the studio, and I could tell that you were singing at the top of your lungs." He smiled slowly. "I've finally accepted that these are perfectly legitimate reasons to love some-one."

My sister was speechless.

All of us were.

Steven tore his gaze from Sofia and reached out to shake Luis's hand. "I'm Steven Cavanaugh," he said. "I don't blame you for want-ing Sofia back. But she's definitely taken."

Luis refused to reciprocate, only folded his arms and glared.

"You didn't ask for my permission," Alameda snapped at Steven. "And Sofia has no ring. There is no engagement without a ring."

Absorbing the information, Steven looked down at Sophia. "You . . . told her about the engagement," he said slowly.

Sofia's head dipped in a nervous bob.

"Technically, they're engaged to be engaged," I broke in. "Steven was planning to discuss it with you tonight, Alameda. After dinner."

"He can't have dinner with us," Alameda said. "I invited Luis."

"I invited Steven first," Sofia said.

"Enough!" Luis growled. He grabbed for Sofia. "I want to talk to you outside. Alone."

Steven blocked the movement with a startling swiftness, knocking Luis's arm away. "Back the fuck off," he said in a tone that raised the hair on the back of my neck. This was not at all like Steven, who prided himself on never losing his cool.

"Steven," Sofia interrupted, trying to keep the situation from getting out of hand. "*Querido mío,* it's fine, I . . . I'll do what he wants. I can talk to him."

Steven stared at Luis, his gaze hard. "She's mine."

Antagonism thickened the air as the two men faced each other. I sorely regretted having sent Tank away. In the past he had done his share of breaking up fights, and this one promised to be a doozy.

"Luis," Alameda said uneasily, "maybe you should go back to the hotel, and I'll handle my daughter."

"No one is going to handle me," Sofia burst out. "I'm not a puppet. *Mamá,* when are you going to accept that I can make decisions for myself?"

Alameda's mouth trembled and her eyes filled with tears. She fished in her handbag for tissues. "I've done everything for you. My whole life has been for you. I'm only trying to stop you from making so many mistakes."

"Mamá," Sofia said in exasperation, "Luis and I are wrong for each

other." Alameda was sobbing too loudly to hear. Sofia turned to Luis. "I'm sorry. I wish all the best for you and your son–"

"Eres babosa," Luis exploded. From the way Sofia stiffened, I knew it was an insult. He gestured toward Steven. "When he finds out how stupid and lazy you are, the way you lie in bed like a dead fish, he'll throw you out. He'll leave you fat and pregnant with his bastard, just like your father left Alameda."

"Luis," Alameda exclaimed, shocked out of her tears.

Luis continued bitterly, "Someday you'll come crawling to me, Sofia, and I'll tell you that it's what you deserved for being so–"

"And that is absolutely all we need to hear about your opinions," I said briskly. Seeing that Steven was about to lose it, I strode to the door and shoved it wide open. "If you need a taxi, I'd be happy to call one for you."

Luis stormed out without another word.

"How will he get back to the hotel?" Alameda asked in a watery voice. "We came in my car."

"He'll figure it out," I said.

Alameda blotted her eyes, which were surrounded with raccoon-like rings of mascara. "Sofia," she whined, "you made Luis so angry. He didn't know what he was saying."

Biting back a sarcastic reply, I put a hand on the older woman's shoulder and guided her toward the back of the studio. "Alameda, there's a powder room past the kitchen, down the hall to the left. You'll probably want to fix your makeup."

With a muffled exclamation, Alameda proceeded to the bathroom.

I turned to discover that Sofia was in Steven's arms. ". . . sorry to involve you," she was saying in a miserable voice. "It was all I could think of."

"Don't be sorry." Bending his head, Steven kissed her fully on the mouth, one hand at the back of her neck in a light cradling hold. I could hear her sharp intake of breath.

Flabbergasted, I walked by them to the kitchen as if nothing untoward were happening. Mechanically, I began to unload the clean dishes from the dishwasher. "I'll help with dinner," I heard Steven say eventually. "What are we having?"

Sofia sounded dazed. "I can't remember."

~◎~

For the rest of the evening, Steven was the picture of the perfect boyfriend. I'd never seen him act like this before. Affectionate. Easygoing. I couldn't tell how much of it, if any, was real. He insisted on helping Sofia cook, and before long Alameda and I were sitting on bar stools at the counter, watching.

Steven and Sofia had spent countless hours working together, but they had never seemed comfortable in each other's company. Until now. They had just discovered a new kind of together. They were finding the right level, warming to each other.

Having worked in her family's restaurant, Sofia was an accomplished cook. Tonight she was making chicken mole, Alameda's favorite dish. For an appetizer, Sofia set out a bowl of home-fried tortilla chips, delicately thin and crisp, along with salsa pureed into a smoky liquid that made my tongue pulse with heat.

While Steven made margaritas, I went to find Coco, and I brought her out to meet Alameda. Although Sofia's mother and I had almost nothing in common, we had finally found something to bond over. Alameda and every one of Sofia's aunts adored Chihuahuas. She held Coco in her lap, cooed over her in Spanish, and admired her pink leather collar studded with rhinestones. Discovering that I was a willing audience on all Chihuahua-related matters, Alameda proceeded to dispense feeding and grooming advice.

Steven tossed a salad made with fresh-roasted corn, crumbled white cheese, chopped cilantro, and a tangy, creamy lime dressing. "How does this look?" he asked Sofia.

She smiled and replied in passing as she went to the refrigerator.

"What was that?" he asked.

Sofia took out a container of coffee-marinated chicken. "I said maybe add a little more dressing."

"I got that part. I was asking about the Spanish words. What did they mean?"

"Oh." Blushing, Sofia set a heavy iron skillet on the cooktop. "Nothing. Just an expression."

Steven put his hands on the counter, caging her from behind. Nuzzling her cheek, he murmured, "You can't call me names and not tell me what they mean."

Her color deepened. "It wasn't a name, it was . . . well, it makes no sense when I translate."

He wouldn't relent. "Tell me anyway."

"Media naranja."

"Which is?"

"Half of the orange," Alameda said. A frown pleated her forehead as she reached for her margarita glass. "We say it to mean 'better half.' Soul mate."

Steven's expression was difficult to interpret. But he lowered his head and kissed Sofia's cheek before moving away. Sofia began to stir the contents of a nearby pot without seeming to be entirely aware of what she was doing.

If Alameda had any doubts about whether or not the relationship was genuine, I was fairly certain they had just vanished. Steven and Sofia were damned convincing as a couple. Which worried me. With the Warner wedding still ahead of us, this was not the time for a tempestuous relationship and all the accompanying Sturm und Drang.

There was also a chance that Steven would revert to his regular self tomorrow morning. As well as I knew Steven, I couldn't tell what was going on in his mind. Would he totally compartmentalize this entire experience? No doubt Sofia was wondering about that, too.

The chicken turned out to be a masterpiece, bathed in a velvety dark sauce of unsweetened Oaxacan chocolate, spices, and the earthy heat of guajillo chiles. Steven exerted himself to be charming, readily answering Alameda's questions about his parents, who lived in Colorado. His mother was a florist and his father was a retired teacher, and they'd been married for thirty years. Under Alameda's probing, Steven admitted that he might not want to stay in event planning forever; he could see himself managing bigger, corporate-related projects or maybe going into public relations. For now, however, he had a lot more to learn at the studio.

"If only I wasn't so incredibly underpaid," he added in a deadpan tone, and both Sofia and I started laughing.

"After your last bonus?" I asked in mock indignation. "And your upgraded health plan?"

"I need more perks," Steven said. "What about a company yoga class?" Comfortably, he slung an arm around the back of Sofia's chair.

Sofia held a folded tortilla up to his mouth to quiet him. Obligingly, he took a bite.

Alameda smiled thinly as she watched them. She would never like Steven, I thought. I felt certain he must have reminded her of my father. Even though Steven didn't technically look like Eli, he was tall and blond and possessed a similar WASPy handsomeness. I could have told Alameda that Steven was cut from an entirely different cloth, but it wouldn't have made a bit of difference. Alameda was determined not to approve of any man Sofia chose for herself.

We had flan for dessert and small, strong cups of cinnamon coffee. Eventually, Alameda announced that it was time to leave. The good-byes were awkward, interpolated with the awareness of what wasn't being said. Alameda wouldn't apologize for having brought Luis to Houston, and Sofia was still inwardly seething about having been ambushed. Alameda was only marginally civil to Steven, who, for his part, was scrupulously polite.

"May I walk you out to the car, Mrs. Cantera?" he asked.

"No, I want Avery to come with me."

"Absolutely," I said, thinking, *Anything. Anything to get you out of here.*

We walked outside to the parking spaces in front of the studio. I stood beside Alameda's car while she climbed into the driver's seat. She sighed heavily and sat with the door open.

"What kind of man is he?" she asked without looking at me.

I answered seriously. "A good man. Steven doesn't bail when things get tough. He's always calm in an emergency. He can drive anything on wheels, and he can do CPR and basic plumbing. He'll work an eighteen-hour day without a word of complaint, longer if necessary. I can promise you this, Alameda: He's not like my father."

A humorless smile flitted through the shadow patterns on her face. "They're all like your father, Avery."

"Then why were you trying to push Sofia and Luis together?" I asked, bewildered.

"Because at least he would bring her back to live close to her family," Alameda said. "Her *real* family."

Infuriated, I strove to keep my voice calm. "You know, Alameda, you have a nasty habit of taking shots at your own daughter, and I'm not sure what that's supposed to accomplish. If you expect it to provide incentive for Sofia to be near you, it doesn't seem to be working. You might want to try another tactic."

Glaring at me, Alameda slammed the car door shut and started the engine. After she drove away, I went back into the studio, where Sofia was closing the dishwasher and Steven was drying the blender pitcher. Both were quiet. I wondered what, if anything, had been said between them while I'd been outside.

I scooped up Coco and turned her to face me. "You behaved very well tonight," I told her. "You're such a good girl." She strained to lick me. "Not on the lips," I said. "I know where that mouth has been."

Steven picked up his keys from the counter. "Time to roll out," he said. "And after that meal, I mean it literally."

I smiled at him. "You saved the day," I said. "Thank you, Steven."

"Yes, thank you," Sofia said in a subdued voice. All the animation had drained from her expression.

Steven's tone was carefully neutral. "Don't mention it."

I pondered how to make a graceful exit. "Would you like me to—"

"No," Steven said quickly. "I'm going now. I'll see you both tomorrow."

"Okay," Sofia and I both said in unison.

We both occupied ourselves with casual tasks while Steven let himself out. I picked up a paper towel and wiped the already clean counter. Sofia sprayed the interior of the sink, which had just been rinsed. As soon as the door closed, we burst into conversation.

"What did he say?" I demanded.

"Nothing special: He asked me if I wanted to save the rest of the salsa, and where did we keep the plastic bags." Sofia covered her face with her hands. "I *hate* him." I was startled to hear a sob escape.

"But," I said, bewildered, "he was really nice to you tonight . . . ."

"Exactly," Sofia said venomously. Another sob. "Like a Disney prince. And I let myself pretend it was real, and it was w-wonderful. But now it's over, and tomorrow he'll turn into a pu-pumpkin."

"The prince doesn't turn into a pumpkin."

"Then I turn into a pumpkin."

I reached for the paper towel stand and tugged one off the roll. "No, you don't turn into a pumpkin, either. The coach turns into a pumpkin. You end up walking home with one shoe and a bunch of traumatized rodents."

A laugh quivered out between Sofia's fingers. She took the paper towel. Wadding it against her wet eyes, she said, "He meant those things he said. He cares about me. I knew it was the truth."

"Everyone knew, Sofia. That's why Luis got pissed off and left so fast."

"But that doesn't mean Steven wants a relationship."

"Maybe you don't either," I said dryly. "Sometimes starting a relationship is the worst thing you can do to someone you love."

"Only one of Eli Crosslin's children would say that" came her voice from behind the paper towel.

"It's probably true, though."

Sofia glared at me over the sodden white pulp of the towel. "Avery," she said vehemently, *"nothing* our father ever said to you was true. Not one promise. Not one word of advice. He's the worst half of each of us. Why does his half always get to win?" Crying, she jumped up and went to her room.

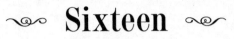

Sixteen

To my satisfaction, not to mention Sofia's, Bethany Warner loved the concept of the Jazz Age wedding at the Filter Building. Hollis was slower to be convinced, worrying that the Art Deco elements might seem too cold. However, once Sofia showed her sketches and samples of lavish details, including fresh flower arrangements ornamented with strings of pearls and glittering crystal brooches, Hollis became more enthused.

"Still, I always imagined Bethany in a traditional wedding gown," Hollis fretted. "Not something trendy."

Bethany frowned. "It's not trendy if it's been around since 1920, Mother."

"I don't want you prancing around in something that looks like a costume," Hollis persisted.

I intervened quickly, grabbing a sketch pad from Sofia and sitting between the Warners. "I understand. We need something classic but not too theme-y. I wasn't thinking about drop-waist for you, Bethany. More something like this . . . ." I picked up a pencil and sketched a slim, high-waisted gown. On impulse, I added a split-front skirt draped in panels of sheer silk and tulle. "Most of the bodice would be done in linear beading and sequins." I filled it in with a light geometric pattern. "And instead of a veil, a double-strand headband of diamonds and pearls going across the forehead. Or if that's a little too dramatic—"

"That's it," Bethany said in excitement, jamming her finger directly on the design. "That's what I want. I love that."

"It's beautiful," Hollis admitted. She gave me a pleased look. "Did you just come up with this, Avery? You're very talented."

I smiled at her. "I'm sure we can have something similar to this made—"

"No, not similar," Bethany interrupted. "I want *this* one."

"Yes, you design it, Avery," Hollis said.

I shook my head, disconcerted. "I haven't designed for a few years. And my old contacts are in New York."

"Find someone to collaborate with," Hollis told me. "We'll take the plane up to New York as often as we need for the fittings."

After the meeting was over and the Warners had left, Sofia exclaimed, "I can't believe they liked the Jazz Age wedding. I thought there was a fifty-fifty chance they'd choose the country club."

"I was pretty certain that Hollis would go for the more stylish option. She wants to be seen as forward-thinking and fashionable."

"But not if it offends the old guard," Sofia said.

I grinned as I went to get Coco from her crate. "I'll bet some of the old guard were there during the original Jazz Age."

"Why did you keep Coco in there while the Warners were here?"

"Some people don't like having a dog wandering around."

"I think you're embarrassed by her."

"Don't say things like that in front of the baby," I protested.

"That dog is not my baby," Sofia said with a reluctant smile.

"Come on, help me do her nails."

We sat side by side at the counter while I held Coco in my lap. "One of us should call Steven and tell him that the Warners liked the Gatsby wedding," I said. I uncapped a puppy-nail-polish pen, the same shade of pink as her rhinestone collar.

"You do it," Sofia said.

So far, Sofia and Steven had been at a stalemate. He had been unusually nice to her the past couple of days, but there had been no sign of the tenderness he had shown the night of Alameda's visit. When I had urged Sofia to say something to him, she had confessed that she was still trying to work up the nerve.

"Sofia, for heaven's sake, go talk to him. Be proactive."

She took one of Coco's delicate paws and held it steady. "Why don't you take your own advice?" she retorted. "You haven't talked to Joe since he took you out to lunch."

"My situation is different."

"How?"

Carefully I applied a coat of polish to Coco's nails. "For one thing, Joe has too much money. There's no way I can go after him without looking like a gold digger."

"Does Joe look at it that way?" Sofia asked dubiously.

"Doesn't matter. It's how everyone else does." The Chihuahua looked solemnly from one of us to the other as we talked. I capped the polish pen and blew gently on Coco's glossy pink nails.

"What if he's decided to outwait you? What if you're both too stubborn to make the next move?"

"Then at least I'll have my pride."

"Pride buys no meat in the market."

"You're hoping I'll ask you what that means, but I'm not going to."

"You might as well start sleeping with him," Sofia said, "since everyone already thinks you are."

My eyes widened. "Why would anyone assume that?"

"Because you bought a dog together."

"No, we didn't! *I* bought the dog. Joe just happened to be there."

"It's a sign of commitment. It shows that you're both thinking about a future together."

"Coco isn't a couples dog," I said heatedly, but as I glanced at her, I realized she was teasing. Rolling my eyes, I relaxed and set Coco carefully on the floor.

As I returned to my chair, Sofia gave me a pensive look. "Avery . . . I've been thinking about a lot of things since I saw Luis the other day. I've decided that bringing him here was one of the nicest things that *Mamá* has ever done for me."

"If so," I said, "trust me, it was purely accidental on her part."

Sofia smiled faintly. "I know. But it helped. Because facing Luis after all this time made me realize something: By not moving on, I've been giving Luis power over me. It's like he's been holding me hostage. He belongs in my past—I can't let him influence my future." Her hazel eyes took in my stricken expression as she continued. "You and I are too much alike, Avery. Thin-skinned people shouldn't feel things as deeply as we do—we bruise too easy."

We were both quiet for a moment.

"Whenever I think about moving on," I eventually said, "it's as terrifying as the idea of parachuting out of a plane. At night. Over a cactus field. I can't seem to make myself do it."

"What if the plane were on fire?" Sofia suggested. "Could you jump out of it then?"

An uneven grin spread across my face. "Well, that would definitely provide some motivation."

"Then the next time you're with Joe," Sofia said, "try telling yourself the plane's on fire. Then the only choice is to jump."

"Over the cactus field?"

"Anything's better than a burning plane," she said reasonably.

"Good point."

"Then you're going to call Joe?"

I hesitated, surprised by the flare of yearning I felt at the question. Two days, and I missed him badly. I didn't just want him, I *needed* him. *I'm doomed,* I thought, and sighed in resignation.

"No," I said, "I'm not going to call him. I'd rather figure out a way to make him come here without having to ask him."

She gave me a bemused glance. "Like fake your own kidnapping or something?"

I laughed. "I wouldn't go that far." After a few seconds of pondering, I said, "But that gives me an idea. . . ."

❧

On Saturday afternoon I closed the studio and took a long, luxurious bath. Afterward I left my hair down in loose waves and misted my wrists and throat with a light cologne. I dressed in lavender silk lounge pants and a matching lace-trimmed top that showed more cleavage than I ever would have displayed in public.

"I'm leaving for a girls' night out" came Sofia's voice as I went downstairs.

"With who?"

"Val and some other friends." Sofia was busy rummaging through her handbag. "Dinner, a movie, and probably drinks afterward." She glanced at me and grinned. "I may crash at Val's place. You'll want the whole house to yourself once Joe sees you in that out-fit."

"He may tell me off for the prank I pulled, and leave right after-ward."

"I don't think so." Sofia blew me a kiss. "Remember the plane," she said, and left.

Wandering around the empty house, I turned down most of the lights, lit some candles in blown-glass votives, and poured a glass of wine. As I sat on the sofa in front of the TV, Coco climbed up a little set of steps to sit next to me.

We were about a third of the way into a movie when the door-bell rang.

Coco trotted down the sofa steps and hurried to the front door with an abbreviated yap. My nerves jangled wildly as I stood and followed, carrying my wineglass. After taking a deep breath, I cracked open the door to find Joe leaning against the door frame. He was heart-stoppingly handsome in a dark suit, dress shirt, and tie.

"Oh, hello," I said in a tone of mild surprise, opening the door a couple of inches wider. "What are you doing here?"

"I'm supposed to take pictures at a fund-raising event tonight. But just as I was leaving, I found out my camera bag was empty. Except for this." Joe held up a piece of paper covered with letters that had been cut from a magazine and arranged ransom-note style. It read:

Call me or the camera gets it.

"Happen to know anything about this?" he asked.

"I might." As I stared into his dark eyes, I saw to my relief that he wasn't angry. In fact, I got the impression that he was considerably entertained.

"This was an inside job," Joe said. "Jack has a key to my place, but he knows better. So it had to be Ella who helped you."

"I admit nothing." I opened the door fully. "Would you like to come in for a glass of wine?"

Joe was about to reply, but his gaze had flickered to the valley of my cleavage and my half-exposed breasts, and then he couldn't seem to look away.

"Wine?" I prompted.

Joe blinked and forced his gaze back up to my face. He had to clear his throat before replying. "Please."

Coco trotted back to the sofa as Joe and I went to the kitchen.

"You were expecting company?" Joe asked, seeing the extra wineglass waiting beside the open bottle.

"One never knows."

"One knows the chances are pretty high when a three-thousand-dollar Nikon is missing."

"It's safe." I poured some chilled pinot grigio and gave it to him.

Joe took a swallow, the crystal stem of the wineglass glimmering in his strong fingers.

Being with him again, having him within arm's reach, filled me with an emotion bordering on exhilaration. For me, happiness was as elusive and fragile as one of those balloons Eli had once brought Sofia. At the moment, however, it seemed to have been woven all through me, stitched deep in my bones and muscles, enriching my blood.

"I hope I'm not making you late for your event," I said.

"It was canceled."

"When?"

A smile touched his lips. "About a minute and a half ago." He set aside his wine, then took off his jacket and draped it over the backrest of a bar stool. Next the shirt cuffs were unbuttoned and rolled up twice, revealing forearms dusted with dark hair. Excited flutters awakened in my stomach as he proceeded to remove his tie.

After unfastening his top shirt button, Joe picked up his wineglass and gave me a level glance. "I haven't called because I've been trying to give you space."

I tried to sound injured. "There's a difference between giving someone space and ignoring them."

"Honey, I'm not ignoring you, I'm trying not to act like a stalker."

"Why didn't you kiss me after we went out the other day?"

The creases at the outer corners of his eyes deepened. "Because I knew that if I started, I wouldn't be able to stop. You may have noticed that I have trouble putting on the brakes with you." He stood and took hold of the sides of my chair, effectively caging me. "Now that you've taken my camera hostage . . . what kind of ransom are we talking about?"

I had to work up my nerve before replying. "I think we should negotiate upstairs. In my bedroom."

Joe contemplated me for a long moment before shaking his head. "Avery . . . when it happens, I'm going to want things that are hard for you to give. It'll be different from the first time. And I can't take the chance that you're not ready."

I rested my hands on his forearms, taut with corded strength. "I've missed you," I said. "I missed talking to you at night and hearing about your day, and telling you about mine. I've even been dreaming about you. Since you're already occupying some of my head space, we might as well sleep together."

Joe was very still, his gaze locked on my reddening face. By now he knew how difficult it was for me to admit how I felt.

"I don't know if I'm ready for this," I continued, "but I know that

I trust you. And I know that I want to wake up with a man in my bed tomorrow morning. Specifically you. So if you–"

Before I could finish, Joe leaned forward and kissed me. My fingers tightened on his arms in a bid for balance. I took an extra breath, another, my lungs striving amid a storm of heartbeats. The kiss turned stronger, more voracious, his mouth opening mine. Without breaking the kiss, he pulled me from the chair and pinned me against the counter, as if I needed to be held in place, restrained, and the hint of male aggression was wildly exciting.

"Joe," I panted when his mouth slid to my throat, "I . . . I have a big bed upstairs, covered with . . . Italian linens and a hand-quilted silk cover . . . and feather and down pillows . . ."

Joe drew his head back to look at me, a dance of laughter in his eyes. "You don't have to sell me on the bed, honey."

He paused at the sound of a phone emanating from his discarded jacket. "Sorry," he said, reaching for the garment. "I only get this ringtone when it's family." He began to hunt through the pockets.

"Of course."

He pulled out the phone and looked at his text messages. "Christ," he said, his expression changing.

Something bad had happened.

"Haven's in the hospital," he said. "I have to go."

"I'm coming too," I said instantly.

Joe shook his head. "You don't have to–"

"Wait two minutes," I said, already running to the stairs. "I'll put on a shirt and some jeans. Don't leave without me."

~∞ Seventeen ∞~

It occurred to me on the way to the hospital that I might have been too pushy, insisting on accompanying Joe. Whatever was wrong with Haven, it was a family matter, and they might not appreciate having an outsider there. On the other hand, I wanted to help in any way possible. And more important, I wanted to be there for Joe. Having gained some understanding of how much the Travises meant to one another, I knew it would devastate him if anything happened to his sister.

"What does the text say about Haven's condition?" I asked.

Wordlessly Joe handed the phone to me.

"Preeclampsia," I said, reading the message from Ella.

"I've never heard of it before."

"I have, but I'm not sure exactly what it is." In a couple of minutes, I'd found a page on preeclampsia. "It's a hypertensive disease. High blood pressure, severe water retention, and toxic buildup in the kidneys and liver."

"How serious is it?"

I hesitated. "It can get really serious."

His hands clenched on the steering wheel. "Life-threatening?"

"Garner is a world-class hospital. I'm sure Haven will be fine." The phone rang, and I looked at the caller ID. "It's Ella. Do you want to–"

"Talk to her while I drive."

I answered the call. "Ella? Hi, it's Avery."

Ella's voice was quiet, but I could hear the stress threaded through her subdued tone. "We're in the waiting room at the neonatal ICU. Are you and Joe headed over?"

"Yes, we're almost there. What's happening?"

"This morning Haven woke up with a headache and nausea, but Jesus, that's routine for her. She couldn't keep anything down, and she went back to bed. When she woke up this afternoon, she was starting to have problems breathing. Hardy brought her to the hospital and they checked her vitals and did some tests. Her blood pressure is through the roof, and her protein levels are triple what they should be, and she's acting confused, which scared the shit out of Hardy. The good news is, the baby's heartbeat is normal."

"How many weeks before the baby is full term?"

"Four, I think. But she'll probably be fine, even being born this early."

"Wait. Are you saying Haven's in labor?"

"They're going to do a C-section. Okay, gotta go–Liberty and Gage are just walking in, and they'll want an update." The call ended.

"They're doing a C-section," I told Joe.

He swore softly.

I looked back at the Web page on the phone. "Preeclampsia is usually resolved within forty-eight hours after the baby's delivered," I said. "They'll give Haven medicine for the hypertension. The baby will be premature, but she's developed enough at this point that there probably won't be any long-term problems. So everything will be okay."

Joe nodded, looking far from reassured.

∽

The waiting room of the NICU was furnished with clusters of blue upholstered chairs and small tables and a sofa. Harsh overhead lighting imparted a lunar whiteness to the atmosphere. The assembled members of the immediate Travis family were understandably tense and subdued as they welcomed Joe and me. Jack, however, summoned a hint of his usual humor. "Hi, Avery," he said, giving me a brief hug, adding in feigned surprise, "You're still hanging out with Joe?"

"I insisted on coming with him," I said. "I hope I'm not barging in, but I thought—"

"Not at all," Liberty interrupted, her green eyes warm.

"We're glad you're here," Gage added. His gaze traveled from my face to Joe's. "No news about Haven yet."

"How's Hardy doing?" Joe asked.

"He's been solid so far," Jack replied. "But if she goes downhill any further . . . he won't take it well."

"None of us will," Joe said, and the group fell silent.

We rearranged a few chairs and settled in the waiting room. Joe and I sat on the sofa. "You sure you want to stay?" Joe asked me sotto voce. "I can have you sent home in the hospital's private car. This won't be over any time soon."

"Do you want me to leave? Is it better for the family if there are no outsiders here? Just be blunt, because I—"

"You're not an outsider. But you don't have to suffer in a hospital waiting room just because I'm here."

"I'm not suffering. And I want to stay, as long as it's okay with you." I curled my legs beneath me and leaned into his side.

"I want you here." He cuddled me closer.

"What did you mean, the hospital's private car?" I asked. "Is that a new service?"

"Not exactly. The hospital has what they call a VIP program for benefactors. The family made some donations in the past, and Dad left them a bequest in his will. So now if any of us comes to the hospital, we're supposed to wait in a VIP room, which is stuck in some distant wing of the hospital, with people hovering over you every minute. We've all agreed to avoid the VIP treatment whenever possible." He paused. "But I'd break the rules if you wanted a ride home in a town car."

"If you're not going to be a VIP," I told him, "don't try to turn me into one."

Joe smiled and pressed his lips to my temple. "Someday," he murmured, "I'm going to take you out for a nice, normal date. No drama. We'll go have dinner at a restaurant like civilized people."

After several long, quiet minutes, Jack said he was going to get some coffee and asked if anyone wanted some. The group shook their heads. He left and returned soon with a Styrofoam cup filled with steaming liquid.

Ella frowned in worry. "Jack, it's not good to drink hot liquid out of those kinds of cups—the chemicals leach into the coffee."

Jack looked sardonic. "I've drunk hot coffee out of Styrofoam for most of my life."

"That explains it," Joe said.

Although Jack sent him a warning glance, there was a betraying twitch at the corner of his mouth as he took his seat beside Ella. He offered her a pack of plastic-wrapped cookies.

"You got that from a vending machine, didn't you?" Ella asked suspiciously.

"I couldn't help myself," Jack said.

"What's wrong with vending machines?" I asked.

"The food is junk," Ella replied, "and the machines themselves are deadly. They kill more people per year than sharks."

"How could a vending machine kill someone?" Liberty asked.

"Fall over and crush them," Ella said earnestly. "It happens."

"There's no vending machine in existence that could take out a Travis," Jack informed her. "We're too hardheaded."

"I'll vouch for that," Ella said. Surreptitiously she took a cookie from the open packet and began to nibble on it.

I smiled and rested my head on Joe's shoulder. His hand began to sift through the loose locks of my hair.

Abruptly, the soothing motion of his hand stopped, a new tension entering his body. Lifting my head, I followed the direction of Joe's gaze.

Hardy had entered the waiting room, not seeming to recognize or notice anyone. His face was haggard and skull white, his eyes electric blue. He went blindly to the farthest corner and sat, his broad shoulders hunched as if he were trying to recover from a mule kick to the chest.

"Hardy—" someone said quietly.

He flinched and gave a little shake of his head.

A doctor had come to the doorway. Gage went to him, and they conferred for a couple of minutes.

Gage's expression was unreadable as he returned. The group leaned in to catch every word as he spoke quietly. "There's a complication with preeclampsia called HELLP syndrome. Basically the red blood cells are rupturing. Haven is heading toward liver failure and a possible stroke." He paused and swallowed hard, his gaze meeting Liberty's. "Delivering the baby is the first step," he continued in an even tone. "After that they'll give her steroids and plasma, and likely a blood transfusion. We'll probably get some news in about an hour. For now, we hunker down and wait."

"Shit," Joe said softly. He glanced at the far corner of the room, where Hardy leaned forward with his forearms braced on his thighs, his head down. "Someone should sit with him. Should I–"

"I will, if you don't mind," Gage murmured.

"Go right ahead."

Gage stood and went to the solitary figure in the corner.

I was surprised by Gage's desire to sit with Hardy, recalling some of what Joe had once told me, that there was no love lost between the two men. Joe had been somewhat vague about the details, but he'd indicated that Hardy had caused some kind of trouble for Gage and Liberty. It seemed there was history between Hardy and Liberty– they had known each other growing up and had even been childhood sweethearts for a time.

"How did Hardy end up marrying Haven?" I had asked.

"Not exactly sure how or when it started," Joe had said. "But once Hardy and Haven took up with each other, it was like trying to stop a runaway train. And eventually we all realized that Hardy loved her, which is all that matters. Still . . . Gage and Hardy generally keep their distance from each other, unless there's an occasion when the entire family gets together."

I stole a discreet glance at the corner of the room, where Gage sat beside Hardy and gave him a rough brotherly pat on the back. Hardy didn't even appear to notice. He was trapped in some private hell, where no one could reach him. In a couple of minutes, however, Hardy's shoulders lifted and fell in a sigh. Gage asked him some-thing, and he shook his head in response.

For the next hour, Gage stayed beside Hardy, murmuring from time to time but mostly offering silent companionship. No one else approached, understanding that Hardy's emotions were too raw, that one person's proximity was all he could handle.

Why that person should be Gage, however, was difficult to understand.

I gave Joe a questioning glance. Leaning close, he murmured, "Haven's always been a favorite of Gage's. Hardy knows if any-thing happens, Gage would be nearly as torn up about it as he would. And besides . . . they're family."

A young nurse entered the waiting room. "Mr. Cates?" He rose to his feet, his face contorted with a raw anguish that I doubted she or anyone else would ever forget. She hurried over to him with her phone. "I have a picture of your daughter," she said. "I took it before they put her in the incubator. She's a perfect four pounds. Seventeen inches long."

The Travises all gathered around the phone with exclamations of excitement and relief.

Hardy took a glance at the image and said hoarsely, "My wife . . ."

"Mrs. Cates came through the surgery without any major issues. She's waking up in recovery—it'll take a little while. The doctor will be here in just a minute, and he'll let you know—"

"I want to see her," Hardy said brusquely.

Before the disconcerted nurse could reply, Gage intervened. "Hardy, I'll talk to the doctor while you're with Haven."

Hardy nodded and strode from the waiting area.

"He really shouldn't be doing that," the nurse fretted. "I'd better go follow him. If y'all want to take a peek at the baby, she's in the special care nursery."

I headed to the nursery with Joe, Ella, and Jack, while Gage and Liberty stayed in the waiting room to talk to the doctor.

"Poor Hardy," Ella murmured as we walked along the hallway. "He's been worried sick."

"My sympathy's with Haven," Joe said. "I don't know the details of what she's been through, and I don't want to. But I do know she's gone through one hell of a battle."

We entered the special care nursery, where the newborn had been placed in an incubator. She had been hooked up to an oxygen tube and monitoring leads, and her midsection was wrapped in a glowing blue pad.

"What is that?" I asked in a hushed voice.

"A biliblanket," Ella replied. "Mia had one after she was born. It's phototherapy for jaundice."

The baby blinked and appeared to drift to sleep, her rosebud mouth opening and closing. Her head was covered with fine dark hair. "Hard to tell what she looks like," Jack commented.

"She'll be beautiful," Ella said. "How could she not be, with Haven and Hardy as parents?"

"Hardy's not what I'd call pretty," Jack said.

"If you did," Joe remarked, "he'd kick your ass."

Jack grinned and asked Ella, "Did Haven tell you what the baby's name was?"

"Not yet."

We returned to the waiting room, where Gage and Liberty had just finished talking with the doctor. "They're cautiously optimistic," Gage reported. "It's going to take three or four days before the HELLP issues are resolved. They've already given her a blood transfusion, and they'll probably do another to help with the platelet count. They're also going to put her on corticosteroid therapy and monitor her closely." He shook his head, looking troubled. "They're keeping her on the magnesium drip to ward off seizures. Apparently it's a son of a bitch."

Liberty rubbed her face and sighed. "Why don't they have a bar in a hospital? It's usually the place you most need a drink."

Gage wrapped his arms around his wife and snuggled her against his chest. "You need to go home and check on the kids. What if Jack and Ella drop you off while I stay here a little while longer? I'm going to stick around and talk to Hardy."

"That sounds good," Liberty said against his shoulder.

"You need me for anything?" Joe asked.

Gage shook his head and smiled. "I think we're fine here. You and Avery go on and get some rest. You've earned it."

~ Eighteen ~

I woke up in the morning with the groggy awareness that I was not
alone. Climbing through the blurred layers of consciousness, I
recalled the events of the previous night…coming home from the
hospital with Joe…inviting him upstairs to sleep with me. We had
both been exhausted, sore from hours spent on uncomfortable
waiting room furniture, emotionally drained. I had changed into a
nightgown and climbed into bed with Joe. The feeling of being held
against his big, warm body had been delicious, and in matter of
seconds I had passed out.

Joe was behind me, one arm tucked beneath my head, his legs
drawn up under mine. I lay quietly and listened to the even cadence
of his breathing. Wondering if he was awake, I let my toes delicately
investigate the contours of his foot. Slowly his mouth came to my
neck, finding a place so sensitive that I felt a shot of delight down to
my stomach.

"There's a man in my bed," I remarked, groping back with my

hand, feeling a hairy muscular thigh, the lean smoothness of a masculine hip. My wrist was gently captured, my hand guided downward until my fingers encountered hard, distended flesh and silky male skin. I took a quick breath, my eyes widening. "Joe . . . it's too early."

His hand traveled to my breast, caressing the shape through the thin knit fabric of my nightgown, softly pinching the nipple, enticing sensation from the stiffening points.

I tried again, sounding ambivalent even to my own ears. "I'm not a fan of morning sex."

But he continued to kiss my neck and pulled the hem of my nightgown up past my knees.

I let out a giggle of nerves and dismay, crawling toward the other side of the bed.

Joe pounced, pushing me back down. He covered me, thighs clamping on my hips, deliberately letting me feel some of his weight, his body charged with lust. The moment was playful, but there was intent in the way he handled me, an assertiveness that stole my breath away.

"At least let me take a shower first," I said plaintively.

"I want you like this."

I began to wriggle. "Later. Please."

Lowering his head, Joe murmured, "You're not in charge. I am."

I went still. For some reason, hearing those soft words while he was pinning me down like that sent a deep, deranged thrill through me. His voice curled hotly in my ear. "You belong to me, and I'm going to have you. Here and now."

I couldn't seem to get enough air. I had never been so intensely aroused.

His position altered, his hand sliding beneath the nightgown and between my thighs, searching intimately. I quivered as he massaged into the wetness, two fingers entering in a gentle glide. My hips began to rock back in a tight, unthinking rhythm, and he matched it exactly, pressing deep into the pulse, building sensation until I began to clench at each impetus.

Turning me to my back, he knelt between my thighs and propped them up so my knees were bent. He kissed my ankle, my calf, working his way upward. I bit my lips and writhed as the kisses crept closer to the juncture of my thigh and groin. "Don't–" I began to protest, right before I felt a hot glassy stroke across my twitching flesh. I couldn't escape the firm wet tug of his mouth. I began to sob, my defenses breaking down beneath the weight of pleasure.

He was unrelenting, concentrating on the shivery-hot place with his tongue, the caresses acquiring a rhythm that guided every impulse and sensation and heartbeat into a single focused current. My legs spread out and I was making sounds like I'd been hurt as the blinding release began. Too much to bear, too intense, my body seized with violent quivers.

Joe spent long minutes drawing out the afterglow even after I quieted, his mouth caressing me with diabolical gentleness. Eventually his head lifted and he kissed my stomach. I was so decimated that I barely registered when he rolled away for a moment and reached for something on the nightstand. He levered himself fully over my body, nudging my legs apart, and I reached up for him with weak arms. Entering me in a demanding drive, he pulled back just enough to thrust again, the deliberate measure of each lunge forcing me deliciously open, my hips lifted with each stroke.

Sometimes the rhythm was teasing and slow, sometimes fast and deep. He paid attention to every response, no matter how subtle, learning what excited me, what gave me pleasure. Joe was making love to me as no one ever had, and although the experience was unfamiliar, I could recognize it for what it was. Devastated, I closed my eyes as he ground into me with a steady circling. Whimpers broke from my throat. There was no holding anything back, no modesty, no control. More racking spasms, my pleasure feeding his. Joe growled in his chest and throat and began to shudder in my arms. I held him, kissing the side of his neck, loving the weight of him on me.

Eventually he turned and pulled me halfway over him, and we lay entangled for a long time afterward. I was in a stupor, random thoughts hovering just out of reach. The smells of sweat and sex mingled in an erotic fragrance, infusing every breath. Beneath my head, Joe's chest lifted and fell in a relaxed pattern. One of his hands wandered over me, stroking gently.

I kissed his shoulder. "I going to take a shower now," I said, my voice husky. "Don't try and stop me."

He smiled and turned to his side, watching me leave the bed.

I went into the bathroom on unsteady legs and started the shower. My throat was tight with the effort to hold back tears. It was difficult to feel so defenseless . . . unguarded . . . and yet at the same time, there was an unspeakable relief in it.

Before the water had heated sufficiently for me to step in, Joe entered the room. His acute gaze caught every nuance of my expression before I could manage to hide it. Reaching a hand into the shower spray, he tested the temperature. He went with me into the glass-fronted stall. Blindly I turned my face into the water.

Joe slicked his hands with soap and began to wash me, his touch tender rather than sexual. I leaned against him passively, making no protest even when his soapy fingers slid between my legs and parted the soft folds for the rinse of hot water. He turned me so the spray was at my back, and I was pressed all along the wet, muscled surface of his front.

"Too soon?" I heard him ask.

I shook my head, arms locked around his waist. "No . . . But it was different from the first time."

"I told you it would be."

"Yes, but I . . . I'm not sure why."

He murmured close to my ear, "Because it means something now."

I could respond only with a shaken nod.

～

After a quick breakfast of coffee and toast, Joe had to leave. He would rush home to change his clothes before meeting with one of the directors of the Travis charitable giving foundation, to discuss the latest initiatives the family had agreed to focus on. "After everything that happened last night," Joe said, "I may be the only Travis who shows up." He stole a quick kiss. "Dinner tonight?" Another kiss before I could answer. "At seven?" One more kiss. "I'll take that as a yes."

I stood there with an idiotic grin on my face as he left.

A little while later, while I was drinking a second cup of coffee, Sofia came downstairs in a pink robe and matching bunny slippers. "Is Joe still here?" she asked in a whisper.

"No, he's gone."

"How was last night?"

I smiled wryly. "Eventful. We spent most of it in a waiting room at Garner Hospital." As we sat next to each other at the counter, I told Sofia all about Haven's pregnancy complications, and the baby's birth, and how the Travises had interacted.

"It was sort of eye-opening," I said. "I've seen families celebrating together, and families on the verge of brawling over incredibly stupid stuff. But I've never actually seen a family, up close, in a situation like that. The way they supported each other . . ." I paused, finding it difficult to put into words. "Well, it surprised me that Gage, who's had problems with Hardy in the past, would be the one to sit with him and comfort him, and Hardy let him, and it was because of the family bond, this . . . this weird connection that's so important to all of them."

"It's not weird," Sofia said. "That's what a family is."

"Yes, I know what a family is, but I've never seen what a family *does*. Not like that." I paused, frowning. "I've never been part of an extended family. I'm not sure I'd like it. They all seem to know each other so well. Too well. There wouldn't be enough privacy for me."

"There are obligations when you're part of a family," Sofia conceded. "And problems. But taking care of each other . . . the feeling of belonging somewhere . . . that part is wonderful."

"Do you miss not being close to your relatives?" I asked.

"Sometimes," Sofia admitted. "But when you're not accepted for who you are, it's not really a family." She shrugged and took a swallow of coffee. "Tell me the rest," she prompted. "When Joe brought you back."

A light blush covered my face. "He spent the night, obviously."

"And?"

"I'm not giving you details," I protested, and Sofia laughed gleefully as my color deepened.

"I can tell it was good just by looking at your face," she said.

I tried to divert her. "Let's figure out our plans for the day. Later this afternoon we need to review what's been done on the Warner wedding so far, and send a report to Ryan. I think he'll be fine with most of it, but I want to make sure–" I broke off as the doorbell rang. "That must be a delivery. Unless you're expecting someone?"

"No." Sofia went to the front entrance and peeked through one of the narrow side windows. She whirled around and plastered her back to the door like a knife thrower's assistant during warm-up practice. "It's Steven," she said, her eyes wide. "Why is he here?"

"I have no idea. Let's ask him."

She didn't move. "What do you think he wants?"

"He works here," I reminded her patiently. "Let him in."

My sister nodded tensely. She turned to unlock the door, then opened it with unnecessary force. "What do you want?" she asked without preamble.

Steven was dressed casually in jeans and a polo shirt. His expression was difficult to interpret as he looked down at her. "I left my phone case here yesterday," he said warily. "I came by to pick it up."

"Hi, Steven," I said. "Your phone case is on the coffee table."

"Thanks." He walked inside with an air of extreme caution, as if he suspected the studio had been booby-trapped.

Coco ascended the steps to the sofa and watched Steven retrieve his phone case. He paused to pet her tiny head and scratch the back of her neck. As soon as he stopped, Coco pawed at his hand and shoved her head beneath his palm, demanding that he continue.

"How's it going?" I asked.

"Fine," Steven replied.

"Would you like some coffee?"

It appeared to be a question with no easy answer. "I'm . . . not sure."

"Okay."

As Steven continued to pet Coco, he stole a glance at Sofia. "You're wearing bunny slippers," he said, as if it confirmed a suspicion he'd had for some time.

"And?" Sofia asked darkly, expecting a sarcastic comment.

"I like them."

Sofia gave him a confused glance.

They were both so focused on each other that neither of them noticed my discreet exit from the kitchen.

"I'm going to the farmer's market," Steven said. "There should be some good peaches. Would you like to come along?"

Sofia replied in a slightly higher-pitched voice than usual. "Okay, why not?"

"Good."

"I just have to change out of my pajamas into some regular clothes and ..." Sofia paused. "Pajamas," she repeated. "That's how to say it. Right?"

Unable to resist, I stopped to glance at them from my vantage on the stairs. I had an unobstructed view of Steven's face. He was smiling down at Sofia, his eyes glowing. "The way you pronounce it," he said, "it always sounds like pa-yamas." He hesitated and lifted his hand to caress her cheek gently.

"Pajamas," Sofia repeated, sounding exactly like before.

Seeming to lose all restraint, Steven pulled her into his arms and murmured something low.

A long silence. A little sobbing breath. "So have I," I heard Sofia say.

He kissed her, and Sofia molded herself against him, her hands climbing into his hair. The two of them seemed overwhelmed with mutual tenderness, clumsy with it as they kissed each other's cheeks, chins, mouths.

Not long ago, I thought as I hurried up the stairs, the sight of Steven and Sofia passionately embracing would have been unthinkable.

Everything was changing so fast. The long, steady road I had plotted out for Sofia and me was turning out to have so many unexpected twists and detours that I found myself wondering if we were going to end up in entirely different places from those we'd originally planned.

I received frequent updates on Haven's condition from Ella and Liberty and, of course, Joe. Although Haven's health was improving rapidly, she wouldn't be well enough to receive visitors outside of immediate family until she was back home. Her daughter, named Rosalie, was thriving and gaining weight and was frequently brought to Haven for what was called "kangaroo time," resting on her chest for skin-to-skin contact.

As I scrolled through photos that Joe had taken and loaded onto his tablet, I paused at a striking image of Hardy cradling Rosalie tenderly in his big hands, his smiling face lowered so that one of her miniature palms rested on his nose.

"Her eyes look blue," I said, zooming in on the picture.

"When Hardy's mom visited yesterday, she said his eyes were exactly that color when he was born."

"When will Haven and Rosalie be able to leave the hospital?"

"One more week, they think. Hardy will be over the moon, bringing his two girls home." Joe paused. "But I hope my sister's not going to want to have any more children. Hardy says he couldn't survive this again, even if Haven wants to take the chance."

"Is there a risk of preeclampsia if she gets pregnant again?"

Joe nodded.

"Haven may be fine with just having one child," I said. "Or Hardy may change his mind. You never can predict what people will do." Having reached the last picture, I handed the tablet back to Joe.

We were at his house in the Old Sixth Ward, a charming bungalow with a slightly smaller companion house in the back. Joe had painted the interiors of both buildings a soft, creamy white and stained the trim a rich walnut. The decor was spare and masculine, with a few pieces of beautifully restored furniture. Joe had spent more time showing me the smaller house, where he worked and kept his photography equipment. To my surprise, there was even a darkroom, which he admitted he seldom used, but would never get rid of.

"Every now and then, I'll shoot a roll of film because there's still something magical about developing a print in the darkroom."

"Magical?" I repeated with a quizzical smile.

"I'll show you sometime. There's nothing like seeing an image appear in the developer tray. And it's all about craft: You can't tell if the exposure is too light or dark, you can't see the details of burning and dodging, so you have to go with what feels right, what past experience has taught you."

"So you prefer that to Photoshop?"

"No, Photoshop has too many advantages. But I still like the idea of having to wait to see a picture in the darkroom. Taking time, and seeing the image with a fresh perspective . . . it's not as practical as digital, but it's more romantic."

I loved his passion for his work. I loved it that he thought of a tiny windowless room filled with trays of caustic chemicals as romantic.

Scrolling through files of photos on a computer monitor, I found a series of shots he'd taken in Afghanistan . . . beautiful, stark, riveting. Some of the landscapes were otherworldly. A pair of old men sitting in front of a turquoise wall . . . a soldier's silhouette against a red sky as he stood on a mountain path . . . a dog, seen from an eye-level perspective with a soldier's booted feet in the foreground.

"How long were you there?" I asked.

"Only a month."

"How did you end up going?"

"A friend from college was filming a documentary. He and his camera crew were embedded with troops at a firebase in Kandahar. But the stills photographer had to leave early. So they asked if I would step in and finish. I was sent to the same two-day training session the rest of the crew had gone through, basically how not to screw things up in a combat environment. The dogs at the front lines were incredible. Not one of them flinched at the sound of a gunshot. One day on patrol, I watched a Lab sniff out an IED that the metal detectors didn't catch."

"That was incredibly dangerous."

"Yes. But she was a smart dog. She knew what she was doing."

"I meant dangerous for you."

"Oh." His lips quirked. "I'm pretty good at staying out of trouble."

I tried to return the smile, but there was a stabbing sensation in my chest as I thought of him taking that kind of risk. "Would you do something like that again?" I couldn't resist asking. "Take a job where you could be hurt or . . . or worse?"

"Any of us could be hurt, no matter where we are," he said. "When your number's up, it's up." His gaze held mine as he added, "But I wouldn't go into a situation like that if you didn't want me to."

The implication that my feelings might sway such a decision was a little unnerving. But part of me responded to it, craved that kind of influence over him. That worried me even more.

"Come on," Joe murmured, leading me out of the small building. "Let's go into the house."

Exploring, I went into the small bedroom. The queen-size bed was covered with simple white sheets and a white quilt. I admired the headboard, a panel made of wooden vertical slats. "Where did you get this?"

"Haven gave it to me. It was the door of an old freight elevator in her apartment building."

Inspecting the piece more closely, I saw a long-faded word sten-ciled in red letters on the side—DANGER—and I smiled. I ran my hand across the smooth surface of a turned-over sheet. "These are nice. Looks like a high thread count."

"I don't know the thread count."

I kicked off my shoes and crawled onto the queen-size bed. Re-clining on my side, I shot him a provocative glance. "Apparently you don't share my appreciation for luxury linens."

Joe lowered himself next to me. "Believe me, you're the most lux-urious thing that's ever been on this bed." Slowly his hand followed the curve of my waist and hip. "Avery . . . I want to take your picture."

My brows lifted. "When?"

"Now."

I looked down at my sleeveless top and jeans. "In this outfit?"

Idly, he traced a pattern on my thigh. "Actually . . . I was think-ing you could take it off."

My eyes turned huge. "Oh, my God. Are you seriously asking me to pose for naked pictures?"

"You can cover yourself with a sheet."

"No."

From the way Joe looked at me, I could tell he was calculating how to get what he wanted.

"What is the point?" I asked anxiously.

"My two favorite things in the world are you, and photography. I want to enjoy both at the same time."

"And then what will happen to these pictures?"

"They're just for me. I won't show them to anyone. Later I'll de-lete every single one if that's what you want."

"Have you done this before?" I asked, suspicious. "Is it some ritual you have with your girlfriends?"

Joe shook his head. "You're the first." He paused. "No, you're the second. Once I was hired to shoot a car ad with a model wearing only silver paint. I went out with her a couple of times after that. She was never actually a girlfriend."

"Why did you break up?"

"After the silver paint came off, she wasn't all that interesting."

I couldn't hold back a reluctant laugh.

"Let me take your picture," Joe coaxed. "Trust me."

I gave him a furiously pleading glance. "Why am I even considering this?"

His eyes flashed with satisfaction. "That means yes." He left the bed.

"It means I'm going to kill you if you betray me," I called after him. Hearing myself, I rolled my eyes. "I'm talking like a telenovela character." I undressed quickly and climbed into bed, shivering at the coolness of the sheets.

In a minute, Joe returned to the room with his Nikon and a small stand-alone flash. He opened the shades, leaving the windows covered with sheers that softened the brilliant afternoon light. As he pulled away the top cover on the bed, I jerked the sheet up high under my chin.

Joe looked at me in a different way from ever before, assessing highlights, shadows, visual geometry.

"I'm not comfortable being naked," I told him.

"The problem is that you're not naked often enough. You need to go without clothes about ninety-five percent of the time, and then you'll get used to it."

"You'd like that," I muttered.

Joe grinned and leaned over to kiss the exposed skin of my shoulder. "You're so pretty without your clothes," he murmured, working his way toward my neck. "Every time I see you in one of those big loose shirts, I think about all those sexy curves underneath, and it makes me as hot as hell."

I slid him a perturbed glance. "You don't like the way I dress?"

He paused in his kissing just long enough to say, "You're beautiful no matter what you wear."

The puzzling thing was, I knew he actually meant it. I could tell it was the truth, had been the truth for him since the beginning. My figure flaws weren't flaws to Joe—he had always regarded my body with a mixture of appreciation and lust that was pretty damned flattering.

I thought it was possible that I'd been testing him without being aware of it, trying to find out if the sack dresses and big tops and baggy pants would make any difference to him. Clearly they hadn't. Joe thought I was beautiful. Why should I think less of myself than he did? What point was there in letting those beautiful clothes hang in my closet unworn?

"I have some really stylish new outfits that Steven helped me pick out," I said. "I just haven't found the right time to start wearing them."

"You don't have to change anything for me."

Perversely, that made me wish I'd worn something new and pretty today, something that measured up to the way he saw me.

At Joe's direction, I lay on my side, awkwardly propping my head on my hand.

Lowering to his haunches, Joe positioned the camera. The shutter clicked and the nightstand unit flashed, covering me with fill light to balance the brilliance from the window behind me. "You've got no reason to be shy," he said. "Every inch of you is luscious." He paused to adjust the stand-alone flash, tested it again, and focused on me. His voice was soft and encouraging. "Can you show me your leg?"

I hesitated.

"One leg," he coaxed.

Cautiously, I slid out my top leg and hooked it over the top of the sheet.

Joe's gaze traveled along my exposed limb, and he shook his head as if presented with more temptation than a man could stand. Setting aside the camera, he bent to kiss my knee.

I reached out to stroke his dark hair. "You're about to drop your camera."

"I don't care."

"You will if it smashes on the floor."

His hand began to insinuate itself beneath the sheet. "Maybe before I start taking pictures, we should—"

"No," I said. "Stay on task."

He withdrew his hand. "After?" he asked hopefully.

I couldn't restrain a grin. "We'll see."

My smile was captured with an immediate click of the shutter. Joe proceeded to shoot pictures from different angles, adjusting the focus ring with expert precision.

"Why do you have it on manual?" I asked, tucking the sheet more securely beneath my arms.

"In this lighting, I can find the right focusing point faster than auto mode can."

It was sexy, watching his hands on the camera, the skillful way he held and manipulated it. There was a particular pleasure in watching a man do something he was that good at. His expression was absorbed and intent as he took a series of shots with me lying on my stomach, my hips covered with the sheet, the length of my back exposed. I rested my head in the crook of my folded arms and gave him a sideways glance. The shutter clicked several times.

"Damn, you're photogenic," he murmured, approaching the bed. "Your skin catches the light like a pearl." As he continued to take shots from various angles, praising and flirting, fondling whenever he got the chance, I found myself beginning to have a good time.

"I'm beginning to think you're just using this as an excuse to feel me up," I commented.

"Side benefit," he said, climbing onto the bed with me. Still holding his camera, he straddled my hips in an easy movement, his denim-clad thighs on either side of me.

"Hey," I protested, tugging the sheet higher over my breasts.

Rising on his knees, Joe angled the camera directly above me and took a few shots. As close as we were, it was impossible not to notice that the button-fly crotch of his jeans was straining. Playfully, I walked my fingers up to his crotch and wiggled them into the spaces between the metal buttons.

Joe fumbled to adjust the focus ring. "Avery, don't distract me."

"I'm trying to help you." I unfastened the top button.

"That's not helping. In fact"–he let out an unsteady breath as I began on the second button–"that's the opposite of helping." He pried my hand from the placket. "Be a good girl and let me take a few more shots. I like this pose." After pressing a kiss into my palm, he positioned my arm up around my head in an abandoned posture. His fingers adjusted my elbow, softening the angle. With every alteration of his weight, I felt the enticing pressure of him against my groin.

Picking up his camera, Joe rose to his knees again. I looked into the lens while he looked at me, and I thought of the last time we'd had sex, how he'd stood at the side of the bed and pulled my legs up to his shoulders, how he'd teased and entered me slowly.

As I lay there, warmed by the erotic memory, I felt a deep, unfa-

miliar sense of ease, of languorous openness. My inhibitions had
dissolved, and for once I wasn't trying to hide anything. It was so
completely the opposite of what I'd expected that my lips parted with
a faint, wondering smile.

The shutter clicked a few more times. "That's it," Joe said softly,
the camera lowering.

"What do you mean?"

"I got the shot I wanted."

I blinked. "How can you tell?"

"Sometimes I can feel it even before I see it. Everything lines up.
The second I push the shutter, I know I've found the sweet spot."

As he stretched to set the camera on the nightstand, I went for
the buttons of his fly again, and I heard his quiet laugh. He stripped
off his T-shirt and tossed it aside. Intent on my task, I worked at the
fastenings, my hair pooling and sliding over his bare stomach. I licked
at the line of crinkled hair leading into his jeans, my tongue sliding
over roughness and silk. He made a fervent sound, his hands coming
to my head, a slight tremor in his fingers. Another button, another,
and then I pulled at the waist of his boxers.

Joe moved to help me. Before he could shove his jeans all the way
off, I was on him, grasping the thick shaft with both hands. It was
scorching hot, the thin skin moving easily over hard flesh. I put my
mouth on him, and he went still, his jeans bunched around his knees,
his lungs working in powerful bursts. I painted him with my tongue,
taking in the salt and satin and a rampaging pulse, his pleasure so
intense that I could feel its echoes in my own body. When I heard
his muffled pleading groan, I lifted my head inch by inch, sucking
wetly all the way. His entire body was rigid, his face flushed.

I crawled over him and he tangled one of his hands in my hair,
forcing my head down to his. As he kicked off his jeans, I straddled

him and reached down to guide him in place. With a hoarse murmur, he moved to help me, his hand closing over mine.

I began to ride fast and hard, pumping in reckless abandon. Wanting to make it last, Joe reached for my hips, forcing me to ease the pace. His hands played over me gently, caressing, coaxing me to lean forward. Lifting his head, he caught my nipple and pulled it deep. I writhed with the heat of him inside me, my body filled and brimming with sensation. He pulled me down farther, and we tried to find ways to pull each other even closer, using arms, legs, hands, mouths, breathing the same air, matching kisses and caresses and heartbeats.

ഇം

Much later, Joe showed me the photo after he'd loaded it onto his laptop. A bright wash of light had imparted a pearly glow to my skin and turned my hair ember red. The eyes were heavy-lidded, the lips full and slightly parted. The woman in the photo was seductive, inviting, radiant.

Me.

As I stared at the image in wonder, Joe wrapped his arms around me from behind and whispered in my ear, "Every time I look at you . . . this is what I see."

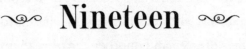

❧ Nineteen ❧

"Everyone be quiet," Sofia said, adjusting the TV volume. "I don't want to miss a word."

"You're recording it, right?" Steven asked.

"I think so, but sometimes I don't get the settings right."

"Let me check," he said, and she handed him the remote.

Everyone in the studio had gathered to watch the broadcast of a local television-magazine show. The producers had sent a camera crew and reporter to the Harlingen wedding we had done recently. The hour-long wedding special featured the latest tips, fashions, and trends, as well as profiling Texas-based businesses. The last segment of the show focused on practical advice for wedding planning. A Houston planner named Judith Lord had been asked to discuss choosing venues and vendors. I had been invited to follow up with advice about day-of preparation and logistics.

The Judith Lord segment was elegant and dignified, exactly what I hoped mine would be like. Judith, a long-established grande dame of the business, possessed a fondant-over-steel composure that I admired immensely. The reporter asked her a few easy questions, the interview cut to a shot of Judith and a client browsing through a row of wedding dresses and another showing them enjoying wedding cake samples, with Mozart playing in the background.

All semblance of dignity vanished, however, as soon as *my* segment started. The music changed to a manic comic-opera piece. "Why are they playing that?" I asked in surprised distaste.

At the same time, Tank exclaimed, "Hey, I like that song. It's the one from the Bugs Bunny cartoon with the barber chairs."

"Otherwise known as Rossini's overture to *The Barber of Seville*," Steven said dryly.

The reporter's voice-over started. *"In the elite world of Texas society weddings, Avery Crosslin has been aggressively building a client list with her take-no-prisoners style—"*

"Aggressive?" I protested.

"That's not a bad word," Steven said.

"Not for a man. But it's bad when they say it about a woman."

"Come here, Avery," Joe murmured. He was half sitting on an arm of the sofa, while Sofia and the rest of the studio team clustered in front of the television.

I went to him, and he slid an arm around my hip. "Am I aggressive?" I asked with a frown.

"'Course not," he replied soothingly, at the same time that everyone else in the room said in unison, *"Yes."*

In the month since Joe and I had started sleeping together, we had grown closer at a rate that would have alarmed me if I'd allowed myself enough time to really think about it. Instead I stayed busy planning two small weddings as well as the Warner extravaganza. Every day was filled with work. My nights, however, belonged to

Joe. Time moved at different pace when I was with him, the hours blazing by at light speed. I always dreaded the shock of the alarm clock in the morning, when we had to go our separate ways.

Joe was a physical man, demanding in bed, endlessly patient and creative. I was never quite certain what to expect from him. Sometimes he was playful and spontaneous, ravishing me against the kitchen counter or on the stairs, doing exactly as he pleased despite my outraged modesty. Other times he would make me lie completely still while he caressed and teased endlessly, his hands so skilled and gentle that it drove me wild. Afterwards we had long, lazy conversations in the darkness, in which I confided things that I would probably regret later. But I couldn't seem to hold anything back with Joe. His attention was like some damned addictive drug that was impossible to kick.

Understanding me far too well, Joe gave my hip a comforting pat as I frowned at the TV. There I was on camera, stressing the importance of maintaining a strict timeline for the wedding day events.

Sofia turned briefly from the television and grinned at me over her shoulder. "You look great on TV," she said.

"Your personality is larger than life," Ree-Ann added.

"So is my ass," I muttered as the television-me walked away and the camera focused on my backside.

Joe, who would tolerate no criticism of my posterior, discreetly pinched my rear. "Hush," he whispered.

For the next four minutes, I watched with growing dismay as my professional image was demolished by quick-cut editing and whimsical music. I looked like a screwball comedy actress as I repositioned microphones, adjusted flower arrangements, and went out to the street to direct traffic so the photographer could get a shot of the wedding party outside the church.

The camera showed me talking to a groomsman who had insisted on wearing a cowboy hat with his tux. He was clutching his hat as if fearing I might rip it from him. As I argued and gestured, Coco stared up at the obstinate groomsman with a grumpy expression, her front paws flopping up and down in perfect timing to the opera music.

Everyone in the room chuckled. "They weren't supposed to film me with Coco," I said with a scowl. "I made that clear. I only brought her because the pet hotel didn't have room that day."

They cut back to the interview. *"You've said that part of your job is to prepare for the unexpected,"* the reporter said. *"How exactly do you do that?"*

"I try to think in terms of worst-case scenarios," I replied. *"Unexpected weather, vendor mistakes, technical difficulties..."*

"Technical difficulties such as..."

"Oh, it could be anything. Issues with the dance floor, problems with zippers or buttons... even an off-center ornament on the wedding cake."

I was shown walking into the reception site kitchen, which had been declared off-limits to the camera crew. But someone had followed me with a head-cam.

"I didn't say anyone could film me with a head-cam," I protested. "They didn't do that to Judith Lord!"

Everyone shushed me again.

On the TV screen, I approached two deliverymen who were settling a four-tiered wedding cake on the counter. I told them they had brought it inside too soon—the cake was supposed to stay in the refrigerated truck or the buttercream would melt.

"No one told us," one of them replied.

"I'm telling you. Take it back to the truck and—" My eyes widened as the heavy wedding cake topper began to slide and tilt. I reached up

and leaned forward to catch it before it could damage all four tiers on the way down.

Someone in editing had bleeped out my swearing.

Noticing the way the deliverymen were staring at me, I followed their avid gazes, discovering I had leaned so close to the cake that my breasts were covered with white buttercream swirls.

By this point, everyone in the room was cracking up. Even Joe was trying manfully to choke back his amusement.

On the TV screen, the reporter asked me a question about the challenges of my job. I paraphrased General Patton, saying you had to accept the challenges so you could experience the exhilaration of victory.

"But what about the romance of the wedding day?" the reporter asked. *"Doesn't that get lost when you treat it like a military campaign?"*

"The bride and groom supply the romance," I replied confidently. *"I worry about every detail, so they don't have to. A wedding is a celebration of love, and that's what they should be free to focus on."*

"And while everyone else is celebrating," the reported said in a voice-over, *"Avery Crosslin is taking care of business."*

I was shown making a beeline to the back of the church, where the chain-smoking father of the bride was lurking with a lit cigarette in his mouth. Without a word, I took the can of Evian from my bag and extinguished the cigarette while he stood there blinking. Next I was kneeling on the floor, duct-taping the torn hem of one of the bridesmaid's dresses. Finally the camera panned to the grooms-man's cowboy hat shoved under a chair, where I'd secretly stashed it.

Someone had turned the hat upside down, and Coco was sitting in it. She stared directly into the camera, her eyes bright, her tongue hanging out, while the piece concluded with a grand orchestral finale.

I picked up the remote controller and turned off the TV. "Who put Coco in that hat?" I demanded. "She couldn't have gotten in there by herself. Sofia, did you do it?"

She shook her head, snickering.

"Then who?"

No one would admit to it. I looked around the room at the entire lot of them. I had never seen them so collectively entertained. "I'm glad you all find this so amusing, since we'll probably be out of business in a matter of days."

"Are you kidding?" Steven asked. "We're going to get more business from this than we can handle."

"They made me look incompetent."

"No, they didn't."

"What about the frosting?" I demanded.

"You saved the cake," Steven pointed out. "While at the same time boosting the testosterone level of every guy in the audience."

"It was a wedding show," I said. "You, Tank, and Joe are the only three straight men in Houston who watched it."

"Give me the remote," Ree-Ann said. "I want to see it again."

I shook my head emphatically. "I'm going to delete it."

"Doesn't matter," Tank told Ree-Ann. "The station will put it on their website."

Joe closed his hand over the remote and removed it carefully from my grip. His gaze was lit with amused sympathy.

"I want to be elegant like Judith Lord," I told him plaintively.

"Avery, there are a million Judith Lords out there, and only one you. You were beautiful and funny on that program, and you gave off the energy of someone who was having a hell of a good time. You accomplished everything Judith Lord did, except that you were a lot more entertaining." Joe handed the remote to Steven and took my hand. "Come on, I'm taking you out for dinner."

By the time he and I had reached the front door, they had rewound the interview and were watching it again.

∽

Returning to the studio a couple of hours later, Joe and I encountered Sofia and Steven, who were on their way out to eat.

Sofia was happy and animated, almost illuminated from within. That undoubtedly had something to do with the fact that she and Steven had recently started sleeping together. Sofia had divulged to me that, unlike Luis, Steven knew about foreplay. I could tell from seeing them together that everything was going very, very well. In fact, Sofia and Steven treated each other with a kindness that I wouldn't have expected, given their past animosity. They had once looked for thousands of small ways to hurt each other, searching for each other's weaknesses. Now they seemed to share an uncomplicated joy in being unguarded with each other.

"Do you feel better?" Sofia asked, hugging me as I walked in.

"Actually, yes," I said. "I've decided to put that stupid television show behind me and pretend it never happened."

"I'm afraid you can't do that," Sofia said, delight glimmering in her hazel eyes. "The producer called this morning and said you're all over their Twitter feed, and everyone loves you. And a half-dozen people have asked about adopting Coco."

I picked up the Chihuahua protectively. Her dry little tongue swiped at my chin.

"I told them we'd think about it," Sofia continued, her gaze teasing.

Within a week, the segment had been picked up by the station's national affiliate. The schedule at the studio was crammed with appointments, and both Steven and Sofia were insisting that we needed to hire more people.

On Friday afternoon, I received a text from my friend Jasmine, a command to call her instantly.

Although I always loved talking with Jasmine and hearing about her life in Manhattan, I was reluctant to dial her. If she'd seen the interview, I was certain she disapproved. Jazz had always said it was imperative that a woman maintain a professional façade no matter what. No crying, no displays of anger, no loss of composure. A television appearance in which I had cursed, carried around a Chihuahua, and ended up with buttercream on my boobs was not what Jazz would consider an appropriate work persona.

"Did you see it?" I asked as soon as Jasmine said hello.

"Yes, you hot shit. I saw it."

That surprised a laugh out of me. "You didn't hate it?"

"It was fabulous. Like a perfectly timed sitcom. You *owned* the screen. You and that little dog—what's her name?"

"Coco."

"I never knew you were a dog person."

"I didn't either."

"The part with the cake—did you plan that?"

"Good Lord, no. I'll never live it down."

"You don't want to live it down. You want to do more of that."

I frowned, puzzled. "What?"

"Remember that opportunity I told you about a while back, the one for *Rock the Wedding*?"

"The Trevor Stearns show."

"Yes. I sent them your résumé and portfolio, and the video, and never heard back from them. They've interviewed dozens of candidates, and as far as I know, they've auditioned three. But they're not one hundred percent happy with any of them, and Trevor is going to freak out if they don't find someone soon. The host not only has to be capable of the job, she also has to have the *thing*. That quality that makes it impossible to take your eyes off her. So a couple days ago, one of the producers, Lois, saw the YouTube video, with you and—sorry, what's the dog's name again?"

"Coco," I said breathlessly.

"Right. Lois saw that and sent the link to Trevor and the others, and they *died*. They took another look at your résumé, and now they think you're *exactly* what they've been looking for. They want to meet you. They're going to bring you up here for an interview." Jasmine paused. "You're quiet," she said impatiently. "What are you thinking?"

"I can't believe it," I managed to say. My heart was pounding.

"Believe it!" Jasmine cried triumphantly. "Now that I've told you, I'll give your contact info to Lois, and she'll arrange a flight. Trevor's in L.A., but the *Rock the Wedding* producers are in Manhattan, and they're the ones you'll talk to initially. We'll have to get you an agent— we won't be able to find anyone in time for the first meeting, but that's okay at this stage. Don't make any commitments or promises. Just let them get to know you, and listen to what they have to say."

"They don't need to fly me to New York, if they can wait a few days," I said. "I'm coming up next Wednesday for a dress fitting with one of my brides."

"You were coming here and you didn't mention it?"

"I've been busy," I protested.

"I'm sure you have. How are things with Joe Travis, by the way?"

I had told her recently about my relationship with Joe, but I hadn't

explained how I really felt about him . . . the deep tenderness and happiness and fear, and the painful ambivalence I felt about becoming
ever more dependent on him. Jasmine wouldn't have understood.
When it came to her own love life, she chose relationships that were
convenient and ultimately disposable. Falling in love was something
she didn't allow herself. "Love doesn't care if you get your work done,"
she had once told me.

In response to her question, I said, "He's divine in bed."

I heard her familiar husky laugh. "Enjoy that hot Texas stud while
you can. You'll be moving back to New York soon."

"I wouldn't count on that just yet," I said. "Trevor and his people
will probably end up deciding not to cast me. Also . . . there's a lot
for me to think about."

"Avery, if this works out, you'll be a celebrity. Everyone will know
you. You can get the best table at any restaurant, the best tickets,
a penthouse apartment . . . what is there to think about?"

"My sister is here."

"She can move up here too. They'll find something for her to do."

"I don't know if that's what she would want. Sofia and I have
worked hard to build this business. It wouldn't be easy for either of
us to abandon it."

"All right. Do your thinking. In the meantime, I'm giving Lois your
info. And I'll see you next week."

"I can't wait," I said. "Jazz . . . I don't know how to thank you for
this."

"Don't be afraid of this chance. It's the right thing for you. New
York is where you belong, and you know it. Things are happening
up here. Bye, sweetie." She ended the call.

Sighing, I plugged my phone back into its charger. "Things are
happening here too," I said.

~ Twenty ~

I've always known you were meant for something like this," Sofia
said after I'd told her about Jazz's call. Her reaction to the news
had been similar to mine: She seemed a little shaken but excited. She
understood the potential of such an opportunity, what it could mean.
Shaking her head slowly, she looked at me with wide eyes. "You're
going to be working with Trevor Stearns."

"It's just a possibility."

"It will happen. I can feel it."

"I would have to move back to New York," I said.

Her smile dimmed a little. "If you do, we'll make it work."

"Would you want to come with me?"

"You mean . . . move to New York with you?"

"I don't think I could ever be happy living away from you," I said.

Sofia reached out and took my hand. "We're sisters," she said
simply. "We're together even when we're not, do you understand, *mi
corazón*? But New York is not the place for me."

"I'm not going to leave you by yourself here."

"I won't be alone. I have the business, and our friends, and . . ." She paused and colored.

"Steven," I said.

Sofia nodded, her eyes sparkling.

"What is it?" I demanded. "What?"

"He loves me. He told me."

"And you said it back?"

"I did."

"Did you say it back because you didn't want to hurt his feelings or because he's the first man you've ever experienced foreplay with, or because you really love him?"

Sofia smiled. "I said it back because I love him for his heart, his soul, and his interesting, complicated brain." She paused. "The foreplay doesn't hurt."

I gave a wondering laugh. "When was the moment you realized you loved him?"

"There wasn't a moment. It was like uncovering something that was there all along."

"It's serious, then? Living-together serious?"

"Talking-about-marriage serious." Sofia hesitated. "Do we have your approval?"

"Of course you do. No one's good enough for you, but Steven's as close as you're going to get." I braced my elbows on the table and pressed my fingertips against my temples. "The two of you could handle the business," I mused aloud. "Steven can do what I do. You're the only truly indispensable person around here–you're the creative engine. All you need are people to make your ideas happen."

"What would it be like for you," Sofia asked, "hosting a show like *Rock the Wedding*? Would you have to come up with ideas?"

I shook my head. "I imagine most of it will be preplanned and staged. My role will be to flail around like Lucy Ricardo and then pull everything together at the end. There'll be pratfalls and manufactured crises, and countless views of my cleavage and my weird dog."

"It's going to be such a big hit," Sofia said in awe.

"I know," I said, and we both squealed.

Sobering after a minute, she asked, "What about Joe?"

The question made my stomach hurt. "I don't know."

"Lots of people do long-distance," Sofia said. "If two people want to make it work, they can."

"That's true," I said. "Joe's got enough money to travel as much as he wants."

"It could make the relationship even better," Sofia volunteered. "You would never get sick of each other."

"Quality time instead of quantity."

Sofia nodded vigorously. "Everything will be fine."

Deep down I knew all of that was bullshit, but it sounded so good that I wanted to believe it. "I don't think there's any need to mention this to Joe until after I go to New York, do you?" I asked. "I don't want to worry him unnecessarily."

"I wouldn't say anything until you know for sure."

ᴏᴇ

I lasted for most of the weekend without saying a word to Joe, but it nagged at me. I wanted to be up front with him, even though I was afraid of what he might say. I had problems sleeping, waking up repeatedly throughout the night and going through the next day exhausted. This cycle was repeated for two more days, until finally Joe turned on the light at midnight. "I feel like I've got a sack of puppies in bed," he said, a note of exasperation in his voice, but his eyes were warm. "What's going on, honey? Why can't you sleep?"

I looked at him in the lamplight, at his concerned face and disheveled hair and that broad chest. I was suffused with a terrible feeling of longing, as if no matter how closely he held me, it would never be close enough. I huddled against him, and he murmured quietly, tucking the covers around us both. "Tell me. Whatever it is, it's okay."

I told him everything, talking so fast that it was a wonder he could follow. I told him everything Jasmine had said about Trevor Stearns and *Rock the Wedding*, and how this was a chance that wouldn't come my way again, and how it was everything I'd ever dreamed of.

Joe listened carefully, interrupting only to ask a question now and then. When I finally paused to take a breath, he eased my face away from his chest and looked down at me. His expression was unreadable. "Of course you have to talk to the producers," he said. "You need to find out what the options are."

"You're not mad? Upset?"

"Hell, no, I'm proud of you. If this is what you want, I'll support you all the way."

I nearly gasped with relief. "Oh, God. I'm so glad to hear you say that. I was so worried. When you think about it, a long-distance relationship doesn't have to be bad at all. As long as the two of us—"

"Avery," he said gently, "I haven't agreed to a long-distance relationship."

Bewildered, I sat up to face him, pulling the silk straps of my nightgown back to my shoulders. "But you just said you'd support me."

"I will. I want you to have whatever makes you happy."

"I'd be happy if I could get this show and move to New York, and also keep my relationship with you." Realizing how selfish that sounded, I added sheepishly, "So basically I want to have my cake, and also have my cake travel back and forth to visit me."

I saw his quick grin, although there wasn't much real amusement in it. "Cake doesn't generally travel well."

"Would you at least be willing to give it a try?" I asked. "With a long-distance relationship, you could have the benefits of being single, but you'd also have the security of—"

"I tried that a long time ago," Joe interrupted quietly. "Never again. There's no benefit, honey. You get tired of being lonely. Tired of all the miles between you. Every time you're together, you're giving a dying relationship CPR. If it's a short-term separation, that's different. But what you're talking about . . . an open-ended arrangement with no stopping point . . . it's a nonstarter."

"You could move. You would have incredible opportunities in New York. Better than here."

"Not better," he countered calmly. "Just different."

"Better," I insisted. "When you consider—"

"Hold on." Joe held up a hand in a staying gesture, a wry smile touching his lips. "First you're going to go talk to those people and find out if you're right for the job, and if the job's right for you. For now, let's get some sleep."

"I can't sleep," I grumbled, dropping to my back, huffing in frustration. "I couldn't sleep last night, either."

"I know," he said. "I was with you."

The light was extinguished, the room so dark that it was shadowless.

"Why didn't this happen three years ago?" I asked aloud. "*That* was when I needed it. Why did it have to be now?"

"Because life has shitty timing. Hush."

My nerves had knotted in agitation. "I refuse to believe you would dump me just because I didn't happen to be conveniently located in Texas."

"Avery, quit working yourself up."

"Sorry." I tried to relax and regulate my breathing. "Let me ask just one thing: Your family has a private plane, right?"

"A Gulfstream. For business."

"Yes, but if you wanted to use it for personal reasons, would your brothers and sister object?"

"*I* would object. It's five thousand bucks per flight hour."

"Is it a light jet, or a midsize, or—"

"It's a Gulfstream large-cabin super-midsize jet."

"How long in advance do you have to call before they can have it ready?"

"For a trip like that, two or three hours." The covers were drawn back from my legs.

"What are you doing?" I couldn't see him, could only feel him moving in the darkness.

"Since you're so interested in my plane, I'm going to tell you all about it."

"Joe—"

"Quiet." The hem of my nightgown inched upward, and I felt a soft, hot kiss on the side of my knee. "The Gulfstream has Internet, TV, a Global Satcom phone system, and the worst coffeemaker in existence." A kiss descended to my other knee, followed by the long ticklish streak of his tongue trailing upward along my thigh. "The two upgraded Rolls-Royce engines," he continued, "provide about fourteen thousand pounds of thrust each." I drew in a sharp breath as I felt the slither of his tongue high on the inside of my leg.

His breath stirred private curls until each hair stood on end, individuate with sensation. "The plane takes about forty-four hundred gallons of fuel."

A single, idle lick. I whimpered, all my focus zinging to that soft place. He nuzzled deeper into the tenderness.

"Fully fueled, it flies nonstop for forty-three hundred nautical miles." His fingertips nudged me open while his lips descended, forming a hot, wet seal. I was dazed and silent, my hips catching a tight upward arch. Just as the pleasure approached an unimaginable spike, his mouth lifted.

"It's been updated with thrust reversers that shorten the landing," he murmured, "and an enhanced vision system with an infrared camera mounted on the front." A long finger slid inside me. "Is there anything else you'd like to know?"

I shook my head, beyond speech. Although he couldn't have seen the movement, he must have felt it, because I heard his quiet sound of amusement. "Avery, honey," he whispered, "you're gonna sleep so good tonight...."

I felt his mouth and tongue again as he worked me with delicately ruthless precision, and I was lost in a tumble of heat. Pleasure gathered, lifted, refracted. When it became too much to bear, I tried to twist away, but Joe wouldn't let me, persisting until my groans had broken into long sighs.

After he was finished with me, I didn't fall asleep so much as I fell unconscious. I slept so long and hard that I barely registered Joe kissing me good-bye the next morning. He leaned over the bed, showered and fully dressed, murmuring that he had to leave.

By the time I was fully awake, Joe was gone.

Two days later, I boarded a private Citation Ultra with Hollis Warner. A flight attendant served us Dr Pepper on ice while we waited
for Bethany, who was running late. Fashionably dressed and heavily
made up, Hollis relaxed in the cream leather seat next to mine. She
explained that her husband, David, offered compensation plans to
some of the top executives in his restaurant and casino businesses
to have the jet for a specified number of personal-use hours, with the
company picking up the tab. Hollis and her friends often used the
Citation for shopping trips and vacations.

"I'm so glad we're staying two nights instead of just one," Hollis
said. "I'm having dinner with some girlfriends tomorrow night. You're
welcome to join us, Avery."

"Thank you so much, but I'm having dinner with friends I haven't
seen in much too long. And there's a meeting I have to attend
tomorrow afternoon." I told her about the meeting with the producers of *Rock the Wedding* and being interviewed as a potential host of
a spin-off. Hollis seemed delighted by the news and said that when
I became a celebrity, she was going to take credit for helping to launch
me. "After all, if I hadn't picked you as Bethany's wedding planner,
you wouldn't have gotten on that show."

"I'll tell everyone it was you," I assured her, and we clinked glasses.

After taking a sip, Hollis tucked a lock of smooth blond hair behind her ear and asked in an offhand tone, "Are you still going out
with Joe?"

"Yes."

"What does he say about this opportunity?"

"Oh, he's being very supportive. He's happy for my sake."

I knew without being told that should the television opportunity
come through, Joe was determined not to influence my decision. He

would not ask me to stay or give up anything. Most of all, he would make no promises. There were no guarantees about what our relationship might become or how long it would last. Whereas there *would* be guarantees, contractual ones, if I was hired by Trevor Stearns's production company. Even in case of failure, I would have some incredible takeaways. Money, connections, a heavily bolstered résumé.

I was spared the necessity of replying when Bethany boarded the plane. She was dressed in a vibrant Tory Burch tunic and capris, her hair gilded with fresh highlights. "Hi, y'all!" she exclaimed. "Isn't this *fun?*"

"Look at how pretty she is," Hollis said with a mixture of pride and rue. "The prettiest girl in Texas, her daddy always says." Hollis's expression went blank as she saw another passenger board after Bethany. "I see you've brought Kolby."

"You said I could bring a friend."

"I sure did, sugar." Hollis flipped open a magazine and began to page through it methodically, her mouth tight. It didn't appear that Kolby, a muscular young man in his twenties, was the kind of friend Hollis had had in mind.

Bethany's companion was dressed in board shorts, a Billabong button-down shirt, and a sports cap from which a shock of sun-bleached hair protruded in the back. He was tanned a deep shade of walnut, his eyes light blue, the teeth toilet-bowl white. From an objective viewpoint, he was handsome in the bland, deeply boring way that only someone with perfectly symmetrical features could be.

"Bethany, you look fabulous, as usual," I said as she leaned down to hug me. "How are you feeling? Are you up to this flight?"

"I sure am!" she exclaimed. "Feeling awesome. My OB-GYN says I'm his star patient. The baby's kicking hard now—sometimes you can see my stomach move."

"Wonderful," I said, smiling. "Was Ryan excited to feel the baby kicking?"

She made a face. "Ryan's so serious about everything. I won't let him come to my checkups, because he brings my mood down."

Hollis spoke while continuing to leaf through the magazine. "Maybe you could work on getting him to smile more often, Bethany."

The young woman laughed. "No, I'll let him fiddle with his drawings and computer designs . . . I've got someone right here who knows how to have a good time." She squeezed the man's arm and smiled at me. "Avery, you don't mind me bringing Kolby on our girls' trip, do you? He won't bother anyone."

The man looked at her with a sly grin. "I'm gonna bother you plenty," he said.

Erupting in a fit of giggles, Bethany dragged him to the bar, where they rummaged through canned beverages. Looking perturbed, the flight attendant tried to persuade them to have a seat and allow her to bring the drinks.

"Who is Kolby?" I dared to ask Hollis.

"No one," she murmured. "A waterskiing instructor Bethany met last summer. They're just friends." She shrugged. "Bethany likes to keep fun people around her. As much as I adore Ryan, he can be a stick-in-the-mud."

I let the comments pass, although I was tempted to point out that it wasn't fair to judge Ryan for not being fun when he was preparing to marry a woman he didn't love and be a father to a baby he didn't want.

"Nothing needs to be mentioned about this," Hollis said after a moment. "Particularly to Joe. He might say something to Ryan and stir up trouble for no reason."

"Hollis, if there's anyone in the world who wants this wedding to go off without a hitch even more than you do, it's me. Trust me, I'm not going to say anything about Kolby to anyone. It's not my place."

Satisfied, Hollis shot me a glance of genuine warmth. "I'm glad we understand each other," she said.

❧

Another disconcerting moment occurred at the hotel reservations desk, where I was checking in. As the desk clerk ran my credit card and we waited for the charge to go through, I glanced at the other clerk at the desk, who had just checked Bethany and Kolby into a single room. I supposed some part of me had hoped that Bethany and Kolby really were just friends. They had behaved like teenagers during the flight from Houston, whispering and giggling, watching a movie together, but there had been nothing overtly sexual in their interactions.

This arrangement, however, left no room for doubt.

I dragged my gaze back to the clerk in front of me. He returned my credit card and gave me a form to initial and sign. I had meant what I'd said to Hollis—I wasn't going to mention anything about this to anyone. But it made me feel guilty and sordid to be part of this secret.

"See y'all later," Bethany said. "Don't expect Kolby and me for lunch—we're ordering room service."

"Let's meet at the concierge desk in two hours," I said. "The fitting appointment is at two o'clock."

"Two o'clock," Bethany repeated, walking to the bank of elevators with Kolby in tow. They paused to look at a display window filled with glittering jewelry.

Hollis came to stand beside me, tucking her phone back into her bag. "You try to raise a daughter someday," she said, sounding tired and a little defensive, "and tell me how easy it is. You'll teach her right from wrong, how to behave, what to believe. You'll do your best. But someday your smart girl will do something stupid. And you'll do anything you can to help her." Hollis sighed and shrugged. "Bethany can do whatever she wants until she's a married woman. She hasn't said any vows yet. When she does, I'll expect her to keep them. Until then, Ryan has the same freedom."

I kept my mouth shut and nodded.

～☙～

At two o'clock on the dot, we were welcomed into Finola Strong's studio and bridal salon on the Upper East Side. The salon was decorated in understated smoky colors, the furniture in the private seating areas upholstered in velvet. Jasmine had referred me to Finola, who had agreed to turn my rough sketches into an appropriate design. Known for her love of clean lines and opulent detail, Finola was well suited to pull off the period beading and intricate paneled construction of the high-waisted skirt. Her team was second to none at creating couture gowns that started at thirty thousand dollars.

Two months earlier, an assistant from the studio had flown to the Warner home in Houston to render the drafted pattern into a muslin mock-up, pinning it meticulously to fit Bethany's body. Since Finola had been told about the pregnancy, she had designed the gown to be easily adjusted to Bethany's changing shape.

This fitting was the first for the actual gown, with much of the beading and trim already added. Today the garment would be adjusted so the fabric would drape and fall perfectly. One of Finola's assistants would fly down with the finished gown a few days before the wedding, for one last fitting. At that time, additional alterations would be made if necessary.

As we lounged in a dressing room with a giant three-way mirror and a private seating area, an assistant brought champagne for Hollis and me and a flute of club soda and juice for Bethany. Soon Finola appeared. She was a slender, fair-haired woman in her thirties, with an easy smile and a lively, discerning gaze. I had met her three or four times during the years I had been in design, but each encounter had lasted for mere seconds during Fashion Week or at some crowded society function.

"Avery Crosslin," Finola exclaimed. "Congratulations on the new gig."

I laughed. "Thank you, but I'm not nearly as convinced as Jazz that I'm going to get it."

"You're no good at modesty," she informed me. "You look positively smug. When do you meet with the producers?"

I grinned at her. "Tomorrow."

After I introduced Finola to the Warners, she pronounced that Bethany would be one of the most beautiful brides she had ever dressed. "I can't wait to see you in this gown," she told Bethany. "It's a global creation: silk from Japan, lining from Korea, beaded embroidery from India, an underlay from Italy, and antique lace from France. We'll leave for a few minutes while you try it on. My assistant Chloe will help you."

After a tour of Finola's salon, we returned to the dressing room. Bethany stood before the mirror, her figure slim and glittering.

The gown was a work of art, the bodice made of antique lace that had been hand-embroidered in a geometric pattern and encrusted with crystal beading as fine as fairy dust. It was held up with thin crystal straps that glittered against Bethany's golden shoulders. The skirt, adorned with scattered beads that caught the light like mist, flowed gently from the high-cut bodice. It was impossible to imagine any bride more beautiful.

Hollis smiled and put her fingers to her mouth. "How magnificent," she gasped.

Bethany smiled and swished her skirts.

However, there was a problem with the dress, and Finola and I both saw it. The drape of the front panels wasn't right. They split much wider over her stomach than I had sketched them. Approaching Bethany, I said with a smile, "You're gorgeous. But we'll have to make a few alterations."

"Where?" Bethany asked, perplexed. "It's already perfect."

"It's the way it drapes," Finola explained. "In the month between now and the wedding, you'll grow enough that the overskirts will fall on either side like theater curtains, which, adorable as your tummy is, will not be flattering."

"I don't know why I've gotten big so fast," Bethany fretted.

"Everyone's pregnancy is different," Hollis told her.

"You're not big at all," Finola soothed. "You're slender everywhere except your stomach, which is just as it should be. Our job is to make this dress fit like a dream, which we will certainly do." She went to Bethany, grasping folds of the paneling, repositioning fabric and viewing the drape with an assessing gaze.

Suddenly Bethany jumped a little and put her hand to the front of her stomach. "Oh!" She laughed. "That was a strong kick."

"It was," Finola said. "I could see it. Do you need to sit down, Bethany?"

"No, I'm fine."

"Good. I'm just figuring out this paneling situation. I'll be done in a second." Finola's gaze was filled with warm interest as she looked at Bethany. "I'm trying to figure out how much your bump will grow in the next month . . . . Are you by chance expecting twins?"

Bethany shook her head.

"Thank goodness. One of my sisters had twins, and that was an unholy challenge. And the due date . . . has that been revised?"

"No," Hollis answered for her.

Finola glanced at her assistant. "Chloe, please help Bethany out of the dress while I talk with Avery about the alterations. Bethany, may we leave your mother here with you?"

"Sure."

Finola went to Hollis and picked up the empty champagne glass on the little table beside her. "More champagne?" she asked. "Coffee?"

"Coffee, please."

"I'll tell one of my assistants. We'll be back soon. Come, Avery."

Obediently, I followed Finola out of the dressing room. She gave the empty flute to a passing assistant and directed her to brew some fresh coffee for Mrs. Warner. We proceeded along a quiet hallway to a corner office lined with windows.

I sat in the chair that Finola indicated. "How tough is the paneling to fix?" I asked in concern. "You won't have to take the whole skirt apart, will you?"

"I'll have my pattern maker and draper take a look at it. For what they're paying, we'll remake the entire fucking dress if necessary." She stretched her shoulders and rubbed the back of her neck. "You know what the problem with the paneling is, don't you?"

I shook my head. "I'd have to take a closer look."

"Here's the cardinal rule of designing for a knocked-up bride: Never trust the due date."

"You think she's off by a little?"

"I think she's off by at least two months."

I gave her a blank stare.

"I see it all the time," Finola said. "Maternity is the fastest-growing department in bridal ready-to-wear. Approximately one in five of my brides are pregnant. And many of them fudge the dates. Even in this day and age, some women worry about their parents' disapproval. And there are other reasons. . . ." She shrugged. "It's not for us to judge or comment. If I'm right about the timing, then Bethany's belly will be considerably larger than we expected when she walks down the aisle."

"Then we should forget the paneling and replace the entire over-lay," I said distractedly. "Although there's probably not enough time to get new beadwork done."

"We'll have some hideously expensive local person do it. How long will Bethany be in town? Can we schedule an additional fitting for her tomorrow?"

"Absolutely. In the morning?"

"No, we'll need more time than that. How about in the afternoon after your meeting?"

"I'm not sure how long it will last."

"If you can't make it, just have Bethany come here by four. I'll take pictures and send jpegs so you can see exactly what we've done."

"Finola . . . are you absolutely sure about the due date?"

"I'm not a doctor. But I guarantee that girl is more than four months pregnant. Her belly button's popped out, which usually doesn't hap-pen until the end of the second trimester. And the way that baby's kicking? Impressive for a fetus that's only supposed to be about five inches long. Even though Bethany's kept her weight down, the bump doesn't lie."

✤

I went out to dinner that night with Jasmine and an assortment of old friends from the fashion industry. We sat at a table for twelve in an Italian restaurant, with at least three or four conversations going on at any given moment. As always, they had the best gossip in the world, exchanging tidbits about designers, celebrities, and society icons. I had forgotten how exciting it was to be in the middle of everything new and fresh, to know things before the rest of the world did.

Plates of beef carpaccio were brought out, the raw meat sliced into translucent sheets even thinner than the scattered flakes of shaved Parmesan on top. Although the waiter tried to bring baskets of bread along with the salad course, everyone at the table shook their heads in unison. I stared forlornly at the retreating bread, which left wafts of sweetly fragrant steam in its wake.

"We could each have just one piece," I said.

"No one eats carbs," replied Siobhan, the beauty director at Jasmine's magazine.

"Still?" I asked. "I was hoping they'd come back by now."

"Carbs will never come back," Jasmine said.

"God, don't say that."

"It's been scientifically proven that eating white bread is so bad for you, you're better off emptying packets of granulated sugar into your mouth."

"Send Avery a copy of the KPD plan," Siobhan said to Jazz. She gave me a significant glance. "I lost twelve pounds in a week."

"From where?" I asked, looking at her rail-thin frame.

"You'll love KPD," Jasmine assured me. "Everyone's doing it. It's a modified ketogenic-Paleo-detox plan, starting with an intervention phase similar to Protein Power. The weight comes off so fast, it's almost as good as having a tapeworm."

When the entrées were brought out, I realized I was the only one in the group who had ordered pasta.

Jett, an accessories designer for a major fashion label, glanced at my penne and said with a sigh, "I haven't eaten pasta since Bush was in office."

"First or second?" Jasmine asked.

"First." Jett looked nostalgic. "I remember that last meal. Carbonara, extra bacon."

Becoming aware of their intent gazes, I paused with my loaded fork halfway up to my mouth. "Sorry," I said sheepishly. "Should I eat this at another table?"

"Since you're technically an out-of-town guest," Jasmine said, "you can keep your penne. When you move back here, however, you'll have to say good-bye to refined carbohydrates."

"If I move back here," I said, "I'll have to say good-bye to a lot of things."

✸

At one o'clock the next afternoon, I took a cab to midtown and walked into the Stearns production offices. After five minutes of waiting, a young woman with a messy bob and a skinny black pantsuit came to escort me to an elevator. We rode a few floors up and entered a reception area with a spectacular ceiling paved in a lavender-and-silver mosaic tile design and furniture upholstered in a deep shade of eggplant.

Three people were there to greet me with such lavish enthusiasm that I relaxed immediately. They were all young and beautifully dressed, smiling widely as they introduced themselves. The woman introduced herself as Lois Ammons, a producer and executive assistant to Trevor Stearns; after that came Tim Watson, a casting producer, and Rudy Winters, a producer and assistant director.

"You didn't bring your sweet little dog?" Lois asked with a laugh as we went into a spacious office with a dazzling view of the Chrysler Building.

"I'm afraid Coco is a little too old and high-maintenance to do much traveling," I said.

"Poor thing. I'm sure she misses you."

"She's in good hands. My sister Sofia is taking care of her."

"You work with your sister, right? Why don't you tell us how that started. Wait, would you mind if we record our chat?"

"Not at all."

The next three hours went so fast that they seemed like three minutes. We started by discussing my past experience in the fashion business and then what it had been like to start the studio with Sofia. As I recounted some of the quirkier weddings we had designed and coordinated, I had to pause while the trio burst out laughing.

"Avery," Lois said, "Jasmine told me that you're still in the process of getting an agent."

"Yes, although I wasn't certain it would even be necessary, so I haven't–"

"It's necessary," Tim said, smiling at me. "If this all works out, Avery, we'll be negotiating issues such as public appearances, licensing and merchandising rights, product endorsements, publishing, residuals . . . So you need to find an agent right away."

"Got it," I said, pulling a tablet from my bag and making a note. "Does this mean we'll be meeting again?"

"Avery," Rudy said, "as far as I'm concerned, you're our girl. We'll have to do some more testing, perhaps send a camera crew to the Warner wedding."

"I'll have to clear it with them," I said breathlessly, "but I don't think they'd object."

"You and this show would be a perfect match," Tim said. "I think you could take Trevor's concept and make it your own. You'll bring great energy. We love the sexy redhead image, love how comfortable you are with the camera. You'll be on a fast learning track, but you can handle it."

"We need to get her together with Trevor and see how they click," Lois said. She smiled at me. "He already loves you. Once you get an agent, we can start talking about tailoring the show to your personality, and working on the pilot treatment. In the first episode we'd like to push the idea that Trevor is mentoring you ... set up some dilemmas and have you call him for advice, which you don't necessarily have to follow. Ideally the dynamic would have hints of tension ... Trevor and his sassy protégée, with a lot of snappy dialogue ... how does that sound?"

"Sounds fun," I said automatically, although I was unnerved by the feeling that a persona was being created for me.

"And there'll have to be a dog," Tim said. "Everyone at the L.A. offices loved seeing you carry that dog around. But a cuter one. What are those fluffy white ones, Lois?"

"Pomeranian?"

Tim shook his head. "No, I don't think that's what I mean ...."

"Coton de Tulear?"

"Maybe ...."

"I'll pull up a list of breeds for you to look at," Lois said, making notes.

"You're getting me another dog?" I asked.

"Just for the show," Lois said. "But you wouldn't have to take it home with you." She laughed lightly. "I'm sure Coco would have something to say about that."

"So," I asked, "the dog would be a prop?"

"A cast member," Tim replied.

While the two men talked, Lois reached out and gripped my nerveless hand, beaming at me.

"Let's make this happen," she said.

∽ə∼

Sitting in the hotel room that night, staring down at my cell phone, I practiced what to say to Joe. I tried a few lines out loud and wrote a few words on a nearby notepad.

When I realized what I was doing . . . *rehearsing* for a conversation with him . . . I pushed away the notepad and made myself dial.

Joe picked up right away. The sound of his voice, that familiar, comforting drawl, made me feel good all over and at the same time filled me with wrenching longing. "Avery, honey. How are you doing?"

"I'm fine. Missing you."

"I miss you too."

"Do you have a few minutes to talk?"

"I've got all night. Tell me what you've been up to."

I sat back farther on the bed and crossed my legs. "Well . . . I had the big meeting today."

"How did it go?"

I described it in detail, everything that had been said, everything I'd thought and felt. While I did most of the talking, Joe was deliberately reserved, refusing to express an opinion one way or the other.

"Did you talk numbers?" he asked eventually.

"No, but I'm pretty sure the money will be big. Maybe life-changing."

He sounded sardonic. "Whether or not the money's life-changing, the job sure as hell will be."

"Joe . . . this is the kind of opportunity I've always dreamed of. It looks like it really could happen. They made it pretty clear that they want to make it work out. If so . . . I don't know how I can turn it down."

"I told you before, I won't stand in your way."

"Yes, I know that," I said with a touch of annoyance. "I'm not worried that you'll try to stand in the way. I'm worried that you won't try to stay in my life."

Joe answered with the weary impatience of someone whose thoughts had been chasing in circles, just like mine. "If your life moves fifteen hundred miles away, Avery, it's not going to be all that easy for me to stay in it."

"What about moving there with me? We could share an apartment. There's nothing tying you to Texas. You could pack everything up and–"

"Nothing except my family, friends, home, business, the foundation I agreed to help manage–"

"People move, Joe. They find ways to stay in touch. They make new beginnings. It's because I'm the woman, isn't it? Most women move when their boyfriends or husbands have a job opportunity, but if the situation's reversed–"

"Avery, don't give me that shit. It has nothing to do with sexism."

"You could be happy anywhere if you make up your mind to be–"

"It's not about that, either. Baby . . ." I heard a short, tense sigh. "You're not just choosing a job, you're choosing a life. A career on rocket fuel. You won't have one damn minute of spare time. I'm not moving to New York so I can see you for half of one day on the weekend, and twenty minutes every night between the time you get home and the time you go to bed. I can't see any room in that life for me, or for kids."

My heart plummeted. "Kids," I echoed numbly.

"Yes. I want kids someday. I want to sit on the front porch and watch them run through the sprinkler. I want to spend time with them, teach them how to play catch. I'm talking about having a family."

It was a long time before I could say anything. "I don't know if I would be a good parent."

"No one does."

"No, I *really* don't. I never had any kind of family. I lived with parts of broken families. One time I came home from school and there was a new man and new kids in the house, and I found out my mother had gotten married again without even telling me. And then one day they all disappeared without warning. Like some magician's trick."

Joe's voice turned gentle. "Avery, listen–"

"If I tried to be a parent and failed, I'd never forgive myself. It's too much of a risk. And it's too soon to be talking about this. For God's sake, we've never even said–" I broke off as my throat closed.

"I know. But I sure as hell can't say it right now, Avery. Because at the moment it would seem like nothing more than a pressure tactic."

I had to end the call. I had to retreat.

"At the very least," I said, "we can make the most of the time we have left. I have a month until Bethany's wedding, and after that–"

"A month of what? Trying not to care about you any more than

I already do? Trying to back away from how I feel?" There was something wrong with his breathing, something broken. His voice was no less intense for its quietness. "A month of checking off the days until the final countdown . . . Damn you, Avery, I can't do that."

Tears brimmed and slid down my cheeks in burning paths.

"What should I say?"

"Tell me how to stop wanting you," he said. "Tell me how to stop—" He broke off and swore. "I'd rather put an end to this right now than drag it out."

The phone was trembling in my grip. I was scared. I was as scared as I'd ever been about anything. "Let's not talk any more tonight," I said breathlessly. "Nothing's changed. Nothing's been decided, okay?"

More silence.

"Joe?"

"I'll talk to you when you get back," he said gruffly. "But I want you to think about something, Avery. When you told me the story about your mom's Chanel bag, you got the metaphor dead wrong. You need to figure out what it really stands for."

Twenty-one

Ravaged and exhausted from a sleepless night, I applied a heavier layer of makeup than usual the next morning. If the hollow-eyed look was in, I thought bleakly, I was definitely on-trend. I packed my bag and went downstairs a few minutes before I was supposed to meet Hollis, Bethany, and Kolby in the lobby. From there we would travel by limo to Teterboro Airport, about twelve miles away. The small airport, located in the New Jersey Meadowlands, was popular for private aircraft.

Heading to a lounge off the lobby, I saw Bethany sitting alone at a small table by a window. "Good morning," I said with a smile. "You're up early too?"

She smiled back at me, looking tired. "Can't sleep too good with all the city noise at night. Kolby's taking a shower. Want to sit with me?"

"Yes, I'll get some coffee."

In a minute, I returned to the table with my coffee and sat opposite Bethany. "I looked at the jpegs Finola sent last night," I said. "What did you think about the skirt redesign?"

"It was pretty. Finola said they would put beading on it."

"So you're happy with it?"

Bethany shrugged. "I liked the panels better. But there's no choice with my bump getting so big."

"It will be a gorgeous dress," I said. "And you'll look like a queen. I'm sorry I wasn't there yesterday."

"You didn't need to be. Finola was real nice to me and Mother." She paused. "She didn't say anything . . . but she knows. I could tell."

"About what?" I asked without expression.

"The due date." Bethany swirled a spoon aimlessly in her coffee cup. "I'm just about to start the last trimester. I may not even fit into that dress by the wedding."

"That's what the last fitting is for," I said automatically. "It'll be fine, Bethany." I drank some coffee and fastened my gaze on the scene outside the window, watching the pedestrians with their necks swathed in stylish scarves . . . a chic woman on a bicycle . . . a pair of elderly men, both in fedoras. "Does your mother know?" I asked.

She nodded. "I tell her everything. I always swear I'm going to keep some things private, and then I end up telling her, and I'm always sorry. But I do it anyway. I guess I always will."

"You may not," I said. "Believe me, I don't do a lot of the things I thought I'd always be doing."

Bethany left the spoon in the mug and pushed it aside. "Mother says you'll keep quiet about Kolby," she said. "Thank you."

"Please don't thank me. It's not my place to say anything."

"You're right. It's not. But I know you like Ryan, and you probably feel sorry for him. You shouldn't, though. He'll be fine."

"Is the baby his?" I asked softly.

Bethany flicked a derisive glance at me. "What do you think?"

"I think it's Kolby's."

Her slight smile faded. She didn't answer.

She didn't have to.

We were both quiet for a minute.

"I love Kolby," Bethany said eventually. "It doesn't make a difference, but I do."

"Have you talked to him about it?"

"Of course."

"What does he say?"

"Stupid stuff. He said he wanted to get married and live in a beach house in Santa Cruz. Like I'd be sending our kid to public school." She let out a little huff of laughter. "Can you imagine me marrying a waterskiing instructor? Kolby has no money. No one would invite me anywhere. I wouldn't be anyone."

"You'd be with the person you love. The father of your child. You'd have to work, but you've got a college degree and connections–"

"Avery, no one makes money from working. Not real money. Even if you get that TV show job, you'll never earn anything close to what a Travis or a Chase or a Warner has. I wasn't raised to live in the top one percent, I was raised to live in the top tenth of the top one percent. That's who I am. You can't go down from that. No one would give up the kind of life I have just because they love someone."

I didn't reply.

"You think I'm a bitch," Bethany said.

"No."

"Well, I am."

"Bethany," I asked, "what are you going to tell Ryan when the baby is born two months early and it's obviously not a preemie?"

"It won't matter then. We'll be legally married. Even if Ryan decides to deny paternity and divorce me, he'll have to pay through the nose. I'll threaten to fight the prenup in court. Mother says Ryan will pay rather than go through a big public embarrassment."

I worked to keep all expression from my face. "Are you sure Kolby won't say anything? He won't cause trouble?"

"No, I told him all he has to do is wait. Once the divorce has gone through and I've got money, Kolby can live with me and the baby."

I couldn't speak for a moment. "What a perfect plan," I finally said.

～◎～

I was quiet for most of the flight back, my thoughts seething. Plugging in a pair of earbuds, I started a movie on my laptop and stared blindly at the screen.

Any trace of compassion or pity I might have felt for Bethany had been obliterated when she had revealed that the wedding was nothing but a means to extort money from Ryan Chase. Bethany and her parents already knew that the marriage wouldn't last. They knew that he wasn't the father of the baby. They were taking advantage of Ryan's innate decency, and he would end up screwed to the wall while Bethany and Kolby lived off his money.

I was pretty sure I couldn't live with that.

In the periphery of my vision, I saw Bethany gesture to Hollis, who joined her on the long sofa at the back of the plane. They whispered together for at least twenty minutes, the discussion becoming increasingly animated, as if the subject were urgent. My guess was that Bethany regretted having told me so much earlier, and she was confessing to her mother. At one point, Hollis looked up and met my gaze directly.

Yes. I had been identified as a potential problem that would have to be addressed.

I returned my gaze to the laptop screen.

Thanks to the time zone change, we arrived at Houston's Hobby Airport at eleven A.M. "How nice," I said with a tacked-on smile, sliding my laptop into my carry-on. "Most of the day is still ahead of us."

Hollis smiled thinly. Bethany didn't respond.

I thanked the pilot and flight attendant while Bethany and Kolby left the plane. Turning toward the exit, I saw that Hollis was waiting for me.

"Avery," she said pleasantly, "before we get off the plane, I want to have a little chat."

"Certainly," I said, equally pleasant.

"I need to explain something because I'm not sure you fully understand our kind of people. The rules are different at our level. If you have any illusions about Ryan Chase, let me tell you something: He's no better than any other man. Don't you realize Ryan's going to keep some sweet young thing on the side? A man with his looks and money, he'll go through three or four wives at least. What do you care if Bethany's one of them?" Her eyes narrowed. "You're not being paid to make judgments or interfere with your clients' personal lives. Your job is to make this wedding happen. And if anything goes wrong . . . I'll make sure no one touches your business. I'll do whatever's necessary to ruin your chances of being on that TV show. David and I have friends who own media empires. Don't even think about crossing me."

My cordial expression didn't falter for one second of her speech.

"As you said at the beginning of the trip, Hollis, we understand each other."

After holding my gaze for a moment, she seemed to relax. "I told Bethany you wouldn't be a problem. A woman in your situation can't afford to act against your own interests."

"My situation?" I echoed, puzzled.

"Working."

Only Hollis Warner could have made that sound like a dirty word.

～⊘～

I deliberately took a roundabout route on the way home from Hobby, so I would have the time I needed. I always did my best thinking in the car, especially on longer drives. Somehow the tortured maze of thoughts at forty thousand feet became miraculously untangled as soon as I set foot on the ground.

There was no denying the importance—the necessity—of having a fulfilling career. But a job was never the most important thing. People were.

The fact was, I already had a career I loved. I had built it from scratch with my sister, and it was all ours, and I was in control of it, and we were damned successful. We could create our own opportunities.

Talking with Trevor Stearns's producers had given me a fleeting taste of what it would be like to be managed and supervised and have everything laid out for me. A fluffy white Pomeranian? . . . No thanks. I was just fine with my toothless Chihuahua, who, although not pretty, was at least not a stage prop.

I realized I had been so swept away by the idea of getting the big break I had always dreamed of, and returning to New York in triumph, that I hadn't paused to consider whether that was still what I wanted.

Sometimes dreams changed when you weren't looking.

The things I'd accomplished and learned, and even lost, had all helped me to look at the world in a different way. But most of all, I had changed because of the people I had chosen to care about. It was as if my heart had been unwrapped and could feel everything more deeply. As if . . .

"My God," I said aloud, swallowing hard as I realized what the Chanel bag metaphor was.

My heart was the carefully protected object on the shelf. I had tried to keep it safe from damage, tried to use it only when necessary.

But some things became more beautiful with frequent use. The nicks and scuffs and cracks, the places that had been worn smooth, the areas that had been broken and repaired . . . all of that meant that an object had served its purpose. What good was a heart that had been grudgingly used? What value did it have if you'd never risked it on anyone? Trying not to feel had never been the right answer to my problems, it *was* the problem.

Happiness and fear were pressed together inside me, a double-sided coin that kept spinning. I wanted to go to Joe right then and make sure I hadn't lost him. I wanted things it was probably better not to think about at the moment.

That life he'd described . . . God help me, I wanted it. All of it, including children. Until this moment, I'd always been too scared to admit that, even to myself. I'd been too encumbered by the fear of turning out like my father.

Except that I wouldn't.

Unlike Eli, I was good at loving people. It was the first time I'd ever realized that.

I had to take off my sunglasses as the bottom rims became slick with tears.

Right now, I had to take care of a couple of urgent matters. Later I would go to Joe when I could find enough time and privacy. His feelings, and mine, were too important to fit in between errands.

I pulled into the drive-through at a Whataburger. Waiting in line to order a Diet Dr Pepper, I fished my phone out of my purse and dialed a number.

"Hello?" came a brusque voice.

"Ryan?" I asked, wiping my wet cheeks. "It's Avery."

His tone warmed. "Back from the big city?"

"I am."

"How was the trip?"

"Even more interesting than I expected," I said. "Ryan, I need to talk to you privately. Is there any way you could take a break and meet me somewhere? Preferably a place with a bar? I wouldn't ask unless it was important."

"Sure, I'll buy you lunch. Where are you?"

I told him, and he gave me directions to a bar and grill not far from Montrose.

I bought a Diet Dr Pepper, bolstered myself with a cold, crackling swallow, and made one more call before leaving the parking lot.

"Lois? Hi, it's Avery Crosslin." I tried to sound regretful. "I'm afraid I've had to make a tough decision about *Rock the Wedding.* . . ."

⁓

For the maximum amount of privacy at a bar and grill, the place had to be either completely packed or mostly empty. The restaurant where I met Ryan was so crowded that we were obliged to occupy two seats at the end of the bar and order our lunch from there. I always liked eating at a bar where the full menu was served, and for this particular conversation, it would be ideal. We could sit close without having to maintain eye contact, which was the perfect way to discuss something this difficult.

"Before I start," I said to Ryan, "I should tell you that it's bad news.

Or maybe it's good news disguised as bad news. Either way, it's going to sound bad when I tell you. If you'd rather not know, I apologize for wasting your time, and lunch is on me, but you're going to know eventually, so–"

"Avery," Ryan interrupted, "slow down, honey. You've been turbocharged."

I smiled crookedly. "New York," I offered by way of explanation. I was surprised but pleased by the endearment, which he'd said in a brotherly way, as if I were part of the family.

The bartender brought a glass of wine for me and a beer for Ryan, and we gave him our orders.

"As far as bad news goes," Ryan told me, "I prefer to have it right away. I don't like it sugarcoated. And don't tell me the bright side. If it's not obvious, it's not a bright side."

"Good point." I considered various ways to break the news, wondering if I should start with Kolby's appearance on the plane or Bethany's fallacious due date. "I'm trying to think of how to explain all of this."

"Try five words or less," Ryan suggested.

"The baby's not yours."

Ryan stared at me blankly.

I repeated it more slowly. "The baby's not yours." I wondered if it was bad that it felt so good to tell him.

With extreme care, Ryan closed his hand around his beer glass and drank the contents without stopping. He signaled the bartender for another. "Go on," he murmured, bracing his forearms on the edge of the bar, looking straight ahead.

For twenty minutes, Ryan listened while I talked. I couldn't read him at all–he was incredibly good at concealing his emotions. But gradually I sensed that he was relaxing, in the deep and elemental way of someone who had carried a heavy burden for months and was finally being allowed to let it go.

Eventually Ryan said, "What Hollis said about hurting your business... don't you worry about that. I'll handle the Warners, so you–"

"Jesus, Ryan, your first concern doesn't have to be for me. Let's talk about you. Are you okay? I was afraid maybe you had feelings for Bethany, and–"

"No, I tried. The best I could do was be kind to her. But I never wanted her." Reaching out, Ryan hugged me while we remained sitting on the bar stools. The embrace was fervent and strong. "Thank you," he murmured in my hair. "God, thank you."

I wasn't certain if he was saying it to me or actually praying.

Drawing back, Ryan looked at me with impossibly blue eyes. "You didn't have to tell me. You could have gone ahead with the wedding and collected your percentage."

"And then stand back and watch the Warners take you to the cleaners? I don't think so." I gave him a concerned glance. "What are you going to do now?"

"I'm going to talk to Bethany as soon as possible. I'll do what I should have done in the first place: tell her we'll wait until after the baby's born, and do a DNA test. In the meantime, I'll demand to meet her doctor and find out the accurate due date."

"So the wedding is off," I said.

"Pull the plug" came his decisive reply. "I'll compensate Hollis for the costs that you can't recoup. And I want to pay you and your people for the hours you've put in."

"That's not necessary."

"Yes, it is."

We talked for a while longer, while the lunch crowd gradually cleared out and the waitstaff was busy running back and forth with credit card folders, cash, and receipts. Ryan paid the check for our lunch and gave the bartender a mammoth tip.

As we left the restaurant, Ryan held the door open for me. "You didn't mention how your meeting with the TV producers went."

"It went well," I said in an offhand tone. "I got the impression they were working up to a nice offer. But I turned them down. They couldn't make me a deal that would top what I've already got here."

"Glad you're going to stay. By the way... are you going to see Joe anytime soon?"

"I expect so."

"He's been as ornery as a two-headed bull while you were gone. Jack says the next time you go anywhere, you have to take Joe with you. None of the rest of us can stand him like this."

I laughed, while nerves fluttered in my stomach. "I'm not sure how things are between Joe and me right now," I confessed. "Our last call didn't end too well."

"I wouldn't worry." Ryan smiled. "But don't put off talking to him. For all our sakes."

I nodded. "I'll get my team started on unplanning the wedding, and then I'll call him." We parted company and headed to our separate cars. "Ryan," I said. He stopped to look back at me. "Someday you're going to hire me to plan another wedding. And the next time, it'll be for the right reasons."

"Avery," he replied sincerely, "I'm going to hire someone to shoot me if I ever get engaged again."

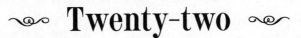

∾ Twenty-two ∾

As soon as I came through the front door, I heard Coco begin to yip frantically. She hurried to me from the main seating area, almost beside herself with excitement. "Coco!" I exclaimed, dropping my bag and scooping her up.

She licked me and tried to cuddle closer while yapping as if to nag me for having been away so long.

I heard a chorus of welcomes from various places around the studio.

It was good to be home.

"Dogs have no sense of time," Sofia said, reaching me in a few strides. "She thinks you were gone for two weeks instead of two days."

"It felt like two weeks," I said.

She kissed me on both cheeks, while Coco wriggled excitedly between us. "Oh, it's good to have you back! I got some of your texts, but you were so quiet yesterday, and nothing at all last night."

"The events of the past two days would surpass even the most overwrought telenovela," I said. "Prepare to be shocked."

Steven laughed and came to me for a hug. After enfolding me in a hearty embrace, he drew back and looked down at me with twinkling blue eyes. "I'm shockproof now," he said. "I've watched enough of those idiotic shows that I can see every plot twist from a mile away."

"Trust me, I'm about to put you to the test." I frowned as Coco kissed my cheek and I felt how raspy her tongue was. "Didn't anyone put coconut oil on her tongue while I was gone?" I demanded. "It's like an emery board."

"She won't let anyone touch it," Sofia protested. "I tried. Tell her, Steven."

"She tried," he acknowledged. "I watched."

"He laughed until he fell off the sofa," Sofia said.

I shook my head and looked into Coco's soulful eyes. "I don't want to think about what you've endured."

"It wasn't that terrible—" Sofia began.

"Sweetheart," Steven interrupted, "I think she's talking to the Chihuahua."

After taking care of Coco's tongue, I asked everyone to stop what they were doing and sit at the long table. "For the rest of the day," I said, "we're all going to be busy with a special project."

"Sounds fun," Val said lightly.

"It's not going to be fun in the least." I looked at Ree-Ann. "Have the Warner wedding invitations gone out yet?" I asked, thinking, *Please say no, please say no . . .*

"Yesterday," she said proudly.

I uttered a word that made her eyes widen.

"You told me to," she protested. "I was only doing what you—"

"I know. It's fine. Unfortunately it means extra work, but we can handle it. I need you to print out the master list, Ree-Ann. We're going to have to contact everyone on it and obtain verbal confirmation of the cancellation."

"What? Why? What are you talking about?"

"We have to unplan the Warner-Chase wedding."

"How much of it?" Steven asked.

"All of it."

Tank looked bewildered. "It's postponed?"

"It's off," I said. "Permanently off."

Everyone looked at me and asked in unison, *"Why?"*

"It doesn't go beyond this room. We do not gossip about clients. Ever."

"Yes, we all know," Steven said. *"Explain,* Avery."

∞

Two hours later, my team still appeared to be dazed by the turn of events. I had assured them that we would all be compensated for the time we'd spent. There would be other weddings, other chances to make our mark. Still, that was small consolation when they had been tasked with unraveling a wedding that was only a month away. Steven had already succeeded in canceling the fleet of Rolls-Royces and one of the wedding favor orders. Sophia had contacted the caterers and the chair and table rental company and was waiting for callbacks. Val and Ree-Ann had both been assigned to call every name on the guest list and inform them of the cancellation, while claiming ignorance as to the reason why.

"How long do we have to do this?" Ree-Ann moaned. "It's five o'clock. I want to go home."

"I'd like you to work until six, if possible," I said. "Depending on how the unplanning goes, we'll all have to put in some overtime this week, so you may want to–" I stopped as I heard a key turn in the front door.

The only people with keys were Sofia, me, Steven . . . and Joe.

He let himself in. His searing gaze found me at once.

A potent silence infused the room.

Joe looked the worse for wear, sleep-deprived, with no reserve of patience left. He was big and brooding and surly . . . and he was all mine.

The sound of my heartbeat filled my head with ragged music.

"Ryan called me." Joe's voice was like gravel in a blender.

The studio was quiet. Everyone listened avidly, making not even the slightest pretense at minding their own business. Even Coco had climbed to the top of the sofa back to watch us with prurient interest.

"Did he tell you–" I began.

"Yes." It was clear that Joe didn't give a damn about who was there or what they saw. His focus was riveted exclusively on me. His color had heightened, and his jaw was hard, and despite his obvious effort at control, I could tell he was on a hair trigger.

I had to get everyone out of the studio. Fast.

"Let me clear a couple of things out of the way," I said distractedly, "and then we can talk."

"I don't want to talk." Joe moved toward me and paused as I stepped back instinctively. "In thirty seconds," he warned, "you're mine. You'll want to be upstairs when it happens." He glanced at his watch.

"Joe . . ." I shook my head with an agitated laugh. "Come on, you can't just–"

"Twenty-five."

Shit. He wasn't kidding.

I cast a wild glance at Ree-Ann and Val, who were having the time of their lives. "You can go home now," I told them curtly. "Good work, everyone. Be back bright and early tomorrow morning."

"I'm going to stay and keep working until six," Ree-Ann said virtuously.

"I'll help," Val chimed in.

Tank shook his head and sent me one of his rare grins. "I'll kick 'em out, Avery."

Steven picked up his keys. "Let's go to dinner," he suggested to Sofia in a casual tone, as if nothing untoward were happening. As if I weren't just about to be ravished in the living room.

"Eighteen seconds," Joe said.

Outraged and giddy, I rushed to the stairs in a panic. "Joe, this is ridiculous—"

"Fifteen." He began to follow me at a measured pace. Feeling like a hunted creature, I scrambled up the steps, which seemed to have turned into an escalator.

By the time I reached my room, Joe had caught up to me. I ran inside and turned to face him as he closed the door. He tensed in readiness to catch me, no matter which direction I bolted. But then I saw the shadows beneath his eyes, and the flush beneath his tan, and my heart ached. I headed straight for him.

His hard arms closed around me. His mouth took mine, and he growled softly in what could have been pleasure or agony. For a few minutes there was nothing but darkness and sensation, those deep kisses demolishing every thought. I was never quite certain how we ended up on the bed. We rolled across the mattress fully clothed, grappling and kissing in a fury, breaking apart only when the need for oxygen was imperative. Joe kissed my neck and tugged at my shirt, more aggressive than he'd ever been before, until I heard threads snapping and felt a button pop off.

With a shaky laugh, I put my hands on either side of his face. "Joe. Take it easy. Hey–"

He kissed me again, shivering with the effort of holding back. I felt the hot, ready pressure of him against me, and I wanted him so badly that a moan rose in my throat. But there were things that needed to be said.

"I'm choosing the life I want," I managed to tell him. "There's no obligation for you. I'm staying because this is my home and I can make my own dreams come true right here, with my sister and my friends and employees and my dog, and all the things I–"

"What about me? Was I a part of your decision?"

"Well . . ."

He frowned, his gaze raking over me as I hesitated.

"Joe, what I'm trying to say is . . . I don't expect a commitment from you because of this. I don't want you to feel pressured in any way. It may be years before we figure out how we feel about each other, so–"

He smothered my words with his mouth, kissing me until I was drunk on the taste and feel of him. After a long time, his head lifted. "You know right now," he whispered, staring at me with those midnight eyes. Tender amusement lurked in the corners of his mouth. This was the Joe I was accustomed to, the one who loved to tease me without mercy. "And you're going to tell me."

My heart began to thump, not in a good way. I wasn't sure I could do what he wanted. "Later."

"Now." He rested more of his weight on me, as if he were settling in for a prolonged siege.

I abandoned all pride. "Joe, please, please don't make me–"

"Say it," he murmured. "Or in about ten minutes you'll be screaming it with me inside you."

"*Jesus.*" I squirmed and fidgeted. "You are the most–"

"Tell me," he insisted.

"Why do I have to be the first?"

Joe held me with his relentless gaze. "Because I want you to."

Realizing there would be no compromise, I began to wheeze as if I'd just run a marathon. Somehow I got out the words in one fraught breath.

To my outrage, Joe began to laugh softly. "Honey . . . you say it like you're confessing to a crime."

I scowled and wriggled beneath him. "If you're going to make fun of me–"

"No," he said tenderly, keeping me pinned in place. He took my head in his hands. A last chuckle escaped, and then he stared into my eyes, seeing everything, hiding nothing. "I love you," he said. His mouth caressed mine, soft as velvet. "Now try it again." Another gentle, smoldering stroke of his lips. "You don't have to be scared."

"I love you," I managed to say, my heart still thundering.

Joe rewarded me by covering my mouth with his, searching deeply. After a kiss that dismantled my brain entirely, he finished with a soft nuzzle. "I can't kiss you enough," he told me. "I'm going to kiss you a million times in our life, and it will never be enough."

Our life.

I had never known a happiness like this, reaching all the way down to the place in my heart where sorrow usually started, siphoning up tears. Joe wiped at the wetness with his fingers and pressed his lips to my cheeks, absorbing the salty taste of joy.

"Let's practice some more," he whispered.

And before long, I discovered that with the right person, saying those three words wasn't difficult at all.

It was the easiest thing in the world.

Epilogue

The Happy Tails Rescue Society has been decorated for Christmas, with lights strung high near the ceiling and a tree in the lobby covered in bone-shaped doggie treats. Although Millie and Dan have enforced a no-adoption policy during the weeks before and after Christmas, to prohibit impulse buying that might lead to later regrets, the shelter and its website have still been busy. People are allowed to visit the dogs and ask for one to be kept on hold until January 1, when adoptions start up again.

Joe sets up his camera in the dogs' exercise room, while I pick out a few toys from the box. We're here for our monthly visit to take pictures of the shelter's newest arrivals. Later in the day, we're going to the Galleria to shop for Christmas presents, which Joe hates nearly as much as I enjoy it. "Shopping is a competitive sport," I'd told him. "Stick with me, pal–I'll show you how it's done."

"Shopping's not a sport."

"It is the way I do it," I had assured him, and he had allowed it was probably worth going just to see me in action.

Even before Dan opens the door to bring in the first dog, I can hear a tumult of high-pitched barking. I make a comical face. "What's going on out there?"

Joe shrugs innocently.

The door opens, and a pack of golden retriever puppies rushes in. I laugh in delight at the roly-poly creatures swarming around us, all bright eyes and wagging tails. Five of them. "All at once?" I ask. "I don't think there's any way I can get them to . . ." My voice fades as I notice that each puppy has a sign tied around its neck. Name tags? Perplexed, I pick up a puppy and read the word printed on its sign while it struggles to lick me. "You," I read aloud. I pick up another. "Me." I glance quickly at Joe, who nudges another puppy in my direction. I look at the sign. "Will."

And then I understand.

I blink against a sudden blur. "Where's the other one?" I ask, sniffling as the rambunctious little bodies scamper around me.

"Guys," Joe says to the yapping, unruly bunch, "let's do it the way we rehearsed." He reaches for the puppies and tries to set them in a line, except the order isn't right.

Will. Me. Marry. You.

The fifth puppy, wearing a ?, has wandered off to investigate the toy box, while the others race around in circles.

"You're proposing with puppies?" I ask, my lips stretched in a crooked smile.

Joe pulls a ring from his pocket. "Bad idea?" he asks.

I love this man beyond reason.

I use my sleeve to blot my eyes. "No, it's wonderful . . . maybe a little ungrammatical, but you can't help it if you lack puppy-herding skills." I move some of the puppies out of the way so I can straddle his lap. My arms link around his neck. "How do I say yes? Do you have any more signs?"

"There was a sixth puppy who was supposed to wear a reversible 'yes' or 'no,' but she was adopted last week."

I kiss him passionately. "The 'no' option wouldn't have been necessary."

"Then..."

"*Yes,* of course it's yes!"

Joe slides the diamond ring on my finger, and I admire the flash of cool, brilliant fire. "I love you," he says, and I say it back with a tremor of emotion. Leaning hard on him, I try to push him to the floor.

Joe eases down obligingly and wraps his arms around me as I lower my mouth to his. After a minute, he rolls me to my back and makes the kiss deeper, more intimate. Our soulful embrace is interrupted as puppies begin to clamber over us, and we discover that it's nearly impossible to kiss when you're laughing.

But we try anyway.